The Wit and Wisdom of Hilda Ffinch

The Bird With All The Answers

by

Juliet Warrington

Clink
Street

London | New York

Published by Clink Street Publishing 2020

Copyright © 2020

First edition.

ISBN:
978-1-913340-88-9 - paperback
978-1-913340-89-6 - ebook

For my Mother

Audrey
(1932–2005)

A child of the Blitz and a lifelong practitioner of British pluck.

I miss you.

The Little Hope Herald

Reader's Letters
Worried, confused, concerned or depressed?
Struggling to keep your pecker up?
Then drop a line to tickety-boo you-know-who

Hilda Ffinch, The Bird With All The Answers
And get it off your chest today!

(Please be aware that letters are sent at your own risk
and that discretion is not guaranteed – Ed.)

Contents

I.

Welcome to Little Hope

*"What do you mean you're 'a little short on communion wine again'?" asked the Bishop, peering over the top of his spectacles at the Reverent Aubrey Fishwick, who appeared to be listing to port a little, "How big **is** your congregation?"*

"Size isn't everything, you know!" replied the Vicar of Little Hope, fingering his cassock nervously and stifling a hiccough, "They're all bonkers, barking, bombed-out! Its only fortified muscatel keeps me going!"

Greetings From A Recent Transplant...

Mrs Prudence Ecclestone
Carnation Cottage
Bushy End
Little Hope

9th April 1940

Dear Mrs Ffinch,

As a recent transplant to Little Hope, I am wondering about the best way to become familiar with the delightful denizens of my new abode. Being naturally a shy and retiring type I am wondering if I need to – dare I even say it – be a little *forward* in my attempts to make friends, or should I wait to be approached as per a 'new hen in an old flock'?

When I hesitantly put my dilemma to the Vicar, he said that you were just the woman to 'steer me straight up the garden path'. I eagerly await your reply.

Yours, in trepidation,

Prudence Ecclestone (Mrs)

The Little Hope Herald
Saturday, 13th April 1940

Dear Mrs Ecclestone,

Might I first take the opportunity to welcome you to Little Hope, one of Yorkshire – nay indeed one of *England's* – finest villages?

We have been sitting atop the moors here since time out of memory and I suspect that the Vicar – the Rev Aubrey Fishwick – has been here since the very beginning. The man is older than he looks and is either preserving (read: pickling) himself with gallons of communion wine or has a terribly degenerate portrait of himself in the attic. Either way, in fairness to the fellow, he delivers a jolly fine sermon (usually outside the Rose and Crown on a Saturday evening just before the blackout, having first imbibed a pint or two himself in order to fit in with his flock) and is always good for an early marrow should you find yourself in need – he's been going at it in the Vicarage garden since the Dig For Victory campaign was first mooted here and without a shadow of a doubt now boasts the finest gourds in Yorkshire.

The villagers are quite lovely but are likely to peer at you suspiciously from behind their lace curtains for the next four hundred years or so unless you set to with a will and a firm handshake and introduce yourself to them. You might consider offering them a Nuttall's Mintoe or a slice of pig's trotter in aspic in order to validate your credentials once you've marched up their garden paths and rattled their knockers. Please be aware that both Ethel Daley and Clara Smallbottom's knockers are loose, so best rap on their doors with your knuckles if at all possible. Should Mr Willie Hardman (number twenty, Goose Lane) invite you in for a cup of tea, do try not to touch his knob with your bare hands as it will be over-greased as usual and you'll end up covered in it, let him open the door for you himself.

You might in addition like to consider joining the Little Hope Women's Institute which meets at the Village Hall on a Thursday evening at half-past seven precisely. It's not all 'Jam and Jerusalem', our ladies also enjoy truffle hunting, competitive strip jack poker (if enough airmen are to be found for an opposing team on the evening in question) and the odd dust-up in the ration queue when Mr Wilf Trotter the butcher puts his special 'thrice stuffed porky banger' on display in his shop window.

We also – should you feel that you'd like to 'do your bit' and give Jerry a bit of a seeing to – have a vacancy for an ARP Warden in the village. The previous incumbent, Mr Roger Golightly, has recently taken up a missionary position in the Belgian Congo along with Mrs Tuppence Boothe-Royde the fallen Salvationist. If interested, please call in at the Little Hope Police Station and ask for Constable Clink, he will happily furnish you with a helmet.

I do hope that this missive aids you in your quest to feel at home here in Little Hope. We're cut off by blizzards of biblical proportions for approximately two months during the wintertime so best make your mind up whether you're going to stay or not by Christmas.

Please do feel free to contact me again should you encounter any problems settling in.

Yours helpfully,

Hilda Ffinch
Hilda Ffinch,
The Bird with All The Answers

Sandy Balls At the Seaside...

Mr Sandy Balls
Dick's End
Greater Hope

15th May 1940

Dear Ms Ffinch,

Bit concerned about the annual holiday. Usually go to Cleethorpes but the beach is jam-packed with crocodile teeth. No chance of getting anything up, deckchair's out of the question, never mind the rest of my paraphernalia to impress the ladies.

Aberystwyth any better?

Yours faithfully,

Mr Sandy Balls

𝕿𝖍𝖊 𝕷𝖎𝖙𝖙𝖑𝖊 𝕳𝖔𝖕𝖊 𝕳𝖊𝖗𝖆𝖑𝖉
Saturday, 18th May 1940

Dear Mr Balls,

I do so hope that you mean 'Dragon's Teeth' my dear man, otherwise, one of us had best telephone the RSPCA and have the entire east coast of England evacuated.

Assuming that you haven't already cracked open your holiday gin (I'm speculating 50/50 on that one at this precise moment in time) or been shot at by the Home Guard for snipping your way through their acres of expertly coiled barbed wire in order to paddle in the brutal North Sea, might I suggest that you perhaps look inland for your summer holiday this year, given that we are at war and the chances of you being surprised by a random periscope whilst taking a dip are greater than ever before?

In my opinion, there is nothing quite so unbecomes a man as the moment when he decides it is acceptable in decent society to casually remove his boots and socks at the seaside and roll both trouser legs up his pale, cadaverous knees, thus causing old maids to blush, dogs to bark and seagulls to swoop in with beaks full of nesting materials.

I wonder, do you perchance remove your shirt to display your string vest in all its glory and pop a knotted handkerchief onto your head when engaging in your particularly uninviting summer ritual? I have to say that if you're after impressing the fairer sex with such a display then you're most certainly barking up the wrong tree, my good man. They'll turn their affections to the aforementioned yapping dog first and you'll find yourself playing second fiddle to it, no matter how big your bone.

In short, Mr Sandy Balls, the seaside look is *not* an attractive look for a fellow. You may well succeed in getting your paraphernalia up, as you put it, but you'll find yourself fiddling with it on your own for the duration of your stay, presupposing that you haven't been collared by the long arm of the law for endangering national security first.

Our prisons are full of felons so desperate for the sight of a bare leg or a pale knee that yours may well set them off and spark a riot, why risk unsettling them?

Take to the open roads, dear man and breathe in the country air instead! Why not get yourself togged up in some sensible plus-fours and a golfing cap and try swinging with a party of friends? It's marvellously invigorating and so much more pleasurable than catching crabs at the beach.

Yours,

Hilda Ffinch
Hilda Ffinch,
The Bird with All The Answers

P.S. Avoid Aberystwyth at all costs, Wales is terribly cold at this time of year and periscope chafing is rife in the Irish Sea at the moment

The Lady Novelist…

Miss Harriet Penn
'Scrivener's Palsy'
Herringbone Lane
Little Hope

25th June 1940

Dear Mrs Ffinch,

I'm a bit bored being just a housewife and think I might like to have a crack at being a lady novelist like yourself. I recently read your book *The Man in the Iron Basque* and enjoyed it very much.

I should so like to see my own tome on sale alongside yours in the bookshop on the High Street and I'm sure that you will agree that there's plenty of room for two literary ladies in Little Hope and who knows, perhaps we might even share a column in the newspaper!

With this in mind, I wonder could you give me some tips on how to write a corker?

Thank you in advance.

Yours,

Miss Harriet Penn

The Little Hope Herald
Saturday, 27th June 1940

Dear Miss Penn,

No.

Yours,

Hilda Ffinch
Hilda Ffinch,
The Bird with All The Answers

The Sausage Queen…

Mrs Hazel Nutter
Bog View Cottage
Bushy End
Little Hope

3rd July 1940

Dear Mrs Ffinch,

My niece is a lovely girl, and everyone says she's the image of me a few years ago (albeit with better hair and teeth). I'd so like to find a social outlet for her as with all the young men away fighting for our freedom as she's become terribly bored and has taken to reading cheap novels.

Might a beauty pageant for our young ladies be a good idea do you think? Would a Victory Sausage Competition pay for the event and the winning banger be given as a prize?

I'm sure that my niece or another nice girl would be honoured to carry the title of Sausage Queen for a year. Is this something you would lend your support to, dear Mrs Ffinch?

Sincerely,

Hazel Nutter

The Little Hope Herald
Saturday, 6th July 1940

Dear Mrs Nutter,

What a splendid idea! It's imperative during these rather trying times that we keep our collective chins up and carry on, regardless of Herr Hitler's attempts to bomb us into submission!

Might I beg to suggest however that the pageant is incorporated into our annual village fete on 21st June? That way we can be reasonably sure of passable weather and the late blackout will ensure that we will still be able to identify those parading their stuff about should the whole thing happen to 'run on a bit' (as these things often do).

I have spoken with the Vicar on this matter, and also with Mrs Agapanthus Crumb – Chair of the Women's Institute of Little Hope – and they are both keen to help out where they possibly can. The Vicar has agreed to open up the church hall for the event but has stipulated that whilst the odd bare calf is acceptable on the stage, he will *not* countenance nudity in the vestry should anyone wish to use it for a change of costume. Mrs Crumb has confirmed that the WI are happy to pitch in and help with hair styling and make up and that they have a glut of beetroot at present which will do nicely instead of lipstick and rouge.

Other villagers have expressed their support for your proposal and have offered to help out where they can – Mr Brewster of Bell End farm has come forward with an offer of some old grain sacks should anyone be short of a frock and dear Constable Clink has offered his services with in respect of drawing stocking seams onto contestants' legs if required, proving that the long arm of the law can certainly come in handy, as it were.

I have also approached Mr Wilf Trotter, the butcher of Little Hope at The Yorkshire Meat Emporium in the High Street and he has confirmed that he is only too happy to provide a fine upstanding sausage for the winner, his only stipulation being that he is permitted to give it to her personally on the stage in front of a large audience in order to advertise his splendid 'Tuesday Tender Touch' of pork loin which he likes to display in his shop window weekly.

Along with Mr Trotter's porky banger and in addition to their help with beautifying contestants, the ladies of the WI would also like very much to extend the offer of a year's free membership of our local branch to the Sausage Queen. I have slight reservations about this as it's likely to put quite a few would-be contenders off, frankly, but hey ho!

I'm rather looking forward to posing with Mr Trotter's sausage at the fete myself, my editor having promised me a front-page spread if it will fit.

Yours, with something approaching mild enthusiasm,

Hilda Ffinch
Hilda Ffinch,
The Bird with All The Answers

That Odd Fellow at the Bus Stop...

Mrs Prudence Ecclestone
Carnation Cottage
Bushy End
Little Hope

15th July 1940

Dear Mrs Ffinch,

Thank you SO much for your letter. I couldn't believe how touched I felt upon receiving your missive and thought to read it on the bus on the way to Sheffield. I was a teensy bit disconcerted to realise however that part of the 'touchiness' was being caused by the strange man sitting next to me in the bus shelter who used my preoccupation to attempt some occupational manoeuvres of his own. A short, sharp stab with a hat pin to his offending digit soon sent him scurrying for cover! Does this sort of thing happen much in Little Hope?

Yours, invigorated by a little prick,

Prudence Ecclestone (Mrs)

The Little Hope Herald
Saturday, 20th July 1940

Dear Mrs Ecclestone,

Thank you for your latest missive, how lovely it is to hear from you again, especially as I learned recently that you *have* decided to stay here in spite of the somewhat inclement Yorkshire weather which we are subject to each year during the festive season.

If I might add as a post-script to my previous reply to you that our heavy/demonic snowfall does in fact provide some The

21

Wit and Wisdom of Hilda Ffinch 22 entertainment in that it brings the community together nicely when we make our daily pilgrimage to the Church of a morning in order to thaw the Vicar's bell clappers out before he mounts his pulpit. As they are ancient and consequently rather delicate, the Vicar prefers his clappers to be thawed gently by hand, in order that no rogue cracks appear, to queer the pitch as it were. Should you decide to join us in this holy endeavour, please do remember to wear gloves on your trek to St Candida's and be prepared to spend a lot of time blowing and rubbing when standing in line waiting your turn. Patience is a virtue, and the Vicar will give you a bunk up into the belfry as soon as he is able.

Now, with regards to the odd fellow with the wandering hands. Without a description I cannot be sure, but when Constable Clink was here giving my Cook a good stuffing (sage and onion, homemade by his sister Connie) on Tuesday last, he did mention that the Bishop of Rotherham progressed through these parts a couple of weeks ago and spent an inordinate amount of time laying hands on anyone who happened to cross his path.

There was an incident in Trotter's Yorkshire Meat Emporium in the High Street when the very reverend gentleman stood side by side with our very own dear Mr Trotter and leaned across the counter to bestow a blessing on the forehead of each lady in the ration queue as they came to the front. Unfortunately, Miss Titty Wainwright's turn at the front coincided with Mr Trotter placing his special thrice stuffed porky banger onto the counter in front of the Bishop at precisely the moment that the latter leaned forward to lay hands on her. This caused him to inadvertently shunt the aforementioned sausage at the good lady with some vigour. Miss Wainwright's delighted shrieks caused a bit of a scuffle to break out and Constable Clink was called in to try to restore order. This was only possible however once Mr Trotter had managed to wrestle his thrice stuffed porky banger - which had become entangled in the Bishop's cincture - away from Miss Wainwright, but not before her frenzied tugging had quite put the Bishop's back out.

I believe that the Bishop removed himself from our midst shortly after this incident, but not before he was seen to inadvertently put his hand on the knee of a 'new lady' at the bus stop on the village green on Tuesday last whilst endeavouring to rise – the latter manoeuvre being a little tricky following the incident with Mr Trotter's sausage. My informant tells me that the 'new lady' had at the Bishop with her hat pin, causing him to spring forward and then genuflect involuntarily in the path of the oncoming bus. Luckily, his current sojourn in the Sheffield Infirmary is not thought to be serious or long term.

Does this ring any secular bells, as it were?

Yours,

Hilda Ffinch
Hilda Ffinch,
The Bird with All The Answers.

A Toggle and Two…

'Esme'
Little Hope

8th August 1940

Dear Mrs Ffinch,

I was in the snug at the local pub with my friend Gertrude when I just happened to hear the village Constable talking to the landlord about a prisoner he'd had to collect from Wales. I wasn't being nosey you understand, but I couldn't help but overhear what they said.

I'd heard rumours that one of the lads from that odd family up near Gallows Hill had run away a bit back in order to avoid his call up papers and nothing was heard of him for a while. Well, from what I overheard, it seems that over in Wales they arrested a woman for being inebriated, and back at the police station her wig fell off. Further examination by the desk sergeant revealed that not only was she was rather well blessed on the bosom side (on account of what turned out to be a brassiere stuffed with hand knitted socks and Murray Mints) but that she also had what I heard the constable refer to as a 'toggle and two'. On top of this, in her handbag they found the Identity Card of the lad from Gallows Hill and checked with Scotland Yard who confirmed that it was him. He's up before the magistrates tomorrow!

All rather tawdry I think, but I'm at a loss to understand what a 'toggle and two' is, although I have a duffle coat myself. Do you have any ideas, and should we be more concerned about that family?

Yours in anticipation, on behalf of all those whom it might affect,

Esme

𝕿𝖍𝖊 𝕷𝖎𝖙𝖙𝖑𝖊 𝕳𝖔𝖕𝖊 𝕳𝖊𝖗𝖆𝖑𝖉
Saturday, 10th August 1940

Dear Esme,

A 'toggle and two' has nothing to do with a duffle coat, let us get that straight from the start.

Now, here's the thing, my dear, I do think that at your age – your joined-up handwriting with its jaunty upward slant leads me to believe that you're most likely to be over thirty, still live at home with Mother, read cheap novels and probably have an abundance of unsightly leg hair poking through your stockings – you really ought to have some idea of the use of slang terminology when it comes the male anatomy.

However, in order to clear the censor and avoid having the Little Hope Herald shut down for smutty publishing, I'll need to tread carefully here, so do try to keep up.

The unclothed male of the species, my dear girl, is <u>quite unlike the female</u>. It gladdens my heart, and gives me some hope for the future of this country that you at least know, judging by your comment about the overstuffed brassier, that men do not have bosoms – the exception to the rule being the Bishop of Llangaff, but his cannonballs are occasioned by nurture rather than nature, and are due entirely to an excess of cake, stuffed goose and communion wine.

Furthermore, men do not sport a 'lower thatched cottage', a 'magic triangle' nor indeed a 'lady's low toupee' as we females do. My dear spouse, Colonel Ffinch, habitually refers to this area of the female anatomy as 'the firing range' but that's quite a rare turn of phrase and one peculiar to his regiment, I believe.

No, my dear, the son of Adam and Eve possesses down below what is sometimes euphemistically termed a 'silent flute', a 'maypole' (albeit not one you'd expect to see on the village green on fete day), a 'gentleman usher', a 'baldheaded friar', an 'old man' or – very rarely, in my experience – a 'kidney prodder'.

Please be aware that these are all polite terms for the <u>single</u> article, as I'm sure you will agree that a fellow boasting all six would have terrible difficulties engaging the services of a decent tailor and would be hounded to the ends of the earth by Messrs Barnum and Bailey (and very possibly one's old friend Miss Violet Millington, too).

I do hope that this has cleared matters up for you, Esme. You may continue to wear your duffle coat with pride. If you're still a little confused, then might I suggest that you pop along (covertly) to The Cat and Cabbage in Hampton Upon Mott on a Tuesday evening after closing time when the regular participants in Mrs Edith Muff-Hawker's Weekly Friendship Gatherings are coming out? Be careful not to snag your stockings on a rogue bush and eat a goodly supply of carrots afterwards, heaven knows you'll need them to restore your eyesight.

Yours knowledgeably,

Hilda Ffinch
Hilda Ffinch,
The Bird with All The Answers

Pulling Like the Clappers…

Miss Isabel Ringer
Handstroke Cottage
Beaver Close
Little Hope

21st August 1940

Dear Mrs Ffinch,

I am at a total loss as to what I am to do now that those nasty Nazis have started their circus tricks and the government has issued an edict banning the ringing of church bells unless the Jerry comes. I mean, what am I to tug on now that the Vicar's bell clappers have been muffled?

I have been pulling on my favourite bell rope for several years and have become something of an expert in manual dexterity. Indeed, I can pull with one hand, both hands or indeed with either hand in rapid succession, such is the muscle strength which I now possess in my upper arms. The Vicar knows that his bells are in safe hands with me tugging away at them.

It's also an excellent way to keep fit and I fear that I may run to fat if I cannot continue.

I am so dejected; what am I to do?

Yours,

Isabel Ringer

𝕿𝖍𝖊 𝕷𝖎𝖙𝖙𝖑𝖊 𝕳𝖔𝖕𝖊 𝕳𝖊𝖗𝖆𝖑𝖉
Saturday, 24th August 1940

Dear Miss Ringer,

Oddly enough, the Vicar and I were discussing your prowess in the pulling department on Tuesday last when we met for our twice weekly tête-à-tête and a quick munch (one has to admire the man, even in these difficult times one never comes away from his front parlour empty-handed, indeed, on this occasion he gave me an excellent spotted dick) and I can confirm that the good man misses having your hands on his bell rope every bit as much as you do.

"Miss Ringer really did have it down to a fine art," he explained. "Bell clappers are terribly delicate things, Mrs Ffinch, and you'd be surprised at the scale of damage which might be occasioned by a rogue tug."

Actually, I wouldn't.

Colonel Ffinch and I went through a phase of frenzied campanology whilst on our honeymoon in the West Country. It came to an abrupt end when my dear spouse gave a gargantuan pull on the Bishop of Exeter's well-hung bell rope causing a frightful commotion in the poor man's upper chamber as his gudgeon dropped out and occasioned his headstock to come adrift. One shredded muffler and a questionable tittums-touch later and a subsequent pull-off was completely out of the question. There was nothing for it but for the assembled ringers to get the Bishop's handbells out for evensong.

The Colonel and I later heard that neither the Bishop nor his congregation were particularly impressed with the state of affairs and that it took several members of the Exeter Women's Institute a great deal of pulling and bunking to get the good man's beam back up again. Fortunately by this time my spouse and I had given up bell-ringing and had moved on to mud-larking in quite another part of the country, something which proved to be much more fun, and so we weren't too concerned about the havoc caused by the Colonel's slightly overzealous hand stroke. We did agree however that the Bishop really ought to have made sure that his gudgeon was fit for purpose before inviting complete strangers in for a quick tug.

But, back to the present and to your dilemma. The Reverend Fishwick and I both agreed that it would be a shame to let your masterful grip weaken through wont of a good jerk of a Sunday morning and so he's wondering if you might like to volunteer to polish his much-loved front knob instead? It is, as you know, rather large and heavy and is handled by parishioners several times a week when calling at the Vicarage for spiritual advice and succour. Impressive though it may be, it is in need of constant attention lest it come off in someone's hand again as was almost the case when I called for tiffin last week.

The Reverend Fishwick asked me to let you know that the job's yours if you want it and blow what the rest of the bell ringers think. Do please let him know your thoughts at your earliest opportunity.

I do hope this helps.

Yours,

Hilda Ffinch
Hilda Ffinch,
The Bird with All The Answers.

P.S. Obviously, polishing the said doorknob will also entail wiping down the Vicarage door and giving it a fresh lick (of paint) as and when required. RSVP ASAP before Miss Fanny Walklate gets to hear of the vacancy and is on it like a rabid ferret.

Taxi!

Mrs Fanny Foot
Mountjoy Cottage
Bushy End
Little Hope
Yorkshire

21st September 1940

Dear Mrs Ffinch,

I know there's a war on but have you seen the price of taxi fares from Little Hope to Hampton Upon Mott these days? Disgraceful!

It used to cost me 2s 6d to visit my sister by this means of transport once a week and now it's shot up to 5s 4d!

Daylight robbery!

Yours furiously,

Mrs Fanny Foot

The Little Hope Herald
Saturday, 28th September 1940

Dear Mrs Foot,

Would it kill you to get the bus like everyone else (except me, of course)? I've had a gander at the local timetable and one can purchase a return ticket from outside The Yorkshire Meat Emporium in the High Street here in Little Hope to Fiddler's End in Hampton Upon Mott for ninepence!

Petrol is *rationed*, madam, and taxi drivers are only permitted to purchase two gallons per day. Is it any wonder that the cost of a ride has shot up like a ferret up a drainpipe? Do pull yourself together and leave taxis vacant for those who really need them.

Apologies for the brevity of my reply, but Hardy's Handsome Cab has just pulled up at the front door with my weekly supply of macaroons and gin on board, it's a long way to Sheffield and back and the driver will expect a tip.

Yours disapprovingly,

Hilda Ffinch
Hilda Ffinch,
The Bird with All The Answers

The String Quartet...

Mr Richard Rimmer
6, Balaclava Street
Little Hope

11th September 1940

Dear Mrs Ffinch,

I do feel that since the war started and most of our Morris men have gone off to fight there's been a lack of proper family entertainment in the village. With this in mind, I've been thinking of starting up a little orchestra or perhaps a string quartet. Problem is, although I've asked around at The Cat and Cabbage and The Royal Oak no one seems very keen?

You have connections, I wonder do you know anyone who might be interested? I'm getting proper deflated and it's upsetting my digestion.

Yours hopefully,

Richard 'Dick' Rimmer

(Still here on account of flat feet.)

The Little Hope Herald
Saturday, 14th September 1940

Dear Dick,

The problem, as you say, lies in the fact that most of our able-bodied men are away giving Jerry a good seeing to somewhere or other, leaving us with a motley crew of elderly or infirm gentlemen who are full of entirely the wrong sort of wind. I do realise that entertainment is in short supply in the village nowadays, but I'm fairly certain that no one really wants to see old Mr Percy Braithwaite's left lung billowing in and out of the end of his trumpet like a half-achieved rubber balloon at the summer fete.

I believe therefore that the way forward for you lies not with our remaining menfolk but in the company of the ladies of the village, many of whom know how to play a good tune on an old fiddle.

To this end, why not take yourself and your quest out of the fuggy little hostelries of Little Hope and have a sniff at the slightly more fragrant ranks of the Women's Institute instead? They meet at the Village Hall at seven o'clock on a Tuesday evening, and I think you will be pleasantly surprised.

I have already made some enquiries on your behalf and recommend that you consider auditioning the following:

- Miss Fanny Mellord of Bushy End. She knows a thing or two about making a French horn rise to the occasion.
- Mrs Mildred Winterbottom of Tart's Hill straddles a cello like Randolph Scott and is already jolly popular down at the local airfield.
- Miss May Day and her twin sister Dee – resident in my own gatehouse along with their mother and two small dogs – have had their bassoons out now on several occasions in order to entertain the troops over at Hillsborough Barracks and they both went down a storm.
- Miss Minnie Beaver of Cock Lane is an accomplished artist on both the piccolo and the clarinet, size being no object.
- Mrs Lavinia Fox, of Fox Hall, is a dab hand at the castanets and is also known to play with Brigadier Fox's maracas when gets them out.
- Mrs Magdalen Craddock of Agincourt Terrace is competent on both the washboard and the comb and paper.

That leaves, to the best of my knowledge, just Miss Virginia Creeper (the lady novelist and author of *The Merry Wives of Whitby*) who resides at Fagg End in this Parish. She is an accomplished violinist and is known to go at it like Paganini if the moon is in the right quarter and one hears that she can also gargle the National Anthem, albeit only with gin.

Last but by no means least comes Mrs Ethel Ricketts, the Reverend Fishwick's housekeeper, who has been known to toot the Vicar's own flute upon occasion and is said to be quite proficient at it.

I mean, I've practically done your work for you there, Dick! Much as I would like to help you further by volunteering for your Orchestra of Little Hope, I'm afraid that the piano is not my forte.

Do let me know how you get on.

Yours,

Hilda Ffinch
Hilda Ffinch,
The Bird with All The Answers

P.S. A word to the wise. Should Mrs Fox's spinster sister-in-law, Miss June Fox, approach you with a harpsichord in tow, please send both her and it back to Fox Hall at once. The harpsichord is worth a fortune and June couldn't carry a tune in a bucket (if she had one, which she doesn't, it's full of sand due to the danger of incendiaries).

That Piano is Driving Me Nuts…

'Mrs Sorely Tried'
Crecy Street
Little Hope

8th October 1940

Dear Mrs Ffinch,

I'm not one to complain usually but I've proper got my nerves on and no matter how much Sanatogen I get down my neck it's never quite enough.

My next-door neighbour (who shall remain nameless but has a wall eye and a limp and is the village undertaker) has seen fit to buy his wife a piano and bugger me (pardon the French) if she ain't banging away on it night and day like Old Nick's blacksmith. I know piano playing ain't easy, but neither is not taking a frying pan to the back of her head when on the rare occasion she gives my ears a rest and pops out into her backyard to peg her drawers out.

Please help before I do something I might regret.

Yours,

'Sorely Tried of Crecy Street'

The Little Hope Herald
Saturday, 12th October 1940

Dear 'Sorely Tried',

My deepest sympathies at this terrible state of affairs, I know only too well how tiresome an inept pianist can prove to be; Many moons ago, when my parents were roughing it in a twelve up, twelve down in Kensington, they retained the services of a pianoforte teacher – Mrs Tabitha Quills – for my sister Cordelia and I. To say that the woman was tone deaf is an understatement, even the footmen took to serving dinner with cotton wool balls in their ears and Falstaff, my Father's basset hound, almost drove him to apoplexy with its incessant howling whenever the blessed woman decided it was time to tickle the old ivories, as it were. Ultimately though, Beethoven's Fifth became Mrs Quills' Last as she contrived to perform it when the Duke of Woking was on the premises. A particularly mournful howl from Falstaff rather took His Grace by surprise and carnage ensued at the dinner table, the grand finale of which proved to be the accidental launch of three French sticks, a bottle of port and a soup tureen through the dining room window.

So trust me, I do know how trying a poor pianist can be.

I have thought long and hard about your situation and, following a consultation with the Vicar over tea and macaroons, I have come up with the following solution which – if properly adhered to – ought to put a stop to your noisy neighbour's shenanigans.

My lame gamekeeper breeds cats in an effort to keep his cottage rodent-free and his prize mouser (Lucrezia Pawsia) was delivered of a litter just three months ago. A finer posse of kittens you never did see and most of them were soon snapped up by villagers in order to keep their cheese rations safe and out of the paws of hungry mice. Even the Vicar invested in one in order to put an end to the shenanigans of a particularly unsociable mouse who had been nibbling at his communion wafers and eyeing up his oats.

As a consequence of the popularity of these little pussies, my gamekeeper is left with just two kittens at home. One, which he intends to keep for himself is coming along very nicely and has already dragged home two bouncy rabbits and an irate badger but the other, a rascally little bundle of black and white fur, really is far too vocal ever to make it as a successful mouser.

This little kitten, fondly known as Furzellini, loves nothing better than to sing for his supper (which starts at six in the morning, apparently) and he will not pipe down until the sun is well over the yardarm and my gamekeeper is too far gone in drink to hear him. Music sets him off too apparently and should his master chance to get his Enrico Caruso out then the little cat goes berserk. One hears that he had my gamekeeper's gramophone horn between his teeth on Tuesday evening last and had to be enticed away with a dish of giblets.

I propose therefore, that you pop round to see Mr Scratcher and tell him that you're the person who has come about the pussy – I've already had a word with him about it – and he'll be only too happy to give it to you, free of charge.

I prophesy that if you put pussy's basket in a room where it can best get an earful of your neighbour's atrocious tinkling then it will become incensed in no time at all, will jump through the nearest window (please be sure to leave it open in readiness) and will shred the washing on madam's line in the blink of an eye. Clothes are rationed, and she won't be able to get her hands on a new pair of drawers daily!

That ought to do the trick. If it doesn't, then I suggest that you get your hands on a French horn and give it a good blow on the hour, every hour, but find the cat a new home first or it'll have your throat out.

I do hope that this helps! Bon chance, 'Sorely Tried', bon chance!

Yours,

Hilda Ffinch
Hilda Ffinch,
The Bird with All The Answers

Sheep...

Col. Clayton Fitzwaffle (Retd)
Fuquham Hall
Greater Hope

19th October 1942

Dear Mrs Ffinch,

What? Took a recce down to the river to check out the lie of the land. Dangerous times, these. Someone has to do it.

Spied Jonny Foreigner on the far bank. Had the lads form a square, unfurled the colours, don't yer know. Turned out to be a damned fool flock of sheep!

And why is whisky so expensive? Never had this problem on the frontier. There were sheep aplenty and cheap hooch to bath 'em in. Never at tiffin though, thank God, what?

Regards, dear lady, regards!

Col. Clayton Fitzwaffle (Retd)

The Little Hope Herald
Saturday, 26th October 1940

Dear Colonel Fitzwaffle,

The arrival of your letter this morning coincided with a visit from Farmer Brewster of Bell End Farm who called in order to use my telephone to alert the Home Guard to suspicious activity in his pasture across the river.

It seems that some doddering old fellow in a nightshirt has been tearing up and down the field waving what appears to be a pair of long johns on a stick whilst shouting "Send for the Dragoons!" at his prized flock of Teeswaters.

Under normal circumstances, Farmer Brewster explained, he would have expected his sheepdogs to see the old bugger off but unfortunately both dogs were fast asleep and snoring soundly, having polished off the best part of a bottle of Old Elgin Scotch Whisky which had mysteriously made its way into a bowl on his front porch just after breakfast whilst he was round the back stroking his ferrets.

Colonel Fitzwaffle, my dear man, I'm assuming that Mrs Fitzwaffle has no idea that you're on the loose from the Sheffield Asylum and is even now out and about getting a good stuffing from the village butcher as she does every Tuesday. This being the case, I have despatched little Fanny Fuller from the Vicarage to warn your dear lady and to alert Constable Clink of your close proximity.

Good luck escaping from Broadmoor.

Yours,

Hilda Ffinch
Hilda Ffinch,
The Bird with All The Answers (and the loaded blunderbuss)

A Bad Case of the Collywobbles…

'Miss Dormouse'
Grope Lane
Higher Hope

22nd October 1940

Dear Mrs Ffinch,

Like other girls in the village, I've volunteered to help wherever I can with the war effort. But when I hear the air raid siren, I'm overcome by the most terrifying panic, and I can't breathe.

I'm afraid that if I tell anyone, they'll think I'm lacking in patriotism. What can I do to show a brave face, or better still, how can I actually *become* brave?

Yours nervously,

'Miss Dormouse'

The Little Hope Herald
Saturday, 26th October 1940

Dear 'Miss Dormouse',

Well, for starters you can come out from behind that teapot. The only thing you have to fear, my dear, is fear itself.

Oh, and the Luftwaffe, obviously. They're out to get you.

And, if you're paddling with your bucket and spade in the North Sea off Bridlington, the German Navy, Portuguese jellyfish and sea mines.

Apart from that, nothing.

Except fifth columnists.
And funny men at large in the blackout.
And Jerry parachutists.
And landing craft.
And incendiaries.
And landmines.
And looters.
And tea shortages.
And faulty prophylactics.

You see? Practically nothing!

So, chin up, and best foot forward. I'm enclosing a packet of cigarette filters for you, they make excellent earplugs and should help you with your siren-induced collywobbles. Be aware obviously that when wearing them you won't be able to hear oncoming traffic in the blackout and so perhaps consider dressing as Queen Boadicea when venturing out to 'do your bit' in the dark, that way if you are inadvertently flattened by the ten o'clock Little Hope to Sheffield bus on account of not having heard it careering up behind you, no one will ever doubt that you were a true patriot.

And please, above all, remember that we are British. We are brave, even when unnerved a bit by Herr Hitler's excitable ejaculations, by our own lost socks, and by a shortage of Huntley and Palmer's bisquits.

Do brace yourself to your task now and keep that upper lip in check, dear! Mr Carstairs in Omdurman Street has a terribly stiff one, and he's ninety-two for heaven's sake.

Now scuttle forth, Miss Dormouse! Scuttle forth and help win the war!

God Save the King etc!

Yours,

Hilda Ffinch
Hilda Ffinch,
The Bird with All The Answers

Colonel Fitzwaffle Flies Again...

Col. Clayton Fitzwaffle (Retd)
Fuquham Hall
Greater Hope
Yorkshire

3rd November 1940

Dear Mrs Ffinch,

Those were not long-johns I was waving about and I am not returning to that asylum. It's full of nutters. I know unhinged sheep when I see them, I've been watching them since the Relief of Mafeking!

As long as I'm camped 40 yards north of the river bend and 217 yards west of the ruined cottage with the limp hollyhocks neither you nor my dear misguided Petunia Mildred will find me.

Regards,

Col Clayton Fitzwaffle (Retd)

The Little Hope Herald
Saturday, 9th November 1940

Dear Colonel Fitzwaffle,

The policeman who has just hand delivered this letter to you will now escort you to the police station in Little Hope, from whence you will be returned to the Sheffield Asylum.

I would advise you, my dear man, not to try anything funny as the Home Guard are lined up on top of Gallows Hill, from where they'll have a clean shot should you endeavour to make a run for it. Their Commanding Officer, Major Jeremy Pratt, has been in disgrace since an incident involving the Chief Constable and a rogue squirrel on Friday last and is now jolly keen to redeem himself.

Take heed, Colonel Fitzwaffle, take heed! I hear that Pratt is a keen shot and has a terribly twitchy trigger finger.

Yours,
Hilda Ffinch
Hilda Ffinch,
The Bird with All The Answers

A Piggin' Bath…

Miss Dora Millington
'Trollop's End'
Slack Bottom
Greater Hope

18th December 1940

Dear Mrs Ffinch,

I share my home with my Great Aunt Doris – a wonderfully stoic lady and an admirably self-sufficient character who can turn her hand to anything. She may be old, but she's not at all infirm and as a result I've never had to worry about her doing strange things like some old people are wont to do.

Until now, anyway. I take that all back as I have just returned home from my weekly WI meeting to be greeted by the hanging corpse of a fully-grown pig over our bathtub!

To say it was a shock to see this big porker hanging in the bathroom is an understatement and I wonder how on earth to broach the subject with my aunt. The thought of wallowing in the bath with pig's trotters dangling over my head makes me feel a bit queasy.

Please help, I don't want to upset my aunt but I work on the land and need a good soak!

Yours sincerely,

Dora Millington (Miss)

The Little Hope Herald
Saturday, 21st December 1940

Dear Dora,

If, as I suspect, your Great Aunt Doris is actually Doris 'Curmudgeon' Millington, the former landlady of The Stoker's Arms up on the moor above Greater Hope then you're skating on very thin ice indeed, my dear.

Let me take you back to the great blizzard of 1913 (long before my time, obviously) to the night when your Great Aunt first appeared at The Stoker's Arms, having travelled alone through deep snow on a mercy mission from her Father, Mr Sweeney Millington of Millington's Pie Shop in Nottingham.

Carrying two barrels of India Pale Ale, a sack of 'meat seasoning' and a crate of candles on her back, Doris had been drafted in at the last minute as Arthur, her father's drayman, had put his back out trying to get his cart up the Great North Road and his horses were having none of it on account of snowballs in their hoofs.

Exhausted and sweating like Jack the Ripper at a surprise party for suspects held by Inspector Abbeline of the Yard, Doris made it through the storm and staggered in to The Stoker's Arms just before nightfall. She was immediately swept off her feet by a grateful landlord and twelve thirsty steelworkers, who had left Sheffield on a charabanc outing three days before and had become prisoners of the storm. None of them had seen a woman for quite some time and so Doris was quite the centre of attention at first until the storm worsened and food began to run out.

For seven days and seven nights the gods raged against mankind. Canals and rivers froze and the handles of village pumps all across Yorkshire came clean off when agitated with too much vigour. The lights of the marooned inn high up on the moor, bright and gay at first and quite magnificent in their Pickwickian splendour, were seen from the church tower in Greater Hope to dim gradually, diminish in number and slowly die away until not a single one remained.

Finally the day came when the storm blew itself out and a small party of men from the Greater Hope Ferret Fanciers Forum wrapped themselves up snugly, prevented their thighs from freezing on the journey across the moor by diligently adhering to the Forum's accepted ferret/trouser leg ratio, and set out on a rescue mission to The Stoker's Arms, dragging a sledge loaded with damson chutney and bread and lard behind them.

For five hours or more they toiled upwards towards the moor, digging through the frozen precipitation like frenzied badger-hogs until at last they reached the door to the inn. Bracing themselves and fully expecting to be confronted with a tableau rivalling Madam Tussaud's 'Last Moments of Robert Falcon Scott and his Unfortunate Friends' (price: two shillings on admission), they pushed the door open cautiously and peered in. To their wide-eyed astonishment, the rescue party found Doris Millington wallowing in a tin bath (a full one with enough steam to preserve her dignity, thankfully) in front of a roaring fire, sipping on half a pint of pale ale and singing 'When the Midnight Choo-Choo Leaves for Alabam'.

"Good evening, gentlemen!" she beamed, gesturing at them through the steam with a slice of toast, heavily topped with brawn, "Do come in! There's nobody else here!"

And it was true. Not a single soul apart from Doris was to be found at The Stoker's Arms that day, although the Ferret Fanciers Forum searched the place from top to bottom. It was no easy undertaking given that their efforts were hampered by the amount of brawn the landlord had clearly stocked up on before his disappearance. There was enough of the stuff to withstand a siege. The inn's larder was overflowing with it and a dinner plate piled high with at least half a pound of the stuff was sat on the table in the kitchen.

Doris explained, when questioned by Constable Crumble (a leading light in the Ferret Fanciers Forum and thus a member of the rescue party) that the landlord and the steelworkers, concerned that they might succumb to starvation at The Stoker's Arms on account of the raging blizzard outside (none of them liked brawn as they were all vegetarians apparently) had set off en masse for the village the morning after her arrival, to try to bring help or at the very least, some lettuce and a bit of cucumber for sandwiches, and that she hadn't seen hide nor hair of them since.

"But there were no footprints outside the inn when we arrived!" frowned Constable Crumb, "Not so much as an indentation or undulation!"

"The snow," replied Doris, "was positively horrid. I shouldn't think they'll be seen again. The landlord left his Last Will and Testament on the bar, just in case, and he absolutely insisted on leaving the Inn to me should he fail to return. Now, would you like a meat pie? I found some pork in the cellar and whipped eighteen of them up this morning. They're delicious..."

Constable Crumble declined the pie, but did have some brawn, liberally topped with the damson chutney the rescue party had bought with them. He always maintained that it was the best brawn he'd ever tasted having a seasoned, interesting texture and – best of all – he was the lucky winner of Doris Millington's 'Find the gold filling in the brawn' competition.

"Do keep it," said Doris, "I always like to pop one in, you may not have any fillings now but you may need it one day, you never know..."

Something was clearly amiss, not everyone in the vicinity swallowed Doris' tale, and there were those who always believed that with her arrival at the inn 'Dingley Dell' had become 'Dingley Hell'. But Constable Crumble always refused to see it and soon afterwards he gave up the police force for a position behind the flap, as it were, in Doris Millington's newly acquired public house, the one with the intriguing doorknobs.

I do hope that you've taken all that in, Dora and will give it some thought. I'll say no more about that terrible snowstorm for now, my dear, but I'd be inclined to keep mum about the swinging porker in the bathroom if I were you. If you feel that you need to have a word with your Great Aunt Doris regarding the same then please, do carry on.

Personally, I would advise you to err on the side of caution however and perhaps just hop on in there, wink at 'Dangling Percy' and use the nearest trotter in lieu of a nail brush.

I do hope that this puts your mind at rest. Good luck living with Mrs Miggins.

Merry Christmas.

Yours,

Hilda Ffinch
Hilda Ffinch,
The Bird with All The Answers

II.

Keep the Home Fires Burning
(Or smouldering a bit, at least)

"You're not terribly domesticated, are you, my dear?" said Colonel Ffinch as Hilda whipped out her divining rods in order to find the kitchen.

"Of course I am!" came the reply, "I have a cook, a housemaid, a gardener and a chauffeur. What more could one want?"

My Fanny Has Been Overdoing It...

Mr John Drake
7 Jutland Terrace
Little Hope

13th November 1939

Dear Ms Ffinch,

I'm very worried about my Fanny on account of her overuse of goose grease! Recently she suffered a slight chill after which begun her frenzied use of the pungent slime, but now that she is better she insists on rubbing it on her chest every evening as a preventative measure!

Our bedroom currently smells like an abattoir and the bacteria from the grease on our mattress has caused the growth of a percurliar species of mushroom.

What am I to do? Please could you advise?

Sincerely yours,

Mr John Drake

The Little Hope Herald
Saturday, 18th November 1939

Dear Mr Drake,

Peculiar, dear, it's *peculiar*

Now, having corrected your grammar, do let us press on.

Having been raised mainly in Mayfair, Buckinghamshire and the Sixteenth Arrondissement (one's Father having been under the British Ambassador in Paris for a while, from which gay old time his French letters are still preserved for posterity in the top drawer of my Mother's bureau) and also in a world in which new-fangled penicillin was passed around the dinner table with the port, one had – until marrying Colonel Ffinch and moving 'to the north' – very little experience with the British working class's preoccupation with applying the rendered fat of a partially domesticated goose to the upper torso in times of crisis. One had heard rumours, of course, and one thought briefly that it might be part of the Colonel's mating ritual (he's been around a bit) on one's wedding night when he whipped his monocle out and bellowed "Right! Let's have a gander then!" but it turned out to be nothing of the sort.

But I digress.

Now, the chances of you actually taking your Fanny in hand are obviously minimal on account of the saponaceous nature of the goosey by-product she's probably glistening with at this very moment. Indeed, one has visions of an unfortunate incident involving a tragic failure to secure a good grip, an open window and a twenty-foot drop onto the cobbled street below should you endeavour to do so and so *extreme* caution is urged in this case.

Might I suggest therefore that you begin by removing all traces of goose fat from the house? Please be aware that after such a prolonged relationship with the fowl (sic) stuff there will undoubtedly be caches of it stowed away in the most unlikely of places. This being the case, you'd do well to search under loose floorboards, to scour the interiors of hatboxes in the attic and to look behind any religious images which might adorn your walls as these addicts become terribly crafty over time and no one would ever suspect the Virgin Mary of fencing a bit of goose grease.

This achieved, you might then have a quiet word with Mr Trotter the butcher, who is to be found at The Yorkshire Meat Emporium in the High Street and to ask him to desist from giving your Fanny any further form of lubricant on the grounds that it's not coming out of your sheets and they're becoming rather stiff as a result. As a single man himself, who must surely do his own laundry, Mr Trotter will understand.

Finally, perhaps pull back the blankets on the bed which you and your Fanny frequent and leave a frying pan, a rasher of bacon (fat trimmed off for obvious reasons) and your weekly egg ration on top of the sheet in question and – when Fanny asks you what you're about – explain that the mushrooms growing therein are just the ticket to finish off your full English breakfast in the morning. Irony, my dear man, often wins the day, as may explaining to Fanny that the olfactory honk of an old bird is actually rather offensive.

I do hope this helps,

Yours with a disapproving glance at your Fanny,

Juliet Warrington

Hilda Ffinch
Hilda Ffinch,
The Bird with All The Answers

He Leaves A Trail of Absolute Chaos!

Mrs Diana Scrubb
Pentecost Cottage
Bell End Lane
Little Hope

1ˢᵗ March 1940

Dear Mrs Ffinch,

My husband Cecil, unable to join the regular army on account of a head wound received at Passchendaele (a game of five aside behind the lines went terribly wrong when Cecil headbutted a low-flying carrier pigeon, thinking it to be a football and was rendered unconscious for quite some time on account of then being potted by a Hun sniper who had been aiming at said bird) has joined the local Home Guard and is, frankly, making my domestic life hell.

I've always been somewhat house-proud, but in these times of austerity it is nigh on impossible to get one's hands on decent cleaning products and Cecil is constantly traipsing remnants of farmyard and woodland into the kitchen after his watch. It's driving me nuts and, to compound matters, most days I am left in sole charge of my eleven-month-old grandson, who is just starting to crawl (his Father is away on active service and his Mother works in munitions) and the child just will not cease and desist from crawling through Cecil's trail of chaos.

Help! What can I do? I'm sick and tired of sniffing my peg rugs for badger spoor!

Yours hopefully,

Diana Scrubb

The Little Hope Herald

Saturday, 2nd March 1940

Dear Mrs Scrubb,

Have you considered modifying the child's rompers somewhat, so that he might inadvertently clean up after your dear Cecil whilst on his perambulatory route of choice?

A single rolled up length of towelling sewn on to each wrist cuff (you might tuck the little one's hands in, like gloves) and dampened before play will enable him to wash the floor as he scoots along on all fours and an old tea towel sewn across the child's romper bottoms at the knees and ankles will ensure that the floor is also dried as he passes over it. You might also add a little tummy pocket, open at the front, with a scrubbing brush inserted (bristles pointing away from the child, for health and safety reasons) for an extra clean shine?

If the child is a 'bottom shuffler' as indeed some are wont to be, then a similar modification might be made to a romper suit by attaching a terry towelling washcloth to the underside of the heels and calves and a tea towel buffer to the bottom – bearing in mind that a less than clean nappy might hinder rather than help the operation in this case.

Alternatively, you could keep your back door locked, as it were, and insist on hosing your spouse down in the yard before letting him into the house. Please be aware however that should you decide to take this course of action then it may prove problematic should Jerry rupture the water mains again 'mid spurt', there's every chance that you might encounter some horrified opposition from female neighbours of a prudish disposition.

I do hope this helps.

Yours,

Hilda Ffinch
Hilda Ffinch,
The Bird with All The Answers (and three small children regularly cleaning the kitchen on account of the housemaid's unenviable fecundity).

All Fours or Kneeling?

'Violet M.'
Harpy Cottage
Bushy End
Little Hope
Yorkshire

8th May 1940

Dear Mrs Ffinch,

Isn't there an alternative to donkey-stoning my step? I am getting calluses on my knees – it's very undignified having my bottom waggling away whilst on all fours. The Vicar's already seen me and tutted, I dread to think what he's had to say about it.

Yours hopefully,

Violet M.

The Little Hope Herald
Saturday, 11th May 1940

Dear Violet M,

The Vicar, my dear, has had plenty to say about it, as indeed have several of your neighbours, the postman, three ARP wardens *and* Mr Peabody the greengrocer. They've all seen you, swinging your derriere like a runaway metronome on that doorstep, with and without your donkey stone!

Now, with regards to an alternative method of scrubbing your step, I feel that it is not so much your equipment which is the problem as the way in which you choose to implement its purpose. One *must* learn to keep the movement of one's bottom when performing on all fours to a gentle, rhythmic tempo – perhaps try Ravel's 'Bolero' rather than 'The Radetzky March' as I fear that going at it like the King's racehorse on Derby Day will not end well for you.

Might I also exhort you to endeavour to go east to west when 'assuming the position', rather than north to south for the sake of the milkman's horse? I hear that the unfortunate beast was quite unsettled by your antics on Tuesday last and took off at a fast trot, causing half the village to have clotted cream delivered rather than milk.

As things stand, you are rather going at it like the galloping major! For heaven's sake woman, it's unseemly, rein it in!

Yours,

Hilda Ffinch
Hilda Ffinch,
The Bird with All The Answers

Kippers...

Mrs E MacDonald
36 Titley Road
Little Hope

15th June 1940

Dear Mrs Ffinch,

My sister Edith is having terrible problems curing her kippers. She has tried many methods but all have failed and now she smells like an old trawlerman and her house is attracting cats. To add insult to injury, no one will sit by her on the bus and she's twice been refused entry to a cinema in Sheffield.

How can she possibly get rid of this fishy smell as no amount of scrubbing will shift it?

Yours faithfully,

Enid MacDonald (Mrs)

The Little Hope Herald
Saturday, 20th June 1940

Dear Mrs MacDonald,

I do believe that I may have encountered your sister – not by sight, you understand, but by olfactory divination – on Tuesday last whilst helping with the flower arranging in church prior to our 'Eat It For England' Festival. Several members of the Little Hope WI had also come along to lend a hand and we were all going at it quite merrily with the Vicar until suddenly the heady perfume of old Mr Thorne's late summer roses was replaced with the unmistakable aroma of the Hull fishing fleet.

The Vicar, unaware that your sister is a kipper curer of epic proportions, experienced a bold but fleeting epiphany at that moment, during the course of which he was quite convinced that St Andrew the Apostle – summoned by the stench of damp trawlerman – was about to manifest and bless our meagre wartime festival table, which was laden with nothing more than three tins of Spam, two boxes of powdered egg and a tablecloth kindly donated by Mrs Minnie Blenkinsop from 23 Omdurman Terrace.

Sadly, the hoped-for epiphany was quickly dismissed by the overwhelming odour of mackerel and the Reverend gentleman rose from his knees just in time to point a shaking digit at a retreating figure at the back of the church, before the door slammed shut and we were left to the cruel and tragic fate of asphyxiation by slightly overdone kipper – or at least we might have been had not the verger appeared swinging a large smoking censer which had only just been returned by the starfish decoy site at Bushy End, where it had been on loan since the outbreak of hostilities.

For goodness sake, Mrs MacDonald, can you not dissuade your sibling from her current obsession with deceased mackerel and perhaps steer her in the less offensive art of mashing dead potatoes instead? Mrs Proctor of the Little Hope WI will be only too happy to instruct her in this gentle art, just say the word and she'll get her Jersey Royals out at once.

Should your sister baulk at this proposal, then might I suggest that you lure her to the crossroads at the end of the village at approximately three o'clock this coming Wednesday when Farmer Brewster of Bell End Farm will be hard at it fertilizing his crop. Get your malodourous sibling to lean against the gate to the open field on the left and then stand well back yourself, Mr Brewster hasn't been able to abide the smell of fish since Mrs Brewster left him for a Danish trawlerman and I'm quite sure that he'll be only too happy to 'accidentally' anoint your kipper of a kinswoman with a large forkful of meadow muffins.

I do hope that this helps.

Yours,

Hilda Ffinch
Hilda Ffinch,
The Bird with All The Answers

P.S. Please be aware that visiting your sister at this time is having an unfortunate knock on effect upon your good self: I could definitely smell kippers on the envelope which contained your letter, a state of affairs which upset my pussy greatly.

Can Jerry See Down My Chimney?

Mrs Alice Potter
Cranberry Cottage
Donkey Trot Lane
Little Hope

25th August 1940

Dear Mrs Ffinch,

Whilst lying in bed the other night, I remembered that I hadn't put the fireguard up and when I went downstairs to do so I suddenly had the most terrifying thought: Supposing a Jerry bomber is able to see down my chimney during the blackout and thus knows exactly where to drop his load?

Is this likely to be the case, and if so did I ought to desist from lighting a fire at night until the war is over? I've no burning desire to make myself and my little cottage a target! I've some excellent cabbages coming up and would dearly like to live to see them through to fruition.

Yours, by candlelight in the pantry,

Alice Potter, Mrs.

The Little Hope Herald
Saturday, 31st August 1940

Dear Mrs Potter,

Have you ever, in all the time you have lived in your little cottage on Donkey Trot Lane, found yourself being rudely swept out of the house and into your foxgloves by a tidal wave of rain thundering down the chimney during a summer storm? Have hailstones ever ricocheted off your fender and landed with a loud splash in your cup of Darjeeling or have you perhaps awoken on a winter's morning to find your little sitting room knee-deep in a snowdrift?

No, of course you haven't, nor are you likely to. Many a century has passed, Mrs Potter, since we English sat cross-legged in a circle about a fire in the middle of our wattle and daub huts eating roasted squirrel and watching the smoke disappear through a simple hole in the roof before idly picking our teeth with a handy bit of deer antler and then popping out to defecate in the lupins.

No indeed, times have changed. Nowadays a chimney such as yours is not simply a vertical gateway to the skies – it is a cunning funnel designed to bend a little on the way up in order to slow the passage of Mother nature's unexpected fits of pique, allowing them to melt away or burn to a crisp before they have time to annoy you, to kill you or to spoil your rag rug. Crucially, this little bend in your brickwork is also keeps peeping toms, cat-burglars and the Luftwaffe at bay.

We are a civilised race, my dear, and our chimneys are the envy of the world. I myself have a couple of particularly impressive examples, one of which is large enough for a string quartet to enter without too much ado, whereupon they might light a few sparklers, bang out a bit of Mozart and still give the Luftwaffe no hint of their presence.

So light your fire of an evening by all means, Mrs Potter, and rest assured that your glowing hole will not be visible from forty-one thousand feet above. Please be sure to put your fireguard up though, as a stray coal may indeed issue forth and land on your rug, setting the whole house ablaze and definitely enabling Herr Goering's henchmen to pinpoint not only your little cottage but indeed the entire village. I'm sure that you don't need me to tell you how unpopular you are likely to be in the vicinity on the back of such a monumental faux pas!

Good luck with the cabbages, dear, adhere to the above advice and you'll probably outlive them.

Yours,

Hilda Ffinch
Hilda Ffinch,
The Bird with All The Answers

How Thick Did It Ought To Be?

Mrs Eva Thorne
10, Kitchener Terrace
Little Hope

30th August 1940

Dear Mrs Ffinch,

How thick does the muck on one's windows need to be before it blocks out the light completely and makes one's blackout blinds redundant?

Asking on behalf of a friend, on account of difficulties of cleaning around blast tape.

Yours,
Eva Thorne

The Little Hope Herald
Saturday, 31st August 1940

Dear Mrs Thorne,

As a rule, one didn't ought to be able to grow potatoes or Webb's Wonderful Lettuce in it. That aside, the thicker the dirt the greater the likelihood of a passing wag writing his (or her) name in it. Worse still it might encourage a miscreant to draw something terribly rude which you yourself may not spot but which might be regarded with horror by the Vicar should he happen to call round rattling his collection box at you.

My advice to you is not to let the dirt build up in the first place, my dear! Many a housemaid has had a ticking off (and a corresponding short wage packet) up at Ffinch Hall in the past on account of neglecting her window cleaning duties. A weekly wipe over with a damp cloth and then a quick polish with a scrunched-up ball of newspaper does the trick nicely (apparently). Do remember to wash your hands afterwards however, as newsprint does rather tend to stain the skin, but don't throw your balls away afterwards as they might still be ironed out, cut into squares and hung in the privy in place of toilet roll.

There is, of course, a rather quirky alternative to cleaning your windows on a regular basis, and that is to let the dirt build up sufficiently so that both glass and blast tape gradually develop an impressive patina (read: coating of grime). When thick enough – and by that I mean when the blast tape is greyer than a Naval dockyard in the rain – take a clean cloth and carefully wipe just the glass panels, leaving the tape in place to fester. This will, from certain angles and in just the right light, give the impression that you possess highly desirable Elizabethan lead panes which will undoubtedly make you the envy of your neighbours.

Please note however that the above tip will greatly reduce visibility within your house, even during the hours of daylight and will therefore increase the risk of barked shins, rogue carpet tripping incidents and accidental pelvic table shunts.

Perhaps, with this in mind, consider the pros and cons of cleaning your windows properly in the first place against the cost of a new insurance premium for use in the event of having to spend six months in traction at the Sheffield Infirmary on account of an unexpected encounter with a rogue bit of carpet in (what should have been) broad daylight?

I do hope this helps, Mrs Thorne. Good luck!

Yours,

Hilda Ffinch
Hilda Ffinch,
The Bird with All The Answers

Is He 'At It' In The Pantry Again?

Mrs Felicity Bugg
Killjoy Cottage
Moorcock Lane
Little Hope

5th September 1940

Dear Mrs Ffinch,

Since marrying my husband George, some twenty or so years ago, I have prided myself in my household management skills. I have never been one to overspend, have always seen to it that even socks and tea towels are ironed and put away nicely and have kept a keen eye on the contents of my larder.

The latter exercise has historically been on account of George's keenness for a bit of spotted dick whenever one is to be had, an unfortunate taste he developed as a young man and which has seen him pile on the pounds over time. I had despaired of his ever again becoming the slim man I married until the outbreak of war bought me hope.

At first, rationing did lead to George losing weight, quite a lot of it actually, and I'd rather started fancying him again. However, over the past month or so I have noticed that he's started looking a bit 'jowly' and something – or some*one* – has been nibbling away at the contents of the larder.

I can't say for certain that it's George (as he hasn't had a spotted dick to tempt him for some time), it may after all be a mouse – but how can I be sure?

Yours,

Felicity Bugg.

The Little Hope Herald
Saturday, 7th September 1940

Dear Mrs Bugg,

Might I begin by stating unequivocally that there is absolutely nothing wrong with a bit of spotted dick – in moderation, of course?

It is a something which Colonel Ffinch and I look forward to indulging in wholeheartedly when he comes back from the front, as it were, although we do tend to go at it in the privacy of our own dining room as it's not something which we care to share with others. As my Great Aunt Alicia used to say "Spotted Dick! Spotted Dick! One gobbles quite a lot of it!" and she was something of an expert, having herself indulged heavily both at home and in continental Europe, too in the past.

Now, might I suggest the following plan be put into place with a view to ascertaining just who or what is helping themselves to the contents of your larder?

1. Gather together the ingredients for a fine spotted dick. This may take you some time, as rationing is playing havoc with grocery shopping nationwide apparently, according to my Cook who takes care of that sort of thing up at the hall, but start now and you should be sufficiently well stocked by Christmas (next year).

2. Choose a moment when you are entirely alone in the house and lock yourself away in the kitchen room thingy place.

3. Weigh out your much sought after (and probably stale, by this time) ingredients and put to one side.

4. Poke about in your dried fruit a little, adding several 'Sure Shield' fruit laxatives (8 1/2d from Dr. Hellebore's

Chemist Shop in the High Street). Mix well and perhaps take just the one yourself should your own bowels be at all sluggish (waste not, want not).

5. Do the whole mixing bits together thing (I myself am unsure as to what to add and when, obviously, but should you chance to slip a small glass of porter in front of my Cook in the snug of The Royal Oak on her night off then she will almost certainly clear up that little mystery for you and see you well on your way).

6. Cook, or boil, or braise, or roast or whatever the whole thing in a suitable receptacle.

7. When cooked, turn your masterpiece out onto a large plate and leave to cool before slipping your dick into the pantry, ensuring that it is spotted side up.

8. *Do not, under any circumstances, forget that there is a Mickey Finn in your spotted dick and accidentally try some yourself.*

9. Keep schtum about what's in the larder and monitor your spouse's bowel movements over the course of the next 48 hours or so. (If he has been 'at it' and has to move into the outside privy for the duration, then perhaps consider sandbagging the roof of the outhouse in question, for Mr Bugg will almost certainly still be in there when the sirens sound of an evening).

10. Should your husband's bowel movements fail to result in demonic rumbles and the manifestation of a brown rain pitiful to behold, then the culprit is almost certainly the small rodent of which you spoke. There will be little point in putting a trap down for it as by this time it will almost certainly have combusted and will be decorating your pantry walls – further proof of your husband's innocence should it be required.

I do hope that this is helpful. With regard to Mr Bugg's weight gain – should pantry burglary prove not to be the cause – then maybe have a quick word with Mr Doris Golightly of Kitchener Terrace, who, local gossip suggests, has been getting her Belgian buns out for your husband on a Tuesday evening when he's out and about with his Home Guard patrol?

I do hope this helps.

Yours,

Hilda Ffinch
Hilda Ffinch,
The Bird with All The Answers

III.

What Shall We Tell the Children?
(The ones who have turned thirty are
particularly problematic)

"The truth," said Hilda, over dinner at The Savoy with Colonel Ffinch who was home on leave from the front, "Is of paramount importance and didn't ever ought to be suppressed."

"In that case, you ought to know that we're not doing terribly well in France at present," replied her erstwhile spouse, "I didn't want to worry you and so…"

"Do be quiet and pass the salt, dear," Hilda brushed his comment aside. "Did you know that old Mr Peabody has taken up Morris dancing?"

Is It Too 'Lardy-Da'?

'Worried Mum'
Wits End

23rd March 1940

Dear Mrs Ffinch,

Teenage son wants to know if lard is a good replacement for Brylcreem as he's expecting his call up papers any time now. He's always been very particular about his appearance and does want to look his best when sallying forth to give Jerry a good seeing to.

Any advice most welcome.

Thanks,

'Worried Mum'

𝔗𝔥𝔢 𝔏𝔦𝔱𝔱𝔩𝔢 𝔥𝔬𝔭𝔢 𝔥𝔢𝔯𝔞𝔩𝔡
Saturday, 30th March 1940

Dear 'Worried Mum',

Firstly, sort your grammar out, one cannot simply start a letter with the words 'Teenage son', one is missing an initial possessive pronoun! (Apologies for being a little short, I've been waiting for a month now for the merchant fleet to make it into Hull with a consignment of coffee beans and I'm getting rather desperate. A quick ruffle through my gardener's chicory and a sniff at his acorns just isn't doing it for me anymore).

Now, down to business. Which regiment will your son be joining? If it's a rufty-tufty desert commando lot then yes, absolutely use lard – it will come in handy for loosening tight nuts and attracting highly nutritious cockroaches should the food situation become dire and the camels take off in the night.

Other than that, the answer is an unequivocal 'No!' on the grounds that no nice girl will want to walk out with a fellow who smells of rancid pork and attracts cats.

The sort of doxy whom your son will undoubtedly attract should he choose not to follow my advice is likely to be wholly unsuitable and in possession of dubious morals. Sex will undoubtedly occur. Do you wish to spend your old age peering closely at your boy's purported offspring wondering if you've willed the family silver to your own flesh and blood or to the grandchild of a gong farmer?

One suspects not!

To that end, take heed, 'Worried Mum', take heed! Set your lad on the right path now, whilst there is still time!

Good luck to your boy and his regiment and God Save The King!

Yours,

Hilda Ffinch
Hilda Ffinch,
The Bird with All The Answers

P.S. Perhaps consider slipping a packet or prophylactics into your boy's tunic pocket before he sets off, just in case. If he does use it for the conventional purpose then all well and good, but if it's looking a little redundant after a month or so then maybe write to him and suggest that he slips it over the end of his weapon just to keep the damp out.

Where Do Babies Come From?

Mrs Edna Muffin
Corkscrew Cottage
Tart's Hill

9th April 1940

Dear Mrs Ffinch,

My daughter, Rosy, is now of an age when she's starting to ask questions about 'where babies come from' and I'm not sure what to tell her. I've always been very shy and self-conscious about – well, you *know,* that sort of thing – and I'm really not sure if I can bring myself to explain the facts of life to her.

Please help!

Yours,

Edna Muffin

The Little Hope Herald
Saturday, 13th April 1940

Dear Mrs Muffin,

Had you asked me this question before the outbreak of war I would have advised you to have a stiff gin and then take your child to the monkey house at the Regent's Park Zoo where you could have merely stood and pointed at any one of a number of suitable tableaux imitating the human condition from A to Z.

As things stand however, you're off the hook. Take your child to Little Hope Station and await the arrival of the next trainload of evacuees from dear old London town, play your cards right and I am sure that Rosy will have no problem accepting the fact that babies arrive on platform two at three in the afternoon.

I do hope this helps.

Yours,

Hilda Ffinch
Hilda Ffinch,
The Bird with All The Answers

About That 'Five Knuckle Shuffler'...

Arabella Sparks
Cook's Cottage
Hollow Bottom
Greater Hope

18th April 1940

Dear Mrs Ffinch,

I do consider myself both well travelled and well educated, but I recently came across a turn of phrase which has me rather perplexed.

My fifteen-year-old son was out late one evening and, on searching the village for him (lest the Luftwaffe catch him in the open), I espied him running from the bus shelter outside The Royal Oak public house, where the local youth tend to congregate. As he made good his getaway, I heard a lad call after him that he was a *'Five Knuckle Shuffler'*?

Now I know Herbert can be a little wild at times, as indeed is the case with many a young man these days, but I am certain that he's no croupier and that his experience of card playing has never really moved on from a quick game of 'Old Maid' with his sister and I on a Sunday evening after tea, and only then if there's nothing interesting on the wireless, so I was wondering if you could help with an explanation of the phrase in question?

Many thanks in anticipation,

Mrs Arabella Sparks

𝕿𝖍𝖊 𝕷𝖎𝖙𝖙𝖑𝖊 𝕳𝖔𝖕𝖊 𝕳𝖊𝖗𝖆𝖑𝖉
Saturday, 20th April 1940

Dear Mrs Sparks,

The male of the species, my dear, can be particularly feral at times, especially when young and caught in the merciless glare of a full moon, and I'm guessing that that was what set these callow rapscallions off. Really, one wonders where it will all end. One pins one's hopes on the local army recruiting office which ought to put a stop to their gallop.

But getting back to your letter and the matter in hand. As I do not wish to offend the sensitive and maidenly (nor indeed those of a more worldly persuasion who find such a topic a little too stimulating for their own good) let me reply to you in couched terms.

If you were to ask me on the 8th of August (for example) why the Bishop of Rochester hadn't appeared to open the village fete as promised, I might give you a sideways glance before nodding towards the Vicarage and replying knowingly:

"Oh, he's sure to come soon dear, he's just in there celebrating Palm Sunday…"

Or possibly:

"He's rather busy auditioning the Arch*deacon* at the moment, tricky when in a hurry, but I'm sure he'll pull it off as quickly as possible…"

You know, that sort of thing?

The above are classic examples of the exquisite art of the euphemism, something at which we British excel on account of our complete inability to openly discuss anything other than the weather and cricket. Our national aversion to the vocal articulation of matters of a sexual nature when in the company of others can be a trifle crippling at times and is occasionally wont to give rise to confusion and misunderstanding. Even Colonel Ffinch and I decline all discussion of an intimate nature other than the former's occasional 'wondering out loud' over dinner whether his billiards cue might borrow my triangle to line his balls up later.

Comprehend?

Another example of the euphemism might be based upon our own Constable Clink's unavoidable male proclivities. Supposing a small crowd of people had gathered outside the Little Hope Police Station and you – unsure of the cause – asked of me "What on earth is going on, Mrs Ffinch?"

I might then raise an eyebrow and tap the side of my nose before replying discretely that the good constable had been caught "Badgering his witness" or was possibly apprehended "Tipping off the Inspector."

Are you following me, my dear?

For additional clarification, should it be required – Mr Peabody the greengrocer might be caught 'Curing his cucumber' or 'Waxing his carrot' upon occasion, Mr Trotter the butcher from the Yorkshire Meat Emporium in the High Street may enjoy 'Wrestling his eel' or very possibly 'Seasoning his sausage' when he has a moment to himself and I think that we all know that dear Major Boothe-Royde from the Salvation Army enjoys 'Blowing his own trumpet' round the back of The Royal Oak at least twice a week.

I do hope that this has cleared matters up for you, Arabella. Five knuckle shuffling has nothing *whatsoever* to do with card games, although one might still categorise it under the heading 'sleight of hand'.

Yours conspiratorially,

Hilda Ffinch
Hilda Ffinch,
The Bird with All The Answers

P.S. If you do happen to come across the Bishop at the cake stall this year and decide to shake hands, perhaps best if you keep your gloves on anyway, just to be on the safe side?

A Worried Mother…

'Ashamed' of Kitchener Close

1st June 1940

Dear Mrs Ffinch,

My unmarried daughter has been having shenanigans with a soldier who has run off! I'm at my wits end. The neighbours aren't talking to me. I've had vicious letters from them posted through my letter box calling *me* a harlot as well AND they're giving me funny looks in the ration queue!

Please *please* help because I think Gloria may be up the spout!

Yours hopefully,

'Ashamed'

𝕿𝖍𝖊 𝕷𝖎𝖙𝖙𝖑𝖊 𝕳𝖔𝖕𝖊 𝕳𝖊𝖗𝖆𝖑𝖉
Saturday, 8th June 1940

Dear Shamed One,

Whilst your daughter's wanton ways leave a sour taste in the mouths of the righteous here in the offices of the local 'rag', I can in part sympathise with you regarding your inquisitive neighbours!

There are instances when the silence (or sudden death) of one's neighbours is to be truly desired! The Colonel and I came to this conclusion in Simla in '31 when our own neighbours, the detestable Much-Flemings' from three villas down (persistent note senders – *"Please do come to tea?"* to which I habitually responded *"I think not!"* in private, before accepting) were detained at His Majesty's Pleasure for an entire week on suspicion of breaking and entering into the tent of the Maharajah of Pungalore.

The tent was a truly magnificent affair, and apparently it was His Highness' unexpected nocturnal arrival and the sudden erection of his sleeping quarters which led the Much-Flemings (who were full of gin at the time) to mistake it for the opening gambit of the annual Simla Scout Jamboree. After a lot of shuffling about with a nightlight and the dangling of a woggle through the Maharajah's flap, the Much-Flemings were carted off by his bodyguards and turned over to the British authorities, who weren't at all impressed with the couple's hijinks.

The silence which settled over those of us dwelling behind the colours in Simla once the Much-Flemings were out of the way for a while was, I have to say, utter bliss and it made life that little bit more bearable in the extreme heat of an Indian summer. One even stopped pining for Fortnum & Mason, briefly.

Thankfully, the Much-Flemings – when finally re-released into the wild – refrained from ever sending a runner to our villa with an invitation to tea again, principally on account of the pair of them being sent home on a very slow steamer – which point brings me back nicely to the content of your missive.

One has to wonder at what point in time, madam, you decided that it wasn't worth telling your hormonally charged daughter that she was of an age when it's wise to keep one's knees together and avoid touching raw meat?

Traditionally, in a decent Christian household, this conversation takes place just prior to The Wanton One reaching puberty. If – and I doubt this very much given that you and your husband have seven and twelve children respectively – you find explaining the sexual act too embarrassing a subject to broach, might you not have considered taking Miss Floosie on an outing to the monkey house at Regent's Park Zoo? She would have got the picture in no time at all then, my dear.

As it stands, you failed. Your daughter is, it seems, to bless you with a grandchild on the strength of a bag of fish and chips and a bottle of Tizer from a passing soldier who is probably halfway to John o' Groats by now. This being the case, might I suggest that you either pack her off 'to the seaside' for the next ten months or so and entrust her to the care of a maiden aunt with a face like a bucket or give in gracefully, have all your teeth removed and purchase a flat cap and brace of ferrets for your husband?

Yours patronisingly,

Hilda Ffinch
Hilda Ffinch,
The Bird with All The Answers

The Golden Rivet...

'Even More Worried Mum'
Lower Purgatory

9th July 1940

Dear Mrs Ffinch,

I read your letter from the worried mum about her son and Brylcreem. Quite worrying for her I'm sure, and now my own son has been called up to join the Royal Navy.

My old grandfather sailed with the fleet before the last war and keeps telling our Percy to watch out for navy cake when he joins up. I am a bit concerned because Percy has to watch his diet or he comes out in hives and is quite unwell for a bit.

Worse still, my boy is not at all mechanically minded and Grandad has also told him to keep a weather eye out for the golden rivet on board his ship?

Do you have any advice for my lad?

Yours hopefully,

'Even More Worried Mum'

𝕿𝖍𝖊 𝕷𝖎𝖙𝖙𝖑𝖊 𝕳𝖔𝖕𝖊 𝕳𝖊𝖗𝖆𝖑𝖉
Saturday, 13th July 1940

Dear 'Even More Worried Mum',

You are right to be concerned, my dear – and not merely on account of the German navy! I speak from experience, coming from an old seafaring family myself, where hair-raising tales of goings-on and derring-do on the high seas were rarely saved for the company of gentlemen alone and quite often made one prod one's pork nervously with a fork over dinner.

Now, 'Rum, sodomy and the lash!' may be something which one titters about with one's friends over a dry sherry or two when discussing both our own Royal and mercantile fleets these days, but take heed dear madam when I say that a life on the ocean wave can be jolly perilous, and unless you sew young Percy firmly into his naval britches for the duration of the war he may well find himself on the receiving end of quite a bit of navy cake, and it may not be entirely to his taste!

You see, your grandsire is clearly aware that on board ship there is a certain type of matelot who is wont to go a bit funny after a while on account of spending too long at sea without female company. This type of fellow may begin to hallucinate – like a man becalmed in the doldrums with nothing but a gramophone and a single Noel Coward record to keep him company for six weeks or so – and he may start to fancy that Percy is, in fact, a young lady in need of wooing. This being the case, he may then ask your boy to bend over and pick up a phantom 'golden rivet' which is nowhere to be seen. Percy will *not* thank you for not warning him about this, Mother!

Might you perhaps consider tattooing your boy with numerous images of scantily dressed ladies and changing his name to 'Bonecrusher' before he sets off to answer his country's call? This worked jolly well for my somewhat effeminate cousin Everard who left the wall with the fleet just after the last war. It certainly kept funny sailors at bay but sadly didn't deter a tribe of frightfully ill-mannered cannibals in Papua New Guinea, but we still drink to him every Christmas Eve before tucking into our roast pork and stuffing.

I do hope that this helps.

Good luck to your darling boy and Rule Britannia, dear!

Yours,

Hilda Ffinch
Hilda Ffinch,
The Bird with All The Answers

Balls…

Mrs Bet R. Swallow
Dick's Mount Cottage
Jolley Bottom
Little Hope

26th August 1940

Dear Mrs Ffinch,

I am of the family Swallow of Swaledale, recently moved into Little Hope due to unforeseen family circumstances. My late husband passed away on active service and as a result of his penchant for gambling, well suffice to say, one has had to downsize to pay his debts.

My daughter Belinda recently started working in 'that factory' on the Bell End Road, doing her bit for the war effort, and has become rather friendly with a Miss Muff-Hawker who apparently hails from nearby and lives on licensed premises.

Now I have nothing against people in the publican trade, being partial to a small libation myself, but I do fear that Belinda's innocence may be becoming compromised. I happened to be walking past a certain local hostelry one evening, having been out to take tea with a friend who lives nearby, when I overheard a partial conversation between two young girls in the blackout. I immediately recognised my daughter's voice and also that of young Miss Muff-Hawker, emanating from a darkened alleyway adjacent to said public house.

I have to say, I was rather shocked when I heard Miss Muff-Hawker say to my daughter "Take it from me Bel, policemen have bigger balls than firemen" and I was even more shocked to hear my daughter ask her to explain the magnitude of the difference – so shocked in fact I didn't stay to hear the answer.

So, in a nutshell, what is the difference between policemen's and firemen's balls?

Yours in shock,

Bet Swallow

The Little Hope Herald
Saturday, 31ˢᵗ August 1940

Dear Mrs Swallow (late of Swaledale),

First of all, might I take the opportunity to welcome you to Little Hope and to offer my deepest condolences on the death of your husband? In these troubled times I fear that the fate of all of us is determined by the roll of a heavenly dice, a thought which – given your late spouse's penchant for gambling – may give you some comfort.

Now that we've got the obligatory commiserations/pleasantries out of the way, on to the subject in hand – balls.

I myself have only ever had anything to do with officers' balls, truth be told, and quite a few of those encounters have been under duress if I'm to be entirely honest. I have lost count of the times Colonel Ffinch has asked me if I fancy holding one of an evening, but frankly, if I am unprepared and already engrossed in a game of backgammon then it's not going to happen..

In my comparative experience however – leaving policemen and firemen aside – I can tell you this much:

- Cavalrymen's balls tend to be the biggest (given that so many members of the aristocracy are fond of a bit of horseplay) but they are certainly not the best. There is obviously an olfactory downside to spending twelve hours a day in the saddle, and it is one which no amount of Ascot Aftershave lotion can cure. Aside from the smell of the stables and terribly rough hands, saddle sores do rather tend to inhibit free movement and render a quick bash at 'The Shag' nigh on impossible.

- Infantrymen's balls tend to be slightly smaller as a rule but do have 'a lot of go' in them given that those fine fellows are used to physical exercise in the field and can keep it up for hours at a time without appearing to tire. Full of derring-do then, one might reasonably expect to enjoy a 'Rhumba' or two in the moonlight with these chaps and possibly a quick 'Bunny Hug' in the orangery afterwards but beware their annoying habit of whipping their bayonets out at the slightest provocation.

- The Gordon Highlander's balls are a little too gay for my liking, I've never been one for fannying about and can't abide all that leaping up and down above unsheathed weapons, far too dangerous given that even a small prick can ladder one's stockings or sever an artery if delivered at high speed. I'll say no more except to add that in my experience, Highland Flings are never as diverting as one might initially hope.

- The Intelligence Corps' balls tend to be the smallest of the lot (positively miniscule by comparison) as they like to keep everything under wraps lest one opens one's mouth and inadvertently lets everything out. Depending on the current state of international affairs and who has made it back from the deserts of North Africa this week one might possibly wrangle a 'Camel Walk' out of a fellow but he may well be plagued with sand-flies and ague.

- I'm not even sure that I've ever really got the point of the Royal Lancer's balls.

Now, returning to the source of your query. I am familiar with the Muff-Hawkers and should warn you that the hostelry to which you allude is not the most salubrious of establishments. That said, I believe that Mrs Edith Muff-Hawker, the mother of your daughter's friend, has held a couple of local policemen's balls there which, obviously, are not going to be quite the handful that the ones I've occasionally held for Colonel Ffinch and his regiment tend to be.

Firemen's balls are a mystery to me I have to admit, never having held one, but I would imagine that they might be deemed rather dangerous given the extreme length of the average fireman's hose, at least one of which is bound to crop up and be waved about for all and sundry to see during the course of the evening.

My advice to you, therefore, would be to take your daughter to one side and gently explain that although all balls are similar, the higher the social position of the individual the more impressive the rhumba is likely to be.

I do hope that this information is helpful.

Yours,

Hilda Ffinch
Hilda Ffinch
The Bird with All The Answers

A Bit of 'Slap and Tickle'

Mrs Dora Brown
Crimea Cottage
Bellows End
Greater Hope

9th September 1940

Dear Mrs Ffinch,

My young lad, too young to follow his brother into uniform, has been telling me that he was scared witless the other night. He was walking past a local hostelry when a scantily clad woman beckoned to him from a nearby alley. Now I know he looks older than his tender years, but thankfully when she offered him "a bit of slap and tickle for a bob" he didn't hang about but ran home and told me what happened (and also asked for a raise in his pocket money, for some reason).

I'm a bit mithered about someone offering to slap and tickle my lad, and I have heard rumours that some of the men in the village have been seen heading down that ginnel after leaving the pub of an evening.

What *is* going on down there?

Yours,
Mrs Dora Brown

The Little Hope Herald
Saturday, 14th September 1940

Dear Mrs Brown,

Was the public house in question 'The Cat and Cabbage' in Hampton Upon Mott, perchance? Rumour has it that the place is an absolute den of iniquity where a lot more than a 'bit of slap and tickle' might be had on a Thursday evening for the price of two pairs of stockings, a packet of Huntley & Palmers biscuits and a jar of imported melon and lemon jam (the latter being extremely rare, given that it has to avoid the erect periscopes of the German navy *and* a rough handling by a beefy docker with terribly impressive thighs in the port of Liverpool before it reaches your pantry).

Now, I'm sure that you do actually know the meaning of 'a bit of slap and tickle' my dear, on the grounds that I don't imagine for one moment that your own child came into the world as the result of a chance encounter with an archangel, a shooting star and three exhausted wise men up to their eyes in brambles and badger spoor in the Bell End Wood. In short, one hears that 'ladies of the evening' have been 'hawking their muffs' (the Colonel's expression, not mine) in Hampton Upon Mott for some time now and something really must be done about it!

With this in mind, Mrs Nelly Covert and Miss Titty Parlour of the Little Hope Women's Institute are planning to picket the place on Thursday next, just before closing time. They will be joined by the Rev Aubrey Fishwick, who is still terribly miffed at having to forgo his regular Tuesday luncheon at The Cat and Cabbage on account of the landlady having taken up with a Jerry prisoner of war, as a consequence of which sauerkraut is now being served in place of Webb's Wonderful Lettuce, much to the Vicar's chagrin.

Major Boothe-Royde of the Salvation Army will also be in attendance, and given that Mrs Boothe-Royde has recently left Little Hope to take up a missionary position in the Belgian Congo with Mr Golightly our former ARP warden, the Major has taken it upon himself to minister to the fallen and ungodly with the impressive vigour of a man possessed.

Should you wish to join in the protest yourself then please do feel free to go along but remember to take your own sandwiches, burning cross, and a thermos flask of tea. You may also wish to equip yourself with a tambourine, triangle or other percussion instrument with a view to drowning out any counter-protest with a rousing chorus of 'Roll out the Barrel (of Hot Tar)' if needs be. Please dress sensibly and modestly yourself as once Major Boothe-Royde gets going there's no stopping the man, and should he mistake you for one of Mrs Muff-Hawker's regulars he'll have you flat on your back for a quick exorcism in the blink of an eye.

As for your boy, please do fight the urge to take him along. I'm sure that you will understand when I say that absolutely no good whatsoever would have come of him having slipped up that particular back passage the other night and no good will come of him witnessing the deliverance of Mrs Edith Muff-Hawker on Thursday evening, particularly if she's forgotten to put her teeth in again and is interrupted during the course of a half achieved victory roll.

Yours in temperance and modesty,

Hilda Ffinch
Hilda Ffinch,
The Bird with All The Answers

A Tale of Two Johnnies…

Mrs F Dither
Nelson's Nest
Little Hope

20th October 1940

Dear Mrs Ffinch,

I'll come straight to the matter in hand as there's no point beating about the bush: My nine-year-old son, little Johnny, marched into the kitchen yesterday with a packet of prophylactics in his hand saying he'd found a packet of balloons and would I help him to blow one up.

What do I tell the child? His Father – Captain Dither – is away on active service with the navy and didn't get around to 'having the talk' with him before departing and I wouldn't know where to start.

Yours,

Frances Dither, Mrs

The Little Hope Herald
Saturday, 26th October 1940

Dear Mrs Dither,

It pains me greatly to once again hear the 'in a sexual pickle' klaxon going, but clearly, I do. I have lost count of the number of times I have exhorted the villagers of Little Hope to take their children to the Regent's Park Zoo in order that the facts of life be – if not exactly explained to them – then certainly most graphically illustrated within the confines of the monkey house. Had you taken heed of my column earlier in life, Mrs Dither, and had Captain Dither kept *his* column under wraps (as the Americans say) in the first place then you would not now find yourself in this awkward position. However, as neither sensible route was taken then it falls to me to guide you out of the woods and back onto the beaten path.

Might I suggest that in this instance you gamely take a prophylactic from the packet and indulge your child's naïve fantasy by blowing one up and exclaiming that yes, it is indeed a very fine balloon? In this manner, you might let the whole matter blow over and avoid having to clear up what Captain Dither ought to have done before leaving the wall with his seamen. If you can let the matter lie then please do and leave your spouse to fill in the sordid details in a manly fashion when he finally comes sailing home.

Do not, however, think to write and admonish your seafaring husband for neglecting his paternal responsibilities at this time, for our brave lions of the sea (not to be confused with the unfortunate circus creatures balancing balls on their noses in their quest for a kipper or two) have quite enough on their plates at present with German naval telescopes popping up willy-nilly all over the place. There will be time enough for recriminations, long silences and planks of wood separating the two halves of your marital bed once the war is won and the fleet is back in port, as it were.

A final thought though – do pop the 'balloon' in question before your child is able to leave the house and skip gaily up the road with it tied to a stick, lest it be thought locally that you are advertising your services to the lovesick and the forlorn. You might also wish to ensure that the remaining prophylactics in the packet 'meet a sticky end' as it were whilst your child is not looking. Out of sight, Mrs Dither, means out of mind. Tell him that the dog ate them, or that they mysteriously self-inflated and blew away overnight like little zeppelins to bomb Herr Hitler. Children love fairy stories, that should do the trick.

I do hope that this helps.

Yours,

Hilda Ffinch
Hilda Ffinch,
The Bird with All The Answers

P.S. Should you decide to reserve one prophylactic for use by your husband upon his return, please be advised that they do have a 'sell-by' date which must be adhered to lest you find yourself lumbered with another little Johnnie and the possibility of this whole scenario repeating itself in a few years' time ad infinitum, until you are quite old and withered and completely devoid of teeth.

'Ben Dover and the Fireman's Helmet'...

Dorothy Prim
Belladonna Cottage
Knob End
Little Hope

4th November 1940

Dear Mrs Ffinch,

My son Edgar, aged nine and a half, came home from the Little Hope Library yesterday with what I consider to be a book very unsuitable for the under tens: *Ben Dover and The Fireman's Helmet*. The language in it is shocking – I've twice come across the word 'dam!' whilst perusing it!

I've confiscated the book for now, but my question is this – should I go and have a word with the librarian?

Yours,

Mrs D. Prim

𝔗𝔥𝔢 𝔏𝔦𝔱𝔱𝔩𝔢 𝔥𝔬𝔭𝔢 𝔥𝔢𝔯𝔞𝔩𝔡
Saturday, 9th November 1940

Dear Mrs Prim,

I have examined the tome in question and no, you didn't ought to go and remonstrate with our village librarian – unless, of course, your primary aim in life is to look a bit of a twit.

Ben Dover, dear Mrs Prim, is England's answer to Hans Brinker (the little boy who put his finger into the Dutch dyke) and is just the sort of role model you ought to be making your child aware of.

Now obviously, here in England we don't have anywhere *near* the number of dykes that our European neighbours do but that's not to say that those which we *do* have don't need plugging occasionally.

Additionally, The Fireman's Helmet in question was that which Ben Dover used to plug the dyke's hole during a downpour of Biblical proportions and that the 'dam' which has rendered you all of a dither was, in fact, the little house of Mr Bush the Beaver, who – had you made it as far as page twenty-two – you would have realised helped to save the day when the floods came by also stuffing his store of foraged mushrooms into the dyke until the local policeman came, which didn't take long, as it happened.

Really, Mrs Prim. Go to the back of the class and stand with your finger on your lips until home time!

Yours,

Hilda Ffinch
Hilda Ffinch,
The Bird with All The Answers

IV.

Fashion on the Ration

"You've never looked lovelier, darling…" said Colonel Ffinch later that evening as he and Hilda stood on the terrace at Ffinch Manor and watched the moon rise over the frozen lake, "but do I detect the faint whiff of mothballs?"

"Yes," Hilda replied, taking his hand and placing it directly onto her muff, "I really ought to have got this out into the fresh air weeks ago…"

A Problematic Muff...

Mrs Agatha Bird
25 Agincourt Avenue
Greater Hope

5th October 1939

Dear Mrs Ffinch,

Could you please advise me on how to keep my muff clean and in pristine condition? I do like to show it off on cold days as it's rather grand and the envy of many of my neighbours!

Sincerely yours,

Mrs Agatha Bird

The Little Hope Herald
Saturday, 7th October 1939

Dear Mrs Bird,

Firstly, might I enquire as to the age and current condition of your muff? I ask simply because there's nothing more profoundly disturbing to the male of our species than accidentally coming across a withering pelt, whether it be sweating its follicles off on display at a Summer fete or keeping out the cold in the bleak midwinter, as it were.

We ladies do of course tend to be a little more forgiving as, let's face it, we sport a muff for most of our adult lives and are therefore privy to the pitfalls of tending to our beloved finger warmers. It isn't always an easy task though and I'm quite sure that most of us have had to resort to mothballs or a fly swat at one point or another.

Do be sure to give your furry friend a good shake from time to time, preferably in the great outdoors (but not in the High Street) as this will help to free any unwanted lodgers, and follow this up with a quick but firm finger ruffle. If you are able, a quick comb through with a little edible oil should prove beneficial but – war or no war – do avoid using lard as a substitute as this will only attract horseflies and cats, neither of which will do your reputation in the village any good and I'm fairly sure that Mr Bird will also be singularly unimpressed.

Self-service is the phrase to remember, my dear, self-service! Be sure to give your muff a regular seeing-to and get plenty of fresh air to it and all will be well!

Yours,

Hilda Ffinch
Hilda Ffinch,
The Bird with All The Answers (and the terribly luxuriant muff)

How Thick Should It Be?

Mrs N. Batt
36, KOYLI Terrace
Greater Hope

1st December 1939

Dear Ms Ffinch,

What consistency do I need for my gravy browning to make the stocking seams on my legs, please?

Thanks in advance,

N. Batt (Mrs)

The Little Hope Herald
Saturday, 2nd December 1939

Dear Mrs Batt,

As a rule of thumb, it needs to be the consistency of the British Restaurants' weekday drivel and absolutely *not* your homemade Sunday best.

Anything stiffer than strong tea and you'll find it will set solid and cause you to goose-step up and down the High Street and really, nobody in this village will suffer such an insult lightly.

Yours,

Hilda Ffinch
Hilda Ffinch,
The Bird with All The Answers

I'm A Little on The Large Side...

Miss Barbara Large
Heaving Croft
Hanger Lane
Greater Hope

9th January 1940

Dear Ms Ffinch,

I am having difficulty in finding an adequately fitting brassiere on account of my fuller figure and rather large bosoms. Sourcing ladies' undergarments is becoming more of an issue by the day, as I am sure you will appreciate.

I've been rather enterprising however and am looking further afield than the ration queue outside the drapers in the High Street and have hit upon an idea. Could you recommend a British army regiment who might give a few yards of parachute material or similar to help me keep my modesty intact? Might the RAF be able to help?

Desperately yours,

Miss Barbara Large

The Little Hope Herald
Saturday, 13th January 1940

Dear Miss Large,

I'm not at all sure, my dear, that even the Parachute Regiment has enough silk in its arsenal to cover your assets this side of our finally winning the war. Without wishing to be overtly personal, I was on hand to witness the hullabaloo caused at the greengrocers on Thursday last when you inadvertently took out two crates of Webb's Wonderful Lettuce and poor Mr Augustus

Peabody the greengrocer himself on account of your sizeable bosom commandeering his shop counter and tipping the scales in his general direction. The poor man cracked his spectacles rather badly, although there's some conjecture as to whether this happened spontaneously on noting your approach or on account of his having come a cropper, as it were, when suffering facial contact with a 2lb brass weight.

That said, one does appreciate the difficulties you must be facing and, after much thought, I think I may have the answer. I am sending you a parcel (second class) containing two old colanders and the front flap of a khaki tent, the latter having been kindly donated by the Girl Guides of Little Hope (Beaver Patrol) that you might construct an original and unique brassiere for yourself.

This will hopefully not only be of use to you but will also enable the girls to attain their bushcraft badges (the tent having been quietly dismantled and removed without the Boy Scouts who were sleeping in it at the time even noticing) thereby killing two birds with one stone. It is key for the safety of the village that the girls get this badge under their belts and out of the way as I know for certain that young Phyllis Creeper (Thrush Patrol) is particularly adept at fire starting and is keen to have her talents acknowledged following the debacle at this summer's village fete where she may, or may not, have set the tombola tent alight as a result of feeling woefully undervalued.

But back to your issue. Obviously, canvas alone will not suffice to keep your barrage balloons tethered to the lawn, as it were, but with a little ingenuity, the aforementioned colanders and some garden twine I think that you may yet have the brass neck to appear in public again and restore at least a little dignity.

Now, obviously, one is aware that we are, as a country, constantly being exhorted by the Government to save our old pots and pans for making spitfires, but Constable Clink assures me that no action will be taken against you for reinforcing a canvas brassiere with said colanders, particularly as – in a tight corner – they might still be used to strain the greens if required, so to speak.

If I might just add a little fashion tip before finishing, do think on and remove the base of each colander before covering them with said charitably donated fabric, otherwise you may inadvertently adopt the aspect of a dreadnought about to fire a couple of broadsides and mass panic and mayhem might ensue.

 I do hope this helps.

Yours,

Hilda Ffinch
Hilda Ffinch,
The Bird with All The Answers

A Shocking Matter…

Mrs Betty Pollock
Dick's Retreat
Little Hope

8th January 1940

Dear Mrs Ffinch,

Of late, I seem to be having problems with my nylon stockings. The static build-up when I have them on is so great that I keep receiving shocks in my privy parts and it's unnerving my husband who is currently home on leave from the RAF.

I suspect that he thinks I am over keen for a bit of 'you-know-what' on account of him being back and that this is at the root of my problem, when in fact my primary concern is that the sparks may cause irreparable smoke damage to my nether regions!

Yours most desperately,

Betty Pollock

The Little Hope Herald
Saturday, 13th January 1940

Dear Mrs Pollock,

What a shocking predicament you find yourself in, might I begin by saying that you have my firm support – which is clearly more than can be said for your choice of hosiery.

May I suggest that you take the following steps in order to ensure that if sparks do fly between your spouse and yourself then they are of the right nature and for reasons of pleasure rather than what could best be described as a half-achieved attempt at self-immolation?

1. Purchase some prophylactics from Mr Leach the chemist in the High Street. (If you're too embarrassed to go in there yourself for a packet then my lame gamekeeper, Dick Scratcher will be more than happy to give you one in the alleyway behind Trotter's Meat Emporium in the High Street, providing that you give him enough time to get up there).

2. Remove your stockings (N.B. if you're still in the alleyway behind the Meat Emporium then please do ensure that Dick isn't still hanging around, his lame appendage is one thing but I have an overgrown bush which requires his attention and I'd rather you didn't endanger his eyesight or interfere with his blood pressure before he's had a chance to see to it).

3. Remove the fabric garter clips from your suspender belt and replace each one with a rubber sheath, taking care to attach each end with a clove hitch, as a sudden twang in the nether regions can quite take one by surprise and lead to a particularly vocal involuntary ejaculation which – whilst it's fine within the confines of one's own home – isn't something you'd want to happen outside the greengrocers or in front of the Vicar.

4. Double-check that your knots are secure and then put your stockings back on and secure them to your garter belt as usual, perhaps adding a dab of heady perfume such as 'Soir de Paris' in order to mask the faint (but inevitable) whiff of rubber.

Et voila! You should now be fully insulated and able to resume intimate relations with your spouse without needing to wear gumboots and a backpack containing a stirrup pump and field dressings.

Yours,

Hilda Ffinch
Hilda Ffinch,
The Bird with All The Answers

P.S. Obviously, if you have no burning desire to procreate at this point, make sure that you have enough prophylactics left after fireproofing your stockings to still give your husband one anyway, as it were.

Did I Ought to Beat Them Off?

Mrs N. Batt
36 KOYLI Terrace
Greater Hope

25th March 1940

Dear Ms Ffinch,

Thank you so much for your recent reply about gravy browning, very useful it was too.

I wonder though, could you further assist me with some advice on how to prevent the local dogs (and the occasional male human) from trying to lick the gravy browning off my legs?

Personally, I'm not too concerned about it but it is very upsetting for my dear husband.

Yours hopefully,

N. Batt (Mrs)

The Little Hope Herald
Saturday, 30th March 1940

Dear Mrs Batt,

It gladdens my heart that our previous correspondence proved useful to you and that as a result of having taken my advice you are not currently incarcerated in Holloway Prison's F-Wing with a particularly riotous mob of socially unacceptable fifth columnists on the back of an inadvertent goose-stepping incident in the High Street as discussed. I believe that your sacroiliac joint will also thank me in later life as strutting about with one's legs above one's 'Mason Dixon Line' is known to wreak havoc on the lower back after a while and may also cause rather debilitating haemorrhoids.

Moving on to the matter in hand though, might I suggest that on this occasion you shoo the local dogs away by giving them a swift nip with your laundry tongs? A sharp pinch on the nose with a pair of those big boys will have even the most ferocious of hounds cowering in fear before running for the hills.

With regard to the somewhat forward fellows who are causing you such consternation in the High Street, might I suggest that you strike up a brief conversation with them after the first lick to ascertain whether or not they might be American? There are a great many journalists from the old colony pottering about here in Blighty at the moment and I don't think that I need to remind you that our transatlantic cousins are always good for stockings, perfume and chocolate, and so think of the old adage about never looking a gift horse in the mouth before rebuffing their attentions entirely.

On the other hand, should the said fellows indeed turn out to be local men from the village, have at them with the laundry tongs at once and show no mercy.

Yours,

Hilda Ffinch
Hilda Ffinch,
The Bird with All The Answers

A Big Head…

Miss Caroline Hepplethwaite
7 Omdurman Street
Little Hope

9th May 1940

Dear Mrs Ffinch,

I have now reached the age where I'd like to wear a nice hat on my weekly visit to the cinema in Sheffield with my boyfriend but unfortunately Mother Nature decided to give me a rather large head. It's not enormous but measures exactly two feet round in circumference and I'm having terrible trouble finding a hat to fit.

I wonder if you might know where I can find one?

Yours hopefully,

C. Hepplethwaite, Miss

The Little Hope Herald
Saturday, 11th May 1940

Dear Miss Hepplethwaite,

I had a cousin who was similarly afflicted back in the day, and in order to make her presentable for church on a Sunday my enterprising aunt had a large cardboard egg tray decorated and finished off with a length of satin ribbon, which tied neatly under the girl's chin. Whilst the rather fragile nature of the titfer in question made perambulating about in the rain somewhat problematic, it did at least mean that it could be easily dismantled and redecorated for high days and holidays as follows:

- The Christmas hat manifestation was particularly impressive in that the length of satin ribbon was replaced by some rather lovely paper chains, and a large origami 'star in the East' was attached to the crown. There was a minor hiccough at Midnight Mass when the star began to smoulder on account of its coming into close contact with a particularly low chandelier in the church porch, but a quick blow from the Vicar avoided a full conflagration, and my dear cousin regained consciousness just in time to get her communion wafer down her throat.
- Easter proved to be a great success for the resurrected egg box as it took on the aspect of a beautifully woven straw bird's nest – again attached to the crown – but this time topped with half a dozen warm hen's eggs, only two of which hatched during the Vicar's sermon.
- Harvest Festival was a little less successful, largely on account of the weight of the two large marrows balanced a little too precariously atop the now slightly battered egg tray, but one can't win them all and fortunately a doctor was on hand to provide a little pain relief to my cousin by way of a morphine pill and a hastily fashioned orthopaedic collar made from two slightly under-stuffed hassocks and a spare length of bell rope.

Does this idea appeal to you, Miss Hepplethwaite? I do hope so, because should it not then we shall have to start exploring the possibilities of old grain sacks or buckets, neither of which are ideal.

Now, assuming that you think my original suggestion to be a good one, let me just say that I do realise that egg trays can be problematic to source during these difficult times with most of them being given over to paper salvage, but my Cook has had a word with Mr Augustus Peabody the greengrocer on your behalf, and he's kindly put one aside for your personal use. If you would care to call in sometime this week and he'll be happy to get it out for you to see if it fits.

Please do not be tempted to look this particular gift horse in the mouth as that egg tray might otherwise have found itself transformed into the smouldering fuse inside the parachute mine which might well have been dropped onto the Reich Chancellery and won the war. Do you really want that on your conscience for the remainder of your days?

I do hope this helps.

Yours,

Hilda Ffinch
Hilda Ffinch,
The Bird with All The Answers (and the cutest little French beret you ever did see!)

He's Tethered Himself to the Bedpost Again...

Mrs Veronica Barraclough
9 Agincourt Street
Little Hope

8th June 1940

Dear Mrs Ffinch,

I married quite recently and whilst I'm lucky that my new husband is in a reserved occupation and won't have to go away to war, I'm afraid that his dress sense is letting him down a bit and is having a detrimental effect on our private life.

You see, Herbert will insist on wearing a string vest at all times, and I find embracing a man who to all intents and purposes is wearing a rather coarse fishing net very unsettling. I've caught my watchstrap in it twice and I'm sick and tired of him accidentally tethering himself to the bedpost and struggling like a hare in a trap.

I don't want to leave him and go home to Mother but I'm really not sure that I can put up with it much longer.

What should I do?

Yours,

Veronica Barraclough

The Little Hope Herald
Saturday, 15th June 1940

Dear Mrs Barraclough,

Let me begin by saying that whilst I sympathise with your predicament, as a married woman myself I am not surprised that you feel a little let down by the side of married life which the fates have decreed is for your eyes alone.

Many ladies find themselves in the same boat when they have perambulated back down the aisle and tossed their bouquet gaily at the first unmarried maiden who chances to cross their path, although to be fair not every bride finds herself in a boat coxswained by Herbert the trawlerman, as you clearly do.

Unlucky you, Mrs Barraclough, very unlucky you. But do not despair! I know not of a woman alive who finds a string vest attractive on a man, and so you are not alone in your plight.

Might I therefore suggest that you follow the example of my second cousin Bunty Beamish, whose own husband, Randolph, was similarly plagued with no fashion sense whatsoever? Bunty's solution was to slip a sleeping draught into her husband's cocoa one evening before bed and, once he was essentially dead to the world, she set to work unravelling all six of his string vests and winding them into a ball.

This achieved, she then set about weaving an impressive spider's web of string all about the bed where her dear spouse slept until he was enclosed in an impenetrable net, like a doomed trout. The plan was that upon his waking, Bunty planned to tell her husband that he had leapt out of bed in the middle of the night and had set to weaving the web himself, a common occurrence amongst the string vest wearing community on account of mild frostbite of the nipples apparently, and that she had had to physically restrain him lest he go a step further and unconsciously weave himself a noose.

Unfortunately however, Bunty's husband failed to regain consciousness on account of the strength of the sleeping draught she had administered (new spectacles) and he is now pushing up daisies in a small churchyard in rural Devonshire.

But that aside, the plan was sound, and I have no reason to suspect that it would not work for you should you choose to give it a bash. I'm also fairly certain that dear Doctor Proctor will supply you with some sleeping pills if you approach him with some cock and bull story about insomnia on account of living so close to the village air raid siren.

Do let me know how you get on, Mrs Barraclough, and remember to re-wind the string from about your bed once your spouse's nerves are suitably shattered and pop it into the War Salvage Bin behind the Village Hall.

I do hope this helps.

Yours,

Hilda Ffinch
Hilda Ffinch,
The Bird with All The Answers

P.S. I have written to my cousin Bunty, who is currently serving out her term at HMP Holloway to let her know that you intend following in her footsteps, and she eagerly awaits news of the successful completion of your task.

Knickers...

'Thrifty and Nifty'
Little Hope

18th June 1940

Dear Mrs Ffinch,

In an effort to make do and mend and on account of a shortage of coupons for new underwear, I've dug out three pairs of my old grandmother's Victorian bloomers from the attic. My question is this though: How can I make them a little more attractive to the opposite sex?

I'm going to a dance at the barracks at the weekend, and on the off chance that I should trip on the dance floor or something,I don't want to be a laughing stock.

Yours,

'Thrifty and Nifty'

The Little Hope Herald
Saturday, 22nd June 1940

Dear 'Thrifty and Nifty',

Might I remind you that Victorian bloomers, on the whole (so to speak), did rather tend to be crotchless and so all you really need to do is perhaps shorten the legs by half a yard or so?

This done, I'm sure that should you chance to trip up on the dance floor wearing a pair of your grandmother's 'modernised' bloomers then you will prove to be very popular indeed with members of the opposite sex.

A word of caution however, do try not to go base over apex in front of the dance band, the horn section is a little over keen at the best of times, tip them the wink and they may come to your aid with indecent haste, if you get my meaning.

Yours,

Hilda Ffinch
Hilda Ffinch,
The Bird with All The Answers

V.

How to Handle Cocks
(And other barnyard animals)

"Whatever is that hullaballoo?" asked Hilda, looking up from her correspondence pile and simultaneously reaching for her gin.

"It does rather look as though your husband has his cock out again," replied Mrs Fox, sipping her own gin thoughtfully before popping on her pince-nez to get a better look. "I don't know that I've ever seen such a big one, it's attracting quite a crowd…"

My Pussy Won't Stop Growling...

Miss Mildred Sparrow
8, Kitchener Close
Little Hope
2nd March 1940

Dear Mrs Ffinch,

I urgently need advice on account of my growling pussy which proper goes at it in the public air raid shelter at night. Some might say it inappropriate to get it out in there at all, but I do ensure that it is bathed, trimmed and free of fleas at all times.

Problem is it doesn't seem to like *men*, which – as you can imagine – causes a dreadful stir amongst those banged up with it of an evening. What can I do?

Yours sincerely,

Miss Mildred Sparrow

The Little Hope Herald
Saturday, 9th March 1940

Dear Miss Sparrow,

May I begin by saying that it's a breath of fresh air to hear from a young lady who is clearly conscious of the need to keep her pussy hale and hearty during these dark days? Time and time again I hear reports of pussies which have been neglected, left to run wild in the street and are host to any one of a number of undesirable parasites.

Now, growling pussies, on the whole, tend to be irascible either on account of underemployment or simply because they are hungry for fresh meat – is yours getting *enough*, dear? I cannot impress upon you sufficiently the need to pander to puss's needs in this department. A yawning pussy is a bored pussy but a growling one can be really quite challenging. Why, my own pussy (Kitchener) – starved of Colonel Ffinch's attentions when he's away at the front – has been known to go for the sofa cushions or the curtains at the drop of a hat and has twice spat at the postman. Such occurrences are rare but do need to be addressed lest one ends up in front of a magistrate and it goes for him too.

I therefore entreat you to handle your pussy firmly but lovingly, Miss Sparrow, do not let it get the upper hand or it will not come good in the end.

In respect of your pussy's dislike of men, there are very few of us my dear who would take kindly to being petted in the dark by a complete stranger (Mrs Edith Muff-Hawker from The Cat and Cabbage in Hampton Upon Mott being a notable exception) and so it's little wonder that yours is getting a little uptight. Perhaps assuage its hunger with a bit of sausage before the sirens go off of an evening, and make sure that you have another banger to hand should the need arise?

I do hope this helps. Keep that pussy well-trimmed and flea-free now!

Yours,

Hilda Ffinch
Hilda Ffinch,
The Bird with All The Answers

A Rather Frisky Goat...

Miss Judith McGinty
Fagg End Farm
Tarts Hill

25th April 1940

Dear Mrs Ffinch,

Nancy, my nanny goat, has recently become rather frisky and I'm unable to find her a billy to 'get it out of her system' as it were.

Nancy is so randy, that she seems to have taken a shine to my grandpa and now the poor old soul is terrified of coming to visit me in case he is subjected to a good seeing to.

Any suggestions?

Yours desperately,

Miss Judith McGinty

𝕿𝖍𝖊 𝕷𝖎𝖙𝖙𝖑𝖊 𝕳𝖔𝖕𝖊 𝕳𝖊𝖗𝖆𝖑𝖉
Saturday, 27th April 1940

Dear Miss McGinty,

Nanny goats, my dear, can be tricky coves at the best of times and tend to be somewhat excitable even when not 'in season', as it were.

I recall my late mother saying that many years ago, during an unusual holiday with my father in darkest Wales, that they had quite a set-to with a goat. Bournemouth was fully booked that year and it was a little late in the season for Rome and so they stayed with Lord and Lady Anthrax at their country pile on the outskirts of a little village out in the sticks. It was a queer place with forty-six letters in its name – thirty-eight of which were consonants – and it was there that my father found himself on the receiving end of the unsolicited and overtly amorous intentions of what he later described as "a particularly rambunctious old goat."

My mother, who had been taking an early morning bath in the upper reaches of the house at the time of the incident, didn't actually witness what occurred but did hear my father shouting "Get out! Get out! Get those teeth away from me, you unhinged abomination! Be off with you I say!" whereupon she heard the bedroom door slam shut and the perpetrator clatter off down the stairs. Clearly, the goat had gained entry to the house by stealth and had accosted my father whilst he was still abed.

"Clarence was in a terrible state," my mother later recalled. "The silly old thing had really gone at him! The poor man had a visible bite mark on his thigh and was drained of all colour. I said as much to the old nanny who looked after the Anthrax children, a peculiar woman with an unpronounceable name and frightfully large incisors."

"Never mind her," I replied, enthralled. "Was the goat apprehended?"

"No, it was long gone by the time Lord Anthrax came thundering along the landing with his blunderbuss fully cocked, but your father did rather keep to his rooms after that and would only come out for tiffin if pressed."

My parents never did go back to that particular house again, although the Anthraxes (Anthraxii?) did come to visit us in Belgravia quite regularly whereupon their children – all eight of them – ran wild and destroyed two Gainsborough's, a sizeable piece of Ming and a Queen Anne armchair. They had been unmanageable, Lady Anthrax explained rather wearily, since she had been forced to let their Nanny go on account of her having irreconcilable issues with holidaymakers in the vicinity and the local constabulary having become involved, whatever that meant.

But I digress. Following the incident in Wales, my mother – fearful of another old goat ever coming across my father in a state of undress – invested heavily in the catnip market and had every window box and flowerpot in the house seeded with it. It is well known that even the most rampant and aggressive of toms have had their ardour dampened by this unassuming little bush and my mother postulated that if it worked for one species of four-legged beast then it would surely work for them all, albeit if administered in a larger dose.

It appears that she was correct, and as a consequence of this horticultural stroke of genius, my father was goat-free for the remainder of his days and her own pussy (an overstuffed Persian by the name of Mr Omdurman) became terribly laid-back, something which she always maintained was an absolute bonus on the back of it.

And so I suspect, Judith dear, that your salvation lies in the common or garden catnip. Stick a little in your grandsire's buttonhole when he comes to stay, and all will be well. Perhaps pop a little into your cup of tea whilst you're at it and you'll find it will be time for him to go home again before you know it.

I do hope this helps.

Yours,

Hilda Ffinch
Hilda Ffinch,
The Bird with All The Answers

P.S. If the catnip thing fails, my Cook has an excellent recipe for goat curry.

A Particularly Rampant Cock...

Mrs R Hole
Cock-a-Hoop Farm
High Hope

9th June 1940

Dear Mrs Finch,

Please, <u>please</u> could you help me?

My husband's cock is keeping our neighbours from getting adequate shuteye and I am inundated with complaints as a result.

The problem is, he likes to 'strut his stuff' as soon as he's up and he frequents most of the houses in the street. Poor old Mrs Brown (the widow two doors down) hasn't had a cock up her back passage since her husband's passing twenty-odd years ago and now finds herself too nervous to open her back door.

I was considering clipping his wings but am unsure if this will help the situation?

Any advice given would be great fully received.

Sincerely,

Rosy Hole (Mrs)

The Little Hope Herald
Saturday, 22nd June 1940

Dear Mrs Hole,

Might I begin, my dear, by reassuring you that you are not alone in your predicament? Since the outbreak of war, many ladies in rural communities have found themselves in sole charge of a rampant cock, which may or indeed may not, belong to their spouse.

Prior to the commencement of hostilities, Colonel Ffinch took immense pride in his own cock – a fine beast which he named 'Gordon of Khartoum' – which he was quite happy to rest on my privet whilst displaying it in the best light for Mrs Ricketts, the Vicar's housekeeper. Mrs Ricketts, who knows a thing or two about cocks apparently, admired it greatly and had great difficulty keeping her hands off it. Such was my dear spouse's admiration for his pride and joy, together with the esteem in which it was held and venerated locally, that he would also sometimes show it off at The Royal Oak on a Saturday night, having first asked the barmaid to hold it steady for him whilst ordering a round of drinks at the bar.

Now, after much 'umming' and 'ahing' upon the outbreak of war – and in spite of my pointing out that Jerry may well take a pot-shot at it if he was spotted in the open with it tucked under his arm – the Colonel elected to take his cock with him when he departed for the front and although this has resulted in my thankfully not having to throw a bucket of cold water over the beast at the crack of dawn each day when it starts performing, I do have to say that I really rather miss having it around.

Have you, I wonder, considered asking your husband to agree to putting a falcon hood on his cock? Whilst this may seem a little unorthodox and indeed slightly cruel at first, it really isn't and one can be had quite cheaply from my lame gamekeeper, Dick Scratcher, who makes his own and prides himself on keeping his own feisty cock under control quite nicely by such means. I am fairly certain that if kept in the dark and deprived of its liberty then your spouse's 'little wandering friend' will cease in its attempts to gain access to old Mrs Brown's back passage and indeed to sundry other of your neighbours' entrances without the need for physical intervention by your good self.

Failing that, and should the complaints continue, perhaps you might consider giving it a swift blow to render it insensible, or perhaps take steps to hobble the beast – think 'ball and chain'?

Obviously, should those measures fail then I fear that you may need to separate your husband from his little friend once and for all and this being the case, then please do give Dick Scratcher a shout and he'll be quite happy to come round and have at it for you. He attends the St John's Ambulance Brigade meetings on a Friday night here at the village hall and has basic first aid training, he'll soon have the brute in hand and will ensure that its predatory days are over.

Do let me know how you get on.

Yours,

Hilda Ffinch
Hilda Ffinch,
The Bird with All The Answers

A Quick Goose up the Allotment…

Walter Smith
Peacock Cottage
Goose Lane
Higher Hope

4th August 1940

Dear Mrs Ffinch,

I hope it is alright for me to write to you. I don't live in Little Hope, but in another village nearby.

As I have severely flat feet I couldn't sign up, but I do my bit. I'm in the Home Guard though and am very happy to help the ladies in the village with digging and weeding their allotments as I know how hard it can be on those of the female persuasion who find themselves left alone in time of war and, to be honest, my own wife is very keen to get me out of the house most days. She says that my flat feet get under her normal ones and I suppose that she does have a point.

The problem is that when I do waddle off to visit one of my ladies, I find myself subjected to a regular goosing!

It's not on you know, it's very unfair. There I am, minding my own business tugging and dabbing away diligently in the undergrowth of the lady in question, when it happens: a sharp nip on my bottom followed by the sound of raucous laughter. Mrs 'Nameless' seems to find these attacks hilarious even though I have told her to keep her goose to herself before I lose patience and give it to my wife, who is well known for her talents in the plucking and stuffing department.

I have to say that it's only one particular goose which has taken to going for me, a big brute with an evil look in her eye and a honk like an omnibus horn, the rest are very well behaved as indeed are the gaggles of my other dear ladies who wouldn't countenance fowl play at any price.

I don't want to have to stay away as I know how quickly a lady's patch can become overgrown and untidy without a man's attention, but this can't go on!

Please help.

Yours Hopefully,

Walter Smith

The Little Hope Herald
Saturday, 10th August 1940

Dear Mr Smith,

I've had a quick gander at your letter and have to say that – flat feet or not – you really do need to stop being such a chicken!

Don't you know that there's a war on? Better by far a quick nip in the allotments (as it were) than several thousand goosesteps up the High Street. England Expects, Mr Smith, England Expects! Now, do pull yourself together at once and get stuck into your ladies' botanical provinces again! Chin up and put your back into it!

With regard to your being singled out by a particularly vexatious goose, I am enclosing a pair of extra-thick hand-knitted socks (usually sent to sailors and other brave men, so think yourself lucky) for your malformed palmate waddlers, these should help stiffen your weak resolve if nothing else. They should also add the best part of half an inch to your height enabling you to look Mother Goose right in the eye before squaring up to her if necessary.

Should you require any handy tips regarding tugging away in the aforementioned lady gardens then please don't hesitate to have a word with my lame gamekeeper, Dick Scratcher, he's awfully good at it and will be up your end on Tuesday week.

Yours,

Hilda Ffinch
Hilda Ffinch,
The Bird with All The Answers

The Pigeon Fancier...

Mrs Mildred Winterbottom
Rookery Nook
Bushy End
Little Hope

15th August 1940

Dear Mrs Ffinch,

I'm terribly worried about my husband's preoccupation with a pigeon that he has recently named Periwinkle. He is convinced that Periwinkle is a blood relative of his favourite carrier pigeon, Winston, who was killed on active service over Kent recently in an unfortunate incident involving a tea cosy, a catapult and a small troop of over-keen boy scouts.

My Hector has taken to bringing Periwinkle into our house at night, has made him his own air raid shelter in the cupboard under the stairs and – to add insult to injury – he even insists on letting him sleep on a specially made perch in our bedroom, which is unnerving to say the least, especially on birthdays and anniversaries!

What should I do?

Yours in desperation,

Mildred Winterbottom

The Little Hope Herald
Saturday, 17th August 1940

Dear Mrs Winterbottom,

I'm very much afraid, my dear, that Mr Winterbottom is what we used to call in peacetime a 'pigeon fancier'.

Now, this may sound innocuous enough but Colonel Ffinch assures me that there's *nothing* rational about a fellow whose life revolves around wicker baskets, ordnance survey maps, vegetarian sandwiches and very powerful binoculars.

Ask yourself this, dear girl – if Mr W is treating Periwinkle as an honoured house guest and piling on the charm when you are *on* the premises with them, then what do you imagine goes on when they are alone together in a hayloft?

It may not hitherto have crossed your mind, but interspecies 'special friendships' do happen you know. Think about it, where do you suppose Icarus got his high-flying ideas from?

Pigeons, my dear, belong in a *pie* and not in the marital home. Might I suggest that you perhaps slip a large nip of gin into Periwinkle's corn early next Wednesday morning and then toss him out of your bedroom window in the general direction of Bell End Farm at sun up? My lame gamekeeper, Dick Scratcher will be out and about just after cock's crow with his weapon pointed skywards in search of well – my dinner, frankly. I'll tip him the nod and he'll have Periwinkle flat on his back and plucked clean for you in no time at all.

I can guarantee that no matter how close the relationship between your husband and Periwinkle has been, the former will not have seen the latter without his feathers on and as a result, he will not recognise his late companion's carcass when it's surrounded by potatoes and a nice gravy on his plate.

I do hope that this proves helpful. Please don't hesitate to contact my Cook for a stuffing guide should you need one as there's every chance that you may need to try something a little different (if you get my drift) in order to distract Mr Winterbottom from the matter in hand, should he take Periwinkle's sudden 'disappearance' badly.

Yours,

Hilda Ffinch
Hilda Ffinch,
The Bird with All The Answers

A Rather Randy Cock...

Mrs Freda Coward
Rooster's Nook
Hooker's Lane
Little Hope

25th September 1940

Dear Mrs Ffinch,

My husband recently acquired some poultry, but his cock seems intent on harassing the hens and leaving them quite dishevelled! Poor things don't seem to be able to bend over to peck corn without the little blighter circling their vents!

What can I do to help the poor girls? If they stop laying, I shall miss my eggy soldiers of a morning.

Yours, a very concerned,

Freda Coward

The Little Hope Herald
Saturday, 28th September 1940

Dear Mrs Coward,

A rogue cock, my dear, can be a tricky cove to deal with at the best of times – no matter who the owner – but the sad fact that this one belongs to your spouse encourages one to extend one's deepest sympathies to your good self as invariably the crimes and misdemeanours of the perpetrator are wont to come home to roost in the family nest, as it were.

Now, I wonder, have you discussed with your husband the possibility of him keeping his cock to himself for a while? You know, perhaps ask him if he objects to spending some time alone with it in say, the potting shed or the attic? I am a firm believer in the old adage 'monkey see, monkey do' and see no reason why a fellow's cock might not learn good behaviour as the result of a bit of firm handling. Perhaps suggest to Mr Coward that he gives it a short, sharp poke in the wattle should it contrive to go its own way and persist in its pursuit of unrequited carnal pleasure or indeed put a hood on the fowl thing until it masters the gentle art of self-control?

In the meantime, in order to preserve your ladies' flustered feminine modesty and for them to avoid having to bend over and put temptation in the way of said cock, might you not consider spreading their kernels at a slightly elevated angle? This would enable a more reserved forward pecking motion to ensue and stop them going full steam ahead and flashing away like the Lundy lighthouse, as it will be that which is giving your husband's cock the green light.

I do hope this helps, please don't hesitate to write again if it doesn't as I am rather partial to a spot of coq au vin and haven't a single bit of coq on the premises for some time now. I'm loathe to wait until Colonel Ffinch is home on leave next to get some in and so I might be able to help you out by facilitating the disappearance of your husband's cock should you require me to do so.

I pay handsomely and will see to it that your husband is recompensed with a jolly good stuffing.

Yours,

Hilda Ffinch
Hilda Ffinch,
The Bird with All The Answers

'Rabbits…'

Miss Marjorie Scratch
22 Mafeking Terrace
Little Hope

7th October 1940

Dear Mrs Ffinch,

We seem to be having a problem with next door's rabbit on account of him making impromptu visits to Dorothy our little doe. The poor girl has had four litters in as many months, and we are now overrun with the little blighters.

What should I do, for this can't go on?!

Sincerely,

Miss Marjorie Scratch

The Little Hope Herald
Saturday, 12th October 1940

Dear Miss Scratch,

My dear girl, please be advised that I have passed your letter on to our local (unofficial) pest control expert, Mr John Thomas Fiddler, who owns the gaily-painted gypsy caravan in Beaver Copse, just off the Bell End Road.

I had my Cook pop your letter down to Mr Fiddler personally earlier today and I am now living in expectation of a fine new rabbit fur hat (sans the ears, obviously, that would just look silly) and also a pair of warm gloves, which the good fellow has promised to send on to Ffinch Hall as a payment for my having passed your missive on to him. Business is slow for the fellow at the moment apparently and consequently he's always on the lookout for a good tip and rewards handsomely. My Cook returned to Ffinch Hall from her mission with a very perky looking muff, even Thorne the gardener asked if he might have a quick stroke and Dick Scratcher, my gamekeeper, jolly nearly had one anyway.

This may come as something of a surprise to you but the fact is that your little bunny is literally sitting on a goldmine. Let me explain.

You may well, in your *naivety*, see pesky rabbits bouncing about all over the place but to the meat-hungry ladies of this parish – sick to the eyeteeth of rationing and coupons – Dorothy's litters are an absolute bounty! Why, my dear girl, you are practically leaning on the counter of your own restaurant and clothing emporium!

The ladies of this village (and one or two of the gentlemen too, by all accounts) will see nothing but an abundance of delicious rabbit pies and fashionable fur hats hopping about in your garden and will be rendered weak at the knees by the very thought! They are yours for the taking, my dear! Coco Chanel would go berserk for such an abundant supply chain.

Now, matters entrepreneurial aside and onto the flip side of the coin. What the devil do you think Lord Woolton (*swoon* still a handsome beast, in spite of his advancing years) would say if word were to reach his ears in the kitchens of power that Miss Marjorie Scratch of Little Hope is dangerously close to depriving her peckish friends and neighbours of gallons of life-preserving stew and tasty pies? I should think the marvellous man would be horrified and might even be driven to ask questions about your allegiance to this country in the House of Lords.

Dear lord! One despairs! Rabbits, my dear girl, are *not* like us. They cannot read books, drink cocoa, knit or enjoy the wireless

– they have nothing other than sex and lettuce to look forward to! What sort of life is that?

Might I suggest then, in the interests of all concerned, that you allow your rabbit to breed at will and leave the subsequent 'adoption process' of her offspring to the aforementioned Mr John Thomas Fiddler? He's terribly good at it and will be up your end (of the village) sometime on Thursday. He'll willingly get his snares out for you, should you wish to have a look at them and won't think twice about letting you handle them. I'm assuming that you've never seen a gentleman's trapping apparatus before but I have to say that I believe it will be something of a treat for you as his is greatly admired locally and is the envy of many a less well-equipped fellow. A word of warning however – don't get too close as such things tend to be jolly sensitive to the touch and may well go off unexpectedly in your hand.

And so Tally Ho, Miss Scratch! Do follow my advice, dear girl, and you'll be rolling in clover in no time, very possibly with Mr John Thomas Fiddler himself.

Yours,

Hilda Ffinch
Hilda Ffinch,
The Bird with All The Answers

An Itchy Pussy…

Miss Lizzy Blight
3 Kitchener Terrace
Little Hope
Yorkshire

19th October 1940

Dear Mrs Ffinch,

I seem to be having a lot of trouble with my little pussy at present. Although bathed and combed regularly, it seems to have rather an issue with fleas! I have attended to it daily for the past week and applied some ointment to a rather reddened area which I believe is due to being bitten by the little buggers.

Do you have any remedies which I may apply to my poor little pussy for its shenanigans is keeping me up at night?

Sincerely yours,

Lizzie Blight (Miss)

𝕿𝖍𝖊 𝕷𝖎𝖙𝖙𝖑𝖊 𝕳𝖔𝖕𝖊 𝕳𝖊𝖗𝖆𝖑𝖉
Saturday, 26th October 1940

Dear Miss Blight,

One hears on the grapevine, as it were, that your pussy has also been keeping Mr Godfrey Cantrell of Trafalgar Cottage up at night too and that his acclaimed bellringing prowess has suffered quite significantly as a result. The dear man needs to be up early, in the conventional sense, Miss Blight, not only on account of his superior knowledge of campanology but also in order to tend to his superb colony of bees.

Now honey (not a term of endearment, lest you take false encouragement) is, as you will be aware, a most valuable commodity in these trying times and Mr Cantrell's hives are the pride of Little Hope. The nectar which is produced as a direct result of the good man's loving attention to his firm, well-structured honeycomb and much practiced cross-pollination technique, has caressed many a lip in this village with its vitamin-rich goodness and has historically been a source of exquisite pleasure to both male and female inhabitants alike.

Your naughty pussy cannot, therefore, be allowed to continue its nocturnal activities unchecked – apart from the fact that the racket emanating from your bedroom window of an evening has twice been confused with the air raid klaxon on top of the Village Hall and has caused panic on the streets – it is clearly on the verge of rendering poor Mr Cantrell completely exhausted and utterly incapable of tugging on his bell rope and straining his bounty into sterilised jars for sale at the church fete.

Therefore, please do make the effort, Miss Minx Blight, to reign it in a little. We all know what's been going on. Might I suggest that you check in future that Mr Cantrell has left all of his bees in the hive before he makes his way unobtrusively up your back passage of an evening to pay court to that rogue little pussy of yours? I suspect that the 'reddened area' of which you speak was rendered thus by sudden employment of one of Mr Cantrell's rogue *Hymenoptera* making a beeline for it.

I'll leave matters there, as I should hate to stir the pot further, but should you require a cat for company of an evening instead of our dear beekeeper and bell ringer, then please do let Mrs Minnie Cooper of 16 Copenhagen Street know. Her little British shorthair, Mrs Pankhurst, has just had another litter and there are quite enough to go around.

Yours judgingly,

Hilda Ffinch
Hilda Ffinch,
The Bird with All The Answers

A Splendid White Cock…

Mr Reginald Catchpole
'Fletcher's Reach'
Balls Road
Little Hope

10th November 1940

Dear Mrs Ffinch,

Our Nellie says you're the lady in the know and that if you can't raise a cure then there's no chuffing hope.

I have a white cock, Percy, beautiful beast. Normally dead proud like, but he's recently started to look a little sad in the masculine department and as a consequence seems to have lost all confidence and 'puff'. Instead of strutting out as 'cock of the walk', he's taken to slouching about in a most deflated manner and is totally neglecting his duties – I mean I rarely get a 'Doodle' out of him at sunrise anymore – and him normally rising and shouting out for attention the moment the sun's up in Tokyo.

The local hens ain't happy about it either, I can tell you. Turns out this fancy for giving white feathers to them lads as is suspected of not being willing to join their mates in the Forces is at the root of the problem. Seems that Percy's been asked to provide for the honour of King and Country one time too many by some of the local ladies and is having trouble regaining form, and as a result I'm starting to get proper worried about him. Will he ever stand tall and erect again?

I don't normally do this sort o' thing but our Nelly says you're The Bird with All The Answers and so can you please tell me how to get a rise out of my Percy? Is there any hope of his recovery or should I put the poor beast out of his misery?

Yours dejectedly,

Reg.

The Little Hope Herald
Saturday, 16th November 1940

Dear Reg,

Wringing your Percy's neck, as it were, may well solve your own problem, my dear man, but it will also almost certainly result in anyone else with a doodler of a similar size and hue to your own being hard-pressed to keep it out of the grasping hands of the harpies of the Little Hope Women's Institute. Those dreadful women are obsessive in their patriotic intent and when it comes to naming and shaming anyone who is just out of short pants but not yet in uniform, they take no prisoners!

Now, it is well known that those be-tweeded termagants will go to *any* length to get their hands on a fine white cock and when one does fall into their clutches then they'll pluck it clean and expose the unfortunate brute to the elements in no time at all, irrespective of ownership. They really aren't at all fussy and as a preventative measure I've even had to stop Colonel Ffinch from balancing his big boy on the front hedge, he hasn't been particularly happy about this but has finally come to understand that it's for his own good and has settled for fondling it in the greenhouse instead.

Would you really wish such an infelicitous providence then upon the likes of our dear Reverend Fishwick who has been raising his cock in Miss Brewster's barn, or Mr Trotter the butcher who has had his up behind his pig-pen for some time now? Both men are veterans of the Great War and boast fine cocks, similar to your own by all accounts and have thus far managed to avoid having them de-feathered by the militant wing of the WI, but the threat of discovery is ever present.

Reginald dear man, I implore you, for the good of all the roosters in the neighbourhood, you *must* take the matter firmly in hand at once and resolve to keep your fine fellow out of the reach of your female neighbours! To the best of my knowledge, there are no cowardly gentlemen who require the ceremonial presentation of a bit of your cock's plumage in Little Hope (the postman has fallen under suspicion once or twice, but I am reassured by his daily flat-footed trampling of my Webb's Wonderful Lettuce and grumpy demeanour whenever a letter from Colonel Ffinch arrives from the front that his bipedal impairment is indeed genuine, and that he'd far rather be giving Jerry a good seeing to than humping his bulging sack up my driveway twice daily).

Might I suggest, therefore, given that the harridans of Little Hope are unlikely to leave your poor little friend alone as matters stand, that you take a leaf out of the book of Mrs Ena Titley-Major the hairdresser of Withering End and indulge your dejected doodle in a little coloured rinse? 'Golden Glint' manufacture an excellent ladies' hair-dye in a shade named 'Gay Red' which – Mrs Titley-Major assures me – will be just the ticket for your old Percy as obviously no one will look twice at a bright red cock which stands out like a sore thumb and sheds like an old anaconda.

Follow this sound advice and I'm certain that everything will be 'Cock-a-doodle-you!' in no time at all Reg!

Yours,

Hilda Ffinch
Hilda Ffinch,
The Bird with All The Answers

Superstitions...

Miss Ena Twitch
2, Agincourt Rise
Little Hope

18th November 1940

Dear Mrs Ffinch,

I've always been very superstitious and worry a lot about the silliest of things. In the summer, I had a thing about seeing only one magpie and lived in fear that something terrible would happen if I didn't spit on the floor, turn around three times (in an anticlockwise direction) and salute it.

I've managed to get over that hurdle now, since my mother-in-law finally owned up to having been substituting magpie for pigeon in our Friday night family pie for the past year or so, and so clearly the only bad luck about has fallen onto the magpie. But now I'm starting to worry about black cats – I always understood them to be lucky, but an American journalist I happen to know said that it's ever such bad luck if one crosses your path.

Please help me, I'm getting hives thinking about it.

Yours,

Ena Twitch

The Little Hope Herald
Saturday, 23rd November 1940

Dear Mrs Twitch,

Superstition, my dear, is the bane of the Little Englander! The very bane, I tell you!

Do you truly believe that rain at a funeral means that the dear departed one is happy and gay and presumably dancing his or her way up to heaven in very much the manner of Fred Astaire or Ginger Rogers?

Do you think that catching a falling leaf in autumn will somehow bring about a desirable change in one's fortunes?

Do you insist upon having at the bottom of your eggshell with your spoon once you've stripped it clean of its hard-boiled contents in order to 'let the devil out'?

Do you court the spectre of apoplexy should an unsuspecting member of your family contrive to place a pair of new shoes upon the dinner table – preferably when not actually wearing them?

Do you worry about leaving a white tablecloth out on the clothesline overnight lest the Grim Reaper exact revenge for your tardiness, and make off with your nearest and dearest?

I wonder also does the squeak of a bat put you in fear of a witch circling overhead (on a broomstick, obviously and not the aforementioned *vespertilio* which would clearly be a little on the small side and rather tricky to straddle)?

One suspects, dear girl, that your American journalist friend is no stranger to black, white, ginger or indeed tortoiseshell pussies and is merely endeavouring to have you jump into his (presumably) manly arms in fright – which apart from anything else is worrying given that you have a mother-in-law.

Pull yourself together dear, for heaven's sake! Superstition is folly!

Eat the faux pigeon pie and stroke that pussy kindly should it chance to come your way. Cut both ends off your British loaf and watch the devil fly over number 2 Agincourt Rise and then decorate your house from attic to cellar with hawthorn – should a witch chance to come calling on account of the latter then please do give her my best regards.

Finally, should you ever develop a ganglion please do fight the urge to batter it with a Bible, a nasty sprain will surely ensue and you may well need to invest in a large number of mothballs on account of an exodus of the infernal things from between the pages of Leviticus.

Yours, with rolling eyes

Hilda Ffinch
Hilda Ffinch,
The Bird with All The Answers

P.S. That said, I myself do rather like to touch a bit of wood upon occasion, but only when Colonel Ffinch is home on leave.

VI.

Matters Horticultural

"Has anyone seen Thorne?" Hilda demanded, marching into the servants' hall (quite accidentally as it happened, she'd been looking for the orangery).

"He's at it in the potting shed again, Mrs Ffinch," replied Cook, rather tersely.

"Who's he potting this time?" asked Hilda.

"No idea," Cook snorted, "but I'd knock before you go in, if I were you…"

A Well-Trimmed Bush...

Mrs A. Crumb
Crumble Cottage
off Armistice Avenue
Little Hope

25th March 1940

Dearest Hilda,

On visiting your very own dwelling recently, I couldn't help but admire your immaculately trimmed bush. With my man away at war, my bush has become terribly overgrown and is completely out of control!

Any bush trimming advice would be most welcome.

Your friend,

Agapanthus.

𝔗𝔥𝔢 𝔏𝔦𝔱𝔱𝔩𝔢 𝔥𝔬𝔭𝔢 𝔥𝔢𝔯𝔞𝔩𝔡
Saturday, 30th March 1940

Dear Agapanthus,

Many thanks indeed for your recent visit but more so for the jolly nice cake you trit-trotted up my garden path with. I know that you appreciated my eating the entire thing in front of you in one sitting and so please don't thank me for doing so. There is a war on after all and it would have been terribly rude of me to put your culinary offering to one side, as doing so might have led you to believe that I'd be giving it to the dog later.

I did notice you eyeing up my exquisite little bush as you arrived, and I can't impress upon you *enough* the need to retain the services of a substitute topiarist in Mr Crumb's absence.

Whilst the man of the house is away it is incumbent upon his lady to keep her garden tidy.

I myself had my lame gamekeeper, Dick Scratcher, round to give my bush a jolly good seeing to on Tuesday last after Colonel Ffinch mentioned that he'd lost both his wristwatch and monocle in there when he was home on leave last and that he would require both items to be sent on to him at his club if he was to carry on giving Jerry a good old bashing. Both pieces were subsequently retrieved by Dick and I gave my word to the Colonel that in future I'd keep my bush well pruned and shaped like a tiger's head if at all possible.

Should you be unable to find a suitable fellow to do the deed then please do let me know and I'll send Dick round to give you an estimate. He's generally up on a Tuesday.

Yours,

Hilda Ffinch
Hilda Ffinch,
The Bird with All The Answers

We're A Bit Stuffed…

Mr Artie Abercrombie
4, Crecy Street
Little Hope
Yorkshire

10th April 1940

Dear Mrs Ffinch,

We Dig for Victory in our house, we do it every day with great gusto. Our backyard is now an allotment (having the outside privy in it helps), our Anderson shelter is covered in cabbages and even the wife's beloved window boxes are full of runner beans.

Problem is, we've run out of growing space. Any ideas, as we're keen to keep expanding our output? There's a war on, you know!

Yours,

Artie Abercrombie

The Little Hope Herald
Saturday, 13th April 1940

Dear Mr Abercrombie,

Well done you on your sterling effort! It is heart-warming to hear that when the chips are down then the brave Little Englander just shovels them up and turns them into compost! I believe that such enthusiasm will help us to win this war and will ensure that we will still have enough meat on us to give the proverbial 'butcher's pencil' a run for its money when it's all over and done with.

I fully understand your current position with regards to growing space, and whilst it is not a problem which we have come across up at Ffinch Hall (200 acres of prime parkland and a terrace grand enough to hold one of the Duke of Wellington's balls on isn't to be sniffed at) yours is a challenge which intrigued me sufficiently for me to rise to the occasion and seek to find a solution to.

Now, whilst having my third morning gin on the aforementioned palatial terrace, I despatched my cook, my housemaid, my gamekeeper and my gardener on a mission into Little Hope to ascertain the cunning means and methods by which other villagers 'keep the home mires churning' as it were when – like yourself – they are faced with a distinct lack of acreage. To wit, I have determined the following, which I hope may provide you with inspiration:

- Mrs Florence Long grows parsley in her stone hot water bottle during the summer months and says that her garden is now much improved and that a small hole in a large vessel is not at all detrimental to the matter in hand. One can, she confirms, stuff more into it than one might initially think possible and it gives one such a feeling of satisfaction when it comes good. Mr Long agrees and says that it comes up nicely and is erect for quite some time before nature runs its course and the inevitable droop sets in. He also added that whilst he's never really been keen on the taste of fish, Mrs Long's well-watered parsley certainly does make it a lot more palatable when nibbled in moderation.
- Mr Ernest Pidcock recommends the use of prophylactics for the germination of seedlings, commenting that whilst Mrs Pidcock isn't too happy about pegging them out on the washing line with her smalls she does tend to come round a bit when sproutage occurs. One presumes – although Dick Scratcher my gamekeeper failed to ask the question of Mr Pidcock – that this is the first outing into the big wide world for said prophylactics and that Mrs Pidcock hasn't had to handle them twice.

- Mrs Lavinia Fox, of Fox Hall, has apparently been experimenting with the growing of botanicals in water in empty gin bottles. Mrs Fox's usefulness to the local 'Dig For Victory' campaign is debatable however given that as soon as her specimens bloom, she simply tips out the water, replaces it with more gin and goes at it like a Dowager Duchess recently returned from trekking across the Kalahari on foot.

- Mr Humphrey Hughes announced proudly that he's growing mushrooms in his old underpants, but again, I would take this with a pinch of salt and recommend that you do not accept an invitation to dinner with him.

- Mrs Marjorie Marsh recommends the removal of several paving slabs in the backyard in order to facilitate the sowing of seed in the open air. Cook presumed that the picnic rug and cushions covering the freshly dug earth were there to serve as a primitive incubator, but reported that she was unable to see as much as she would have liked to as Private Marsh (who has recently arrived home on leave) was standing in the yard in just his underpants and was clutching an empty beer bottle in one hand and a prophylactic in the other – clearly he and Mrs Marsh have been talking to the Pidcocks.

- Mrs Elvira Clark, whose husband has been missing for some time (not on active service, you understand, but who apparently left the marital home quite suddenly following an argument and went to live with an old aunt in the Orkneys) recommends the use of a home-made fertiliser. She showed my housemaid, Daisy, the wonders it has worked on the six feet by two feet area of backyard which she cleared herself in under three hours in a single night following Mr Clark's departure. Daisy reported that Mrs Clark's potatoes are 'growing like buggery' and so clearly the fertiliser is excellent, although Mrs C refuses outright to reveal its genesis.

- Finally, Miss Titty Wainwright, stalwart of the local Women's Institute heartily recommends the use of an old brassiere for the growing of beetroot. Thorne, my gardener, had clearly arrived at just the right moment with his clipboard and pen and was asked by Miss Green Fingers herself to help her off with the one she was wearing as it was a little tight and high time she had it off. Thorne, ever the gentleman, didn't like to say no and now goes as red as the planted beetroot in question whenever the point is raised.

I do hope that these suggestions prove useful to you, Mr Abercrombie. I look forward to seeing the fruits of your labours at this year's village fete.

Yours,

Hilda Ffinch
Hilda Ffinch,
The Bird with All The Answers

Might I Borrow Your Dick?

Ethel Winterbottom
Wisteria House
Hangman's Hill
Little Hope

25th April 1940

Dear Mrs Ffinch,

I was wondering if you would take it upon yourself to manage your gamekeeper, Mr Dick Scratcher?

With most of the men in the village away fighting Jerry, it is left to us women to tend our own patches and it's all well and good being asked to Dig for Victory, but I for one struggle for a dibber.

Now, I know that the man in question helps you out with your bits and pieces and I was thinking that a lady of your formidable talents would be just the person to arrange for all the ladies in the village to have a bit of Dick on a sort of rota? After all, there is a war on and I think that with our men away it's only fair that all we ladies get our fair share of him to ease the frustration of having to fiddle about with our own patches.

Thank you in advance dear Mrs Ffinch.

Yours expectantly,

Ethel

𝕿𝖍𝖊 𝕷𝖎𝖙𝖙𝖑𝖊 𝕳𝖔𝖕𝖊 𝕳𝖊𝖗𝖆𝖑𝖉
Saturday, 27th April 1940

Dear Ethel,

Managing the Dick in question, my dear, isn't as easy as it sounds. For one thing, my undergrowth is extensive and requires constant attention if Colonel Ffinch's rhubarb is to come up at all this year, and for another Dick needs to be constantly on hand here to encourage the Colonel's gourds to come good, if they are to come at all.

I've tried everything, but clearly I don't have the special touch that Dick does. The Colonel swears by him, even going so far as to invite him round for the occasional stiff one on the terrace (providing that we don't have any house guests of note, obviously) and maintains that he's a far better sower of seed than any he's come across this side of Kew Gardens, and to be entirely fair, he's come across a few in his time.

I do appreciate that the shortage of men in Little Hope and the surrounding villages has led to a surge in the growth rate of ladies' gardens and that obviously it's nigh on impossible (not to mention terribly tiresome) having to go at it constantly on one's own, but perhaps a raised bed might help your endeavours and make it easier to find the odd broad bean amongst the lettuce, as it were? Heaven knows, Dick's a dab hand at it but he can't be everywhere.

Might you consider perhaps banding together with another lady (or two) in the village and going at it *en masse*, as it were? They do say that many hands make light work, and I'm sure that Fanny Cox and Dotty Fishburn from the Women's Institute would jump at the chance to help out. Lord knows they spend enough time fiddling about in one another's foliage and one imagines that a change of parsley, as it were, might be just the ticket for all three of you.

In short then, Ethel, you really don't need a Dick to keep on top of things in your lonely patch, a Fanny's just as good and she'll invariably bring her own kippers.

Yours,

Hilda Ffinch
Hilda Ffinch,
The Bird with All The Answers

I Can't Seem to Get A Decent Mouthful...

Mrs Doreen Spiggot
Elderberry Cottage
Tart's Hill

16th June 1940

Dear Mrs Ffinch,

I am having so many problems with my vegetables. It doesn't matter how much care I lavish on them; my carrots turn out thin, limp and weedy.

Can you tell me how I can get a decent mouthful, nice and firm with a satisfying girth?

Yours hopefully,

Doreen

The Little Hope Herald
Saturday, 22nd June 1940

Dear Doreen,

When, on the outbreak of war, Colonel Ffinch had a mad five minutes and actually began Digging for Victory and tending his gourds himself (rather than just sitting on the terrace with a stiff one in his hand watching our gardener going at it hammer and tongs) I was approached by my Cook who wasn't at all backward at coming forward when voicing concerns about my dear husband's shortcomings with regard to rearing a passable firm one.

Harbouring similar concerns myself – the Colonel has had his moments in the past – and rather than just sit and wait for the inevitable limp one to be dangled enticingly round the side of the drawing room door, I decided to take action. To this end,

I set about studying the art and science of vegetable gardening (a fascinating subject when one gets into it) and spent the best part of four months with my cardigan sleeves rolled up hoeing about the place helping Thorne, my gardener, to give my own little garden the good old seeing-to which it desperately needed.

Now, I have learned that keeping one's garden somewhat moist but not too damp when waiting for things to come up is key, as is keeping the growing root warm and resisting the urge to give it a good tug until the time is just right. Thorne, who has been at it for years, came up with several fine specimens for me to have a gander at in next to no time at all. They were rather impressive on the whole bar a couple which were – I have to say – just a little bit too woody for my taste.

I also learned from my erstwhile gardener that he's raised a purple one before now as well as a brittle French-looking one which sported a terribly blunt tip and an abundance of bright foliage. His advice however, is to stick with what one knows; a tried and tested British one which – whilst it may look a little sad and lack the size and flair of its continental cousins – is full of vitamins and consequently far better for one's eyesight. It is for this reason, Thorne confirmed, that a regular mouthful of our home-grown gardener's delight may go some way towards avoiding accidental contact with the Vicar's Riley Gamecock during the blackout.

I do hope that this helps, sorry for the short reply but typing and holding Thorne's gourds at the same time is proving to be rather tricky.

Yours,

Hilda Ffinch
Hilda Ffinch,
The Bird with All The Answers

My Undergrowth is Out of Control...

Mrs Doris Groom
5, Agincourt Street
Little Hope

4th July 1940

Dear Mrs Ffinch,

My husband Harold, a keen gardener in peacetime, recently returned from active service for a week's leave and I could tell from the outset that something was bothering him. At first, he kept denying that anything was wrong, but on the morning after his arrival when we were still abed he came clean and said to me "Doris, your undergrowth is out of control, just because I'm not here to give it a seeing to myself, doesn't mean that you should let yourself go."

I do feel rather hurt, as I do my best to keep my garden tidy, but with the war on there's always something else to do!

Please advise, I should hate for Harold to go back to the front with a strop on.

Yours,

Doris Groom, Mrs.

The Little Hope Herald
Saturday, 6th July 1940

Dear Mrs Groom,

You are not alone, my dear, many a man has come back from the front, as it were, to find that all is not rosy in his lady's garden. I am inundated with tales of conquering heroes returning to their familiar patches to find them either overgrown or entirely devoid of nature's natural covering or indeed – worst of all – being tended by someone else.

It is difficult for a fellow who is away endeavouring to give Jerry one, to understand that life back on the homefront can also be jolly hard at times, and so I do urge caution in your response to your husband's complaints. Fighting the urge to go at him with your handbag will go some way towards winning the war as, should he lose an eye for example, that would be one less man at the front and a definite point in Jerry's favour.

When Colonel Ffinch leaves the marital home to return to his regiment after a period of leave (having first exhorted one to keep one's garden tidy in his absence) I always endeavour to ensure that he departs secure in the knowledge that upon his return everything will be as shipshape and Bristol fashion as it was when he departed. Now, as I am sure you will be aware from village gossip, I am not one to exert myself needlessly and – if I might be honest with you – whilst I have reared an impressive number of cucumbers in my time I have never *ever* trimmed back my own undergrowth. It is to this end that I employ the services of Mr Aloysius Thorne, gardener of this parish, to surreptitiously keep an eye on things in Colonel Ffinch's absence and – should things become a little untidy – to get stuck in as necessary.

I am assuming, without prejudice Mrs Groom, that you do not have a gardener of your own to hand and to be honest, I'm a little sensitive when it comes to my own being coveted by others, but I have it on good authority that the services of Mr Archibald Cummings of Kitchener Terrace might be had quite cheaply. One hears that the man is a dab hand with a dibber and the shrieks of delight from his lady customers when undergoing 'a good seeing-to' are to be heard as far afield as Harrogate. Verily I say unto you, even Mrs Ricketts, the Vicar's housekeeper has had him in when the Reverend Fishwick has been called away to help the Bishop of Rotherham sort his canonicals out.

I do hope this helps, Mrs Groom, and I exhort you to employ the services of Mr Cummings before your brave spouse returns on leave next. I'm sure that you will not regret doing so and your husband's delight when he claps eyes on your beautifully manicured lawn will be evident for all to see.

Yours,

Hilda Ffinch
Hilda Ffinch,
The Bird with All The Answers

A Bit of a Limp One...

Dicky Rutter
Bog View Cottage
Spanker Lane
Little Hope

5th September 1940

Dear Mrs Ffinch,

My veg patch is tickety-boo. Tomatoes are firm and round, sprouts hard with a good body. My problem is my marrows – a bit limp and no 'go' in them – they're only good for the compost heap or the pig bin really, and I can't abide waste!

Any horticultural tips for a firmer one?

Bless you (Keep Thingingy On!)

Reg Rutter (Dicky to my friends).

The Little Hope Herald
Saturday, 7th September 1940

Dear Dicky,

Marrows are devilishly tricky things to raise – I speak from experience having attempted to rear the Colonel's on several occasions when he's been unable to manage it himself.

You really must handle your gourds with care, dear man, otherwise they'll come to nothing. I find doing it in the comparative comfort of a sturdy greenhouse preferable to giving it a bash in the great outdoors, and perhaps do it on a bed of straw rather than a recently hoed bit of garden?

Do let me know how you get on.

Good luck!

Buggering on as always!

Hilda Ffinch
Hilda Ffinch,
The Bird with All The Answers

They're Going At It Hammer and Tongs!

Edgar Grump
Manor Farm
Little Hope

12th October 1940

Dear Mrs Ffinch,

As a farmer of many years standing, I have to say that I am not at all happy with the current state of affairs in which I find myself, thanks entirely to the Ministry of Agriculture!

Three months ago I found myself saddled with three young 'Land Army' fillies who are making my life terribly difficult. One of them, who shall remain nameless, has muscles like a Victorian strongman and makes me look a complete idiot when she marches off with a bale of hay under each arm, leaving me to follow on dragging just the one behind me. The second young lady has taken to driving my Fordson tractor around my top field as though she's in pole position at Brooklands Race Track and the third – well, I spotted her milking a cow with lipstick on the other day.

I'm obliged to put them up in the house as it's deemed big enough on account of having nine chimneys and five bedrooms but I'm at my wits' end as to how to reign these mad mares in. I'm starting to doubt my own masculinity as a vase of wildflowers has appeared on the windowsill in the parlour and there's a cloth on the table in the kitchen for the first time since 1926.

What's to do, Mrs Ffinch, what's to do?

Yours,

Edgar Grump

𝕿𝖍𝖊 𝕷𝖎𝖙𝖙𝖑𝖊 𝕳𝖔𝖕𝖊 𝕳𝖊𝖗𝖆𝖑𝖉

Saturday, 19th October 1940

Dear Mr Grump,

Might I first of all ask; who was wearing the lipstick, the Land Army girl or the cow, as the truth of that particular matter isn't immediately apparent from your letter?

Now, you appear to all intents and purposes my fine fellow, to be labouring under the misapprehension that a woman's place is in the home, doing little more than the everyday household tasks which have been the lot of the distaff side for time out of memory on account of the posturing and pontificating of a particular breed of alpha male (read: much like yourself).

Must I point out, Mr Grump, that the womenfolk of this realm are – and always have been – brave and stoic and quite a fellow's equal when push comes to shove and the balloon goes up?

What fate do you suppose might have befallen this country had Boudicea elected to stay at home ironing her horsehair unmentionables and cooking badger chops instead of going to war with Imperial Rome and giving Tacitus something to write home about?

Do you think that the manhood of England would have stood to attention quite so readily at Tilbury Dock had Sir Francis Walsingham tottered along down there in his little tights and wittered about the price of castanets in place of the armour-clad Good Queen Bess, who reigned in her mighty steed and vowed to lay down her life in the mud ere she would let her country fall?

And what of young Grace Darling, the lighthouse keeper's daughter, who took her little rowing boat out into a furious storm and fought her way through the raging sea to the wreck of the *Forfarshire* and the salvation of those souls still aboard?

Did she ought to have stayed home and washed the dishes and left them to it?

Really, Mr Grump. *Really*. A true gentleman would not baulk at the comradeship and help offered by the gentler sex in hard times. Why, my own husband now forbears to argue about who carries his travelling trunk up the grand staircase back at Ffinch Hall when he comes home on leave. Neither he nor his man can get it up on their own whereas I soon have the matter in hand and it's all over and done with next to no time. In a similar vein, the Colonel is under no illusions about the superiority of my technique against to his when it comes to firing his motor up, a firm grip and a quick crank from me and the old Bentley comes good.

And so I urge you to stop snivelling at once! Think yourself lucky to have any help at all in these trying times!

Moan and tug at your bales and give yourself a hernia if you must but at least do it with good grace as you follow in the wake of the mighty Land Army lass who undoubtedly has most of the job done whilst you are still pulling your boots on!

Do make an effort and trot about on foot after your speeding tractor and toss your turnips into those freshly turned furrows with all the strength and speed you can muster!

Do at least try to be a gentleman and tell the girl who is milking your cow – or indeed the cow itself, whichever one of them does turn out to be wearing the lipstick – that the colour reminds you of Flanders poppies and the last time we fought and won a war together!

And finally, sniff the wildflowers on the windowsill appreciatively, but don't under any circumstances get crumbs on that nice new tablecloth ere I send my little housemaid down to your farm to arm wrestle you into submission, you ungrateful brute!

Yours,

Hilda Ffinch
Hilda Ffinch,
The Bird with All The Answers

"Not in My (Onion) Bed!"

Dicky Rutter
Bog View Cottage
Spanker Lane
Little Hope

8th November 1940

Dear Mrs Ffinch,

Thank you for your recent help with my limp marrow, all good now and a joy to behold.

I have another problem however, which may well be a police matter rather than 'one for you' but I'll run it past you anyway if that's alright.

I was out a night or two ago taking my evening walk down by my 'Dig for Victory' patch (it's looking marvellous) in the allotments when I thought I spied a vandal wheeling a barrow across my veg patch and so I went to have a gander. On drawing closer I was horrified to see a courting couple in an act of…well modesty forbids me…but, *you know…*'

I didn't recognise the couple as they made a very quick exit when they heard me blundering towards them. Is this a police matter?

Either way, I've been taking my fouling piece with me over the past few nights since, prepared to let them have it should they return – eight square feet of damaged spring onions in wartime – it's not on!

Exasperated,

Reg 'Dicky' Rutter

𝕿𝖍𝖊 𝕷𝖎𝖙𝖙𝖑𝖊 𝕳𝖔𝖕𝖊 𝕳𝖊𝖗𝖆𝖑𝖉
Saturday, 9th November 1940

Dear Dicky,

Thank you for your latest communiqué, I am terribly pleased that you are no longer experiencing gardener's droop and that you are now in possession of a prize specimen which stands a good chance of having someone's eye out at the forthcoming Little Hope Village Fete. Well done, dear man, well done!

A word of friendly advice regarding your pride and joy however, if I may? Do keep it under wraps until the last possible moment in order to avoid the green-eyed spectre of jealousy which is rampant amongst men with withered gourds at such an event. I should hate to see Mr Percy Filch take a rubber mallet to it in a fit of pique similar to that which he demonstrated in 1936 when he mistook Mr Trotter's 'thrice stuffed porky banger' for a new variety of aubergine and made a complete fool of himself in front of the His Grace the Duke of Kent. The man's shame was legion and eternal.

Now, with regard to your nocturnal visitors, please do not turn your fouling piece on them lest you yourself be arrested, tried and hanged like a pheasant! That is not the way, my dear man, not the way! That said, I do understand and sympathise with your outrage and frustration at being rudely exposed to the mating rituals of others. The Colonel and I frequently have to close the French windows during the summertime when the cries of joy (at least we think that's what they are) emanating from our gamekeeper's cottage during a full moon when he and Mrs Scratcher are indulging in a bit of what my dear husband refers to (in their case) as 'potting the partridge' all gets to be a bit too much. Why, I have often said to the Colonel that unwary travellers in these parts harking to that racket might well believe a banshee to be at large in the Bell End Wood and may need to turn to the church for succour and reassurance as a result. It really is most unsettling, and the sound carries a good half mile on a still night with no wind.

But I digress. For a less 'terminal' outcome, might you consider filling your wheelbarrow with three pints of gum Arabic topped with a sack or two of chicken feathers and leaving it in the middle of your onion patch overnight? The lure of a comfortable bunk (as it were) will surely be too great a temptation for your mysterious lothario and his doxy and they'll be tarred and feathered in next to no time. Identifying them afterwards will be an absolute piece of cake!

With this in mind, I will have a word with Constable Clink this evening (he generally calls in for a quick one with my Cook during the course of his beat, tea being a great stimulant) and will tell him to be on the lookout for two extraordinarily large (and exceedingly game) birds in the vicinity of your allotment. He has a keen eye and knows precisely what to do with his truncheon when the need arises.

I do hope this helps.

Yours,

Hilda Ffinch
Hilda Ffinch,
The Bird with All The Answers

P.S. Should you have any spare onions please do drop them round, my Cook has plenty of sage and does rather enjoy a good stuffing.

What Does He Feed That Beast?

Mrs Thora Pyle
Hunter's Cottage
Bell End Road
Little Hope

12th November 1940

Dear Mrs Ffinch,

How much manure is the average horse supposed to produce under its own steam, as it were, and are horses creatures of habit when it comes to, you know, 'doing their business'? I ask because the milkman's horse which trots past my cottage daily seems to produce an awful lot of manure and usually deposits it right outside my front gate.

I have to confess that I do use some of it for my vegetable garden but even so, there's usually enough to fertilise half the county.

Yours,

Thora Pyle

The Little Hope Herald
Saturday, 16th November 1940

Dear Mrs Pyle,

Nobody, but *nobody*, quite knows what Mr Tupper the milkman feeds that beast in order for it to produce the ungodly quantities of manure that it does.

Some say that the curious mushrooms which grow in Farmer Brewster's field are to blame, for its certain that the beast is put out to graze there regularly of an evening and is wont to munch its way through the hedgerow before night falls, often appearing amiable and gay the following morning.

Others blame the quality of the oats available for equine ingestion in these trying times, stating that they're not nearly as robust as they used to be and that consequently the creatures in question feel the need to go more regularly, as it were.

Whatever the cause, you are not alone in your dismay at the piles of dung festering in our streets and so I have arranged for the Boy Scouts to trot along on a twice daily basis to collect the stuff in buckets and to distribute it in equal shares to the following bodies:

- The Allotments of Little Hope Association, for use on the weird and wonderful varieties of vegetables which, as part of our Dig for Victory campaign, are currently springing up from the good earth of Yorkshire in search of sunlight and full-bodied sustenance.
- The Little Hope Historical Society, who have recently embarked on a mission to build eight mediaeval trebuchets for the village for the purposes of civil defence should Jerry make it across the channel. Given that plague-ridden cow carcasses and rocks of sufficient dimensions and weight are likely to be in short supply in the event of an invasion, Miss Amphora Long-Barrow – the eminent archaeologist who dwells hereabouts – has agreed to begin experimenting with large manure balls which, if dried out and then soaked in paraffin and set alight before being launched, may well serve to take out a Panzer division or two.
- The Traditional Crafters of Little Hope. This splendid group of artisans who meet at the Village Hall on a Wednesday evening appear to have run out of potters clay, which is a terrible shame given that their grand project for this year was to have fashioned a life-sized nativity of the entire Holy Family along with their animals and esteemed visitors, for display in the knave at St Candida's this Christmas. The

Crafter's chairman, Mr Enoch Westmacott, has welcomed the chance to 'work with a new medium' and is confident that the odour of the church crypt combined with the aroma of the Vicar's seasonal mulled communion wine (he brews it by the vat full every year, as you know) will counteract any residual horsey smell floating about the place quite nicely.

- Mr Albert Crumbleholme the local builder who, having spent a great deal of time in Natal Colony in his youth, is confident that he remembers how to convert dried dung into house bricks and has submitted plans to the village council for the construction of several new outhouses in Agincourt Street, to replace the ones which were flattened by a rogue parachute mine last month. Work has already begun on a prototype in his own backyard and, if successful, materials for 'Crumbleholme's Do It Yourself Shit-House' will be delivered to the residents of Agincourt Street for self-assembly in very much the same way as our beloved Anderson shelters were.

In the meantime, Mrs Pyle, do please continue to rake up as much muck as you can – my sources tell me that you are very good at this and would win a medal for it were one to be up for grabs.

I do hope this helps.

Yours,

Hilda Ffinch
Hilda Ffinch,
The Bird with All The Answers

P.S. Obviously, I have reservations about Mr Crumbleholme's choice of name for his 'do it yourself' outhouses on the grounds that it outrages common decency and has given the Vicar a headache. But that said, one has to be glad that the Anglo-Saxon vernacular is alive and well in these difficult times, and it may well flourish further and give a good account of itself should Jerry arrive unexpectedly.

VII.

Gentlemen's Problems
(Or, Man Up and Shut Up!)

*Having come a cropper in an unfortunate incident involving
a rhubarb forcer behind the cake stall at the Little Hope Village
Fete, Colonel Ffinch limped across to the Vicarage where he
knew Hilda and the Reverend Aubrey Fishwick would be gamely
manning the refreshments tent. En route, he caught his fingers
in the gate, sprained an ankle on a rogue croquet hoop and
was rather badly goosed by Miss Titty Wainwright (who did
love a man in uniform and was slightly the worse for wear on
account of the Vicar's apple cider).*

*"Are you quite alright?" asked Hilda, as the unfortunate fellow
limped into the home straights. "You're a little late, dear."*

*"Yes, yes, quite alright, thank you," replied the Colonel, glancing
hopefully towards a vacant chair in the hope that he might sit
down before he fell down.*

*"Good idea," Hilda followed his glance. "Might you take that
over to the church hall and give the verger a hand with his
bunting?" she paused, "You're not limping, are you?"*

"Well, I..."

*"Oh good. Hurry along now, dear, the sheepdog trials begin
in five minutes."*

Once A Thespian...

Mr Hilary Hopcock
Maypole House
Fiddler's End
Little Hope

May Day (literally), 1940

Dear Mrs Ffinch,

I recently made the mistake of telling my sister Dorothy that during my time at university I played one of the two principal roles in the amateur dramatic society's production of *Romeo and Juliet*. Had I been 'Romeo' then this letter would not be winging its way to you now, however as I was chosen to play 'Juliet' (on account of lack of interest in the part by the predominantly blue-stocking/suffragette types in my year) I now regret opening my mouth and fear that my shame will be eternal. My sister has, in a fit of pique following an incident involving a small pot of rouge (which I mistook for bunion ointment), told everyone at The Royal Oak that I'm rather partial to a man in tights and like to wear corsets.

My concern is that this might have given some of the remaining chaps in the vicinity completely the wrong idea about me – the postman has winked at me twice now whilst fiddling with his sack, the butcher has waved at me with a large sausage in his hand and, most alarmingly, Akala from the local Boy Scout troop has twice signalled the offer of a night under canvas with him by semaphore.

Each to his own, Mrs Ffinch, each to his own. But my own *is* my own and I'm hoping to give it to Miss Rosy Pole after the Harvest Festival Supper.

Short of actually killing my sister, what can I do to resolve the situation? I need to reclaim my masculinity, post haste!

Yours,

Hilary Hopcock (<u>MISTER</u>)

𝕿𝖍𝖊 𝕷𝖎𝖙𝖙𝖑𝖊 𝕳𝖔𝖕𝖊 𝕳𝖊𝖗𝖆𝖑𝖉
Saturday, 4th May 1940

My Dear Mr Hopcock,

Please do resist the temptation to murder your sibling, as doing so may well attract the attention of entirely the wrong sort of woman, the type whose definition of 'well-hung' is wont to tally with the occupation of Mr Albert Pierrepoint the Crown Executioner who – as we all know – is able to indulge in the despatching act within the confines of the law, and you don't want to end up dangling from the end of *his* rope.

Should you wish to avoid notoriety in the short to medium term then and live to plight your troth to Miss Rosy Pole at the village Harvest Festival Supper, it's best to do so as a fine, upstanding member of the community. No nice girl really wants a marriage proposal from a man straining to be heard above the howls of a baying mob at the foot of the scaffold, many of whom would no doubt be knitting frantically after the French fashion or eating roasted pig's tails on sticks.

In order to reassert yourself as an alpha male, Mr Hopcock, you must make it *blatantly* obvious to even the most innocent of bystanders that you are as red-blooded as the next man, and in order for this to happen I believe that you must be seen walking abroad with ladies of the opposite sex.

Now, I use 'ladies' in the plural term here as with your current reputation as 'the Oscar Wilde of Fiddler's End' (that's what they call you at the local book club) you stand little chance of convincing anyone at all that you are God's gift to the fairer sex by being seen in the company of just one young lady – people will think that she's a close friend doing you a favour in order to save your reputation.

Might I suggest therefore, that you avail yourself of the services of Mrs Edith Muff-Hawker, landlady of The Cat and Cabbage over in Hampton Upon Mott? For a couple of bob she will arrange for a variety of young ladies of her acquaintance to be seen up and down the High Street on your arm, and I believe that an extra tuppence upfront will encourage one of them to hold your hand outside the Post Office or possibly even kiss you on the butcher's porch, as it were.

Your reputation will then become positively Byronesque. Leave a sonnet or two (dedicated to Miss Rosy Pole) on a park bench – anchored by a house brick should the weather be a little inclement – and you'll soon have the fairer sex of Little Hope eating out of your hand. Give it a week or so, enough time for sexual tension in the village to build, and then throw yourself at the dainty feet of Miss Rosy Pole declaring (with as much passion as you can possibly muster) that you'll give every last one of those cheap women up for her. With any luck she'll have fallen for the above ruse and will believe herself blessed to be the only woman that the Casanova of Little Hope really desires.

Please be aware however that there is a slight chance that she may think you a complete cad at this point and hi away to a nunnery, or something equally melodramatic. Terms and conditions obviously apply.

Just before I end my letter, might I bring to your attention the fact that our very own village theatre company – The Dreary Lane Players – are currently auditioning for the part of Heathcliff in their forthcoming attempt at *Wuthering Heights*? Local critics have already dubbed it 'Withering Frights' on account of the role of Cathy having gone to Miss Hetty Mayflower, who has few teeth to speak of and feminine attributes which began heading south in the same week as Captain Scott and Titus Oates, but beggars can't be choosers in your dubious position, dear man, perhaps have a crack at it/her?

Bon chance then, Mr Hopcock! Break a leg!

Yours winsomely,

Hilda Ffinch
Hilda Ffinch,
The Bird with All The Answers (and the love letter from Rudolf Valentino in the safe)

And Then There Were None…

'Devoutly Anonymous'
Yorkshire

9th June 1940

Dear Mrs Ffinch,

I am writing to you anonymously and in 'couched terms' as the problem I have is of a rather delicate nature and plain speaking might affront/terrify some of your less worldly spinster readers.

Before the war, I was a great admirer of most British biscuits, but Huntley & Palmers in particular. I didn't fully realise the depth of my love for them until rationing came along and well – in the words of dear Mrs Agatha Christie – *'then there were none'*. The problem I now have, is that on the rare occasion my housekeeper does manage to get her hands on a packet for me I find myself greatly embarrassed on account of my 'Old Man' standing to attention of his own accord. Whilst this is manageable within the confines of my locked study, it's rather more of a problem over the dinner table and has me seriously thinking twice about attending this year's church fete, as there's bound to be a packet up for grabs in the tombola.

Please advise.

Yours,

'Devoutly Anonymous'

P.S. I've tried prayer and a little gentle flagellation but to no avail.

𝕮𝖍𝖊 𝕷𝖎𝖙𝖙𝖑𝖊 𝕳𝖔𝖕𝖊 𝕳𝖊𝖗𝖆𝖑𝖉
Saturday, 15th June 1940

Dear 'Devoutly Anonymous',

Fear not, dear man, fear not! This is not the first time I have come across a problematic 'gentleman's region' I can assure you!

Colonel Ffinch, my dear spouse, had a similar issue before the war whenever he clapped eyes on a Bakewell tart. Fortunately, his current posting overseas keeps him well away from Derbyshire in general and the aforementioned tarts in particular, and so for the time being it's a case of problem solved.

In the interim period however, whilst the Colonel was awaiting his orders, we did risk a brief foray out to Chatsworth House, where His Grace the Duke of Devonshire was holding one of his balls and requested that we join him. Being wise to my dear spouse's shortcomings in the pie and pastry department and not wishing to let His Grace down, I undertook the following precautionary measure: I had Mr Tack, the village saddler, discretely craft a pair of gentleman's blinkers for our journey through the open countryside where the slightest whiff of a Bakewell tart creeping in through the glove compartment of the Bentley might set the Colonel off. Made from the softest leather and embellished with discrete Whitby jet cameos of the steaming Bakewell tarts, the blinkers were such that a fellow might wear them with the minimum of discomfort and without attracting much attention at all. The latter point was fully addressed by my muffling much of the Colonel's head and jaw with a simple silk paisley scarf, (such as one commonly wears when afflicted with a toothache) and pulling his top hat well down so that the brim rested snugly on the top of his blinkers. An absolute coup was achieved!

Fortunately, Mr Tack is still in business – his flat feet, rendered so by the hoof of many a clumsy carthorse, have put paid to any notion of military service which he might have entertained – and he's always willing to take on a private commission. A set of made-to-measure 'male blinkers' might be had from him in under a week at the very reasonable rate of one guinea and I believe that he also offers a repair service should the thought of your Huntley & Palmers lead to an unforeseen mishap.

I do hope this helps you, 'Devoutly Anonymous', please don't hesitate to write again should your 'Old Man' persist in going his own way.

Yours confidently,

Hilda Ffinch
Hilda Ffinch,
The Bird with All The Answers

P.S. One hears that leather face masks and discreet whips might also be had from Mr Tack at a terribly reasonable price. A set of handcuffs for chaining yourself to a radiator in order to resist the lure of the bisquit siren should her song become too unbearable can also be had (under the counter, as it were) from Mr Hardman the village blacksmith upon request.

Am I Inadequate?

Mr A. Lister
Sunrise Cottage
Cock-a-Hoop Lane
Little Hope

14th July 1940

Dear Mrs Ffinch,

I find myself writing to you in a greatly dejected state occasioned by an encounter with Ernie, the milkman's horse. Please allow me to explain:

On Tuesday last, I was walking out with my girl along the canal bridle path next to the meadow where Ernie hangs out when he's not trotting up and down the high street when we chanced to see 'Big Boy' himself standing there in all his glory, munching on a bit of hedge.

"Oh my!" said my girl, "Would you look at that!"

And I did look, and look again.

"Are…you know…are *men* like that?" my girl asked, blushing and giving me a sideways glance.

"Oh yes," I replied without thinking, "Very much so."

We're to be married in the autumn and I'm obviously worried that when my new wife sees plainly that I'm not like Ernie at all, she'll pack her bags and go home to her mother post haste. Such is my anxiety that my 'Ernie appendage' has gone on strike and it is of use to neither man nor beast (figuratively speaking, of course) at present.

What, oh what, can I do?

Yours deflatedly,

Arnold Lister.

𝕿𝖍𝖊 𝕷𝖎𝖙𝖙𝖑𝖊 𝕳𝖔𝖕𝖊 𝕳𝖊𝖗𝖆𝖑𝖉
Saturday, 20th July 1940

Dear Mr Lister,

Oh dear, you have got yourself into a bit of a sticky situation, haven't you? Such is the cost of the male propensity to exaggerate the scale and range of his gentleman's artillery that it is an account which most men find themselves unable to settle decently when push comes to shove.

But take heart, oh exaggerating one, in that you will not be the first fellow to have to ring the handbell of shame on his wedding night when, failing to live up to the expectations of his beloved, he finds himself forlorn, woebegone, alone and sent to sleep on a horsehair sofa in the cruel moonlight. Many have come before you. Or not, as the case may be.

Ask yourself this, however – would you really wish to be encumbered by a male member of such magnitude that you involuntarily leapfrog over it whilst perambulating down the street? Would not it make stepping off the kerb particularly difficult and increase the risk of turning an ankle badly? True, it might increase your chances of winning the three-legged race at the village fete, but it certainly won't improve your chances in the sack race, if you get my meaning.

Be of reasonable cheer then, Mr Lister, and perhaps take your beloved on a day trip to the Regent's Park Zoo in dear old London town where, I'm sure, during the course of the day you will be able to point to a masculine creature displaying credentials more comparable with your own? That should lower your girl's expectations somewhat.

Perhaps give the Hedgehog enclosure some serious consideration?

I do hope this helps,

Yours,

Hilda Ffinch
Hilda Ffinch.
The Bird with All The Answers (and the husband who is hung like a bull elephant)

The Menstrual Cycle...

Private 'Nobby' Rott
'Somewhere in England'

15th August, 1940

Dear Mrs Ffinch,

On returning home recently for a five-day recovery leave following an unfortunate incident with a bit of rogue shrapnel at the front, I suggested to the dear wife that it might be pleasant to cycle into the countryside on our Raleigh bikes so that we could enjoy a loving moment or two in a warm meadow which we used to frequent before the war. However, my Bet just shrugged her shoulders and replied "No, I have my menstrual cycle, so it would be a waste of time..."

I thought this was a strange thing to say on account of us both definitely having Raleigh cycles, so I asked her where they were, and she explained that both were required for use by the Home Guard and had been requisitioned until the war ends. She went on to say that the two Home Guard members who use our bikes like to call in regularly so that she can see that they're being looked after properly and also so that she's able to give them a bit of a seeing to, if needs be. Somewhat confused, I let matters lie and saw out my leave on foot before returning to my unit.

What do you think? Is it me? I never did manage to find the wife's menstrual cycle, despite having had the shed out and I'm tempted to ask the Home Guard for compensation on account of having missed my moment in the meadow with the Mrs?

Sincerely yours,

'Nobby' Rott, Private,
King's Own Yorkshire Light Infantry

The Little Hope Herald
Saturday, 17th August 1940

Dear Private Rott,

One presumes, dear man, given that you and Mrs Rott have been frequenting 'a warm meadow' in this vicinity since before the war, that you have been intimately acquainted with your spouse for more than a month and that your union was not a sudden one occasioned by our current national alarm level of bristling pike shafts at noon!

Have you not noticed that at a certain time of each month your wife is wont to eschew intimate relations with you and prefers instead the company of several bars of Cadbury's Ration Chocolate (obtained at knifepoint if necessary), hourly nips of gin, endless plates of Huntley & Palmers bisquits and the comforting purr of her own pussy (cat)?

The menstrual cycle, you dolt, is not a two-wheeled perambulating vehicle but a monthly state of female preparation for the perpetuation of the human race. It is a metaphor for 'the arrival of the crimson tide', for 'riding the cotton donkey', 'having the Red Baron to stay' (don't take that one too literally) or for 'displaying the Red Badge of courage' when the deluge begins. Some ladies refer to this period (see what I did there?) as the time when 'Aunt Rose comes to stay' or may allude casually to 'having the painters in' despite the house being in a reasonable state of repair with an excellent coat of gloss on the banisters. My own dear spouse, Colonel Ffinch, who is clearly a little more worldly-wise than yourself, refers to my own monthly bout of 'red moon rising' as "Right then, I'll shut up and decamp to my club until you're alright again" which, whilst displaying a certain lack of empathy for my own situation, has undoubtedly saved his life on more than one occasion.

If I am to be honest with you, Private Rott, my real concern with your issue is that at least two members (sic) of the Home Guard appear to be better acquainted with your wife's menstrual cycle than you are and to this end I would advise that you have a 'frank and fearless' with Mrs Rott (when she's not 'staying at the red roof hotel' or 'flying the Japanese flag') and ascertain just what has been going on in your absence!

On a positive note however, rest assured that both of your pushbikes are probably safe. I myself was almost rendered unconscious on Tuesday evening last when Mrs Rott, accompanied by Angus Pike, the well-known (and rather burly) merchant seaman from Hull, hurtled past me on a pair of matching Raleighs in the general direction of Bushy End, leaving behind them so pungent an odour of North Sea trawler decking that it is probably illegal under the terms of the Geneva Convention. Nothing for you to worry about though, my sources tell me that Mr Pike calls in once a week just to drop his pollocks off.

In the meantime, I am enclosing a copy of Miss Virginia Creeper's classic novel *A Bird in the Hand or a Quick One in the Bush* which will tell you all you need to know about the dangers of attempting to mount the menstrual cycle, as it were.

I do hope this helps. Good luck to you Private Rott! Keep your head down and God Save the King!

Yours,

Hilda Ffinch
Hilda Ffinch,
The Bird with All The Answers

The Menacing Miss Mayflower...

Mr Alfred Cummings
2, Verdun Passage
Greater Hope

9th September 1940

Dear Mrs Ffinch,

I seem to have an issue with a lady called Miss Mayflower, the church verger, who is constantly giving me the eye. Forty years ago, I may have been flattered, but at the age of seventy-six I can hardly tie my own shoelaces, never mind fiddle with anything else.

I realise that I am one of the very few men left in our village with most of our brave fellows away fighting the good fight and I am happy to do my bit for the war effort, but I do have my limits!

Please advise, what should I do?

Yours desperately,

Alfred Cummings

The Little Hope Herald
Saturday, 14th September 1940

Dear Mr Cummings,

Oh come, come now, sir! Do get a firm grip on yourself and endeavour to man up! If the Reverend Aubrey Fishwick can gamely fend off the sex-starved harpies of Little Hope – admittedly with help from a bell, book and candle in his case – then I'm sure that you can give an equally good account of yourself!

Are you not, after all (as local legend has it), the sterling fellow who gave our dear Mr Churchill a bunk up so that he could get his leg over during his escape from the Boers in Pretoria in 1899? If so, you do yourself a grave misservice, Sir! Why, without your impressive upward thrust we might even now be watching Herr Hitler and Lord Halifax shopping for lederhosen and a bit of spiced-up sausage together in Oxford Street!

Now, seventy-six is no age at all, my good man, there's many a good tune played on an old trombone, as the saying goes, and I'll wager that in years to come a song will be written about just that.

With regards to Miss Mayflower herself, I'd take her name with a pinch of salt and stop worrying. She blossomed just before the Titanic went down and has been all talk and no action ever since.

Be of good cheer now and perhaps consider taking a gentle stroll with the ladies of the Women's Institute when they sally forth gathering nuts in the greenwood on Tuesday next? It's that time of year again and I'm sure that they'll be only too happy to take it in turns to hold your sack for you should it become a little full.

Good luck with those nuts now, female and otherwise! Do let me know how you get on!

Yours,

Hilda Ffinch
Hilda Ffinch,
The Bird with All The Answers

P.S. If the more militant members of the WI do happen to slip their hands into your pockets and offer to lighten your load do say "No!" and endeavour to make good your getaway. It won't be the odd tanner they're after and at your age you need to watch it.

A Dirty Great Bayonet…

'Charles'
21 Kitchener Close
Little Hope

1ˢᵗ October 1940

Dear Mrs Ffinch,

If I may be so bold – I have a dirty bayonet and no matter how much I rub it I cannot get the blessed thing to shine these days! My good old wife has had a bash at it too, she's tried spitting on it and then getting a bit of muslin and rubbing vigorously, but without success!

I do like to keep it in good state of repair, you know, just in case. I've heard the Jerries don't like it up 'em and who knows what tomorrow might bring?

Please advise.

Yours, most respectfully,

Charles

The Little Hope Herald
Saturday, 5ᵗʰ October 1940

Dear Charles,

I do sympathise with your problem and would like to assure you that you are not the only fellow afflicted by this plight in wartime.

It is common knowledge that when all is peaceful and rosy in the garden a fellow is wont to take his weapon for granted and often neglects to give the entire shaft a thorough rinse with a good sharp vinegar at least once a week in order to keep it in tiptop condition, indeed, it is often only when the Hun starts trying to kick a fellow's back door in that his mind turns to the state of his lance.

Colonel Ffinch regularly dips his bayonet into my Tiger Claw (a particularly sharp brand of vinegar which we imported regularly from the Chap Matahari Trading Post in Malacca Street, Singapore, before the war) but I fear that it is both exhausted and hard to come by these days, otherwise you'd be quite welcome to dunk yours in too. Might I suggest therefore that you thrust your dirty old bayonet into a bucket of horse urine? The ammonia ought to get a reaction going in next to no time and I'm confident that it'll come up a treat. Don't let Mrs Charles endeavour to spit on it afterwards however as it may be sharper than she thinks after a good seeing to and there's every chance that she'll have her eye out.

Incidentally, the information you have received pertaining to whether or not Jerry likes it up him is indeed correct, I can confirm (from personal experience during a particularly riotous Oktoberfest in Munich in 1928) that Jerry most certainly does not like it up him and assuming the polar opposite has led to the downfall of many an unfortunate submariner.

Yours,

Hilda Ffinch
Hilda Ffinch,
The Bird with All The Answers

Night Blindness...

Mr Brian Pugh
Dick's End Cottage
Bushy Gap
2nd October 1940

Dear Mrs Ffinch,

I recently joined the Royal Observer Corps and passed all the entrance tests with flying colours. Trouble is, at night I can't see a thing through me binoculars and am a bit worried that I might have night blindness.

Do I own up or keep winging it? I do so want to help win the war.

Yours anxiously,

Brian Pugh

𝕿𝖍𝖊 𝕷𝖎𝖙𝖙𝖑𝖊 𝕳𝖔𝖕𝖊 𝕳𝖊𝖗𝖆𝖑𝖉
Saturday, 5th October 1940

Dear Blind Pew,

After receiving your letter this morning, I telephoned that terribly dashing local Observer Corps Captain, William Bligh who is – he confirmed – your commanding officer. He suggests, as do I, that you try removing the lens caps from your binoculars before endeavouring to look through them. We both agreed that this will significantly improve Britain's chances of spotting an incoming Jerry or two in the short term and ultimately, in the long term, it may help to actually win the war.

Now, I have a favour to ask. Captain Bligh has requested that you perform your hilarious 'nightly vigil routine' in the local airmen's mess at eight o'clock sharp on Tuesday evening next as it will do wonders for 'The Chaps' morale. They could do with a good laugh and with you out of the way for the night the citizens of the north might stand a fighting chance of reaching their shelters before Jerry is directly overhead.

I do hope this helps. Don't be downhearted, I'm a huge fan of accidental comedy and you, my dear fellow, are positively hysterical.

Yours,

Hilda Ffinch
Hilda Ffinch,
The Bird with All The Answers

Might I Borrow your Tiger Claw?

'Charles'
21 Kitchener Close
Little Hope

15th October 1940

Dear Mrs Ffinch,

Thanks so much for your recent advice regarding my dodgy bayonet, it was very helpful. I wonder if I might be so bold as to ask if you might now have any spare 'Tiger Claw' at all that you wouldn't mind parting with? Perhaps a consignment has made it to the docks?

I'm becoming a little desperate as I fear that in my case, horses' urine may be rather hard to get. Due to a complete misunderstanding between me and the local constabulary I now have a court restriction stopping me from going within two miles of anything on four legs, all I was doing was checking to see if Farmer Brewster's carthorse needed new back shoes but nobody will listen.

Also, before I go, would a cork in the keyhole help to stop Jerry smashing Mrs Charles's back door in if he comes when I'm not here? She has already greased the knob with dripping in an effort to thwart him, but I fear it won't be enough.

Yours hopefully,

Charles

The Little Hope Herald
Saturday, 19th October 1940

Dear Charles,

How lovely to hear from you again and to learn that, although you are unable to get your hands on any horse urine at this time, you have at least been taking on some of Mr Hardman the blacksmith's work now that he is away at the front. Remember, for want of a nail the shoe was lost, and if Roger the Carthorse at Bell End Farm should happen to cast a shoe then there may well be no harvest in Little Hope this year! Constable Clink has clearly got the wrong end of the stick, I will ask Colonel Ffinch to have a word with him. Should that fail then I'll be playing whist with Lord Anthrax, the chairman of the local magistrates on Friday next and I'll see if I can't pull something off for you.

I fear, however, that I am still unable to supply you with any 'Tiger Claw' as mine has practically dried up and I really can't see the Colonel being able to do much about it until we're able to get it in again. Only last week the poor fellow was reduced to greasing his bayonet with what was left of his 'Beake's Stacholine' (again, terribly difficult to come by), leaving his notoriously stiff moustache most awfully droopy and resulting in him sporting a look of Fu Manchu. This – alas – resulted in an altercation with Cook in the early hours of Wednesday morning when she caught him creeping into her pantry for a spot of tiffin and mistook him for an oriental assassin. We were able to salvage most of the stuffed marrow that she went at him with, but I fear that the Colonel's scallops were done for.

With regard to Mrs Charles's back door, Jerry's a slippery one at the best of times and I'm fairly certain that he won't be put off by a bit of dripping, might I therefore suggest that you board it up for the duration of the war and only use her front entrance?

I do hope this helps.

Yours,

Hilda Ffinch
Hilda Ffinch,
The Bird with All The Answers

A Bit Short on The Old Shag...

'Charles'
21 Kitchener Close
Little Hope

9th November 1940

Dear Mrs Ffinch,

I have the most frightful problem! My pipe hasn't had a sniff of British Oak rough shag for a while now and I am simply gasping for it. I've tried and tried but I just can't get my hands on any for love nor money!

Any ideas for a substitution? Mrs Charles is a bit concerned as she has noticed a change in my behaviour, she says I've become terribly sullen and miserable and that she too misses the days when I had a full pipe thrice daily.

Please help!

Yours,

Charles

P.S. I've tried smoking bay leaves, but find them a bit 'minty'.

The Little Hope Herald
Saturday, 16th November 1940

Dear Charles,

This is not my area of speciality. However, undeterred and determined to help you in your hour of need if at all possible, I telephoned Colonel Ffinch at the War Office to enquire whether he knows anything at all about rough shags. I wasn't particularly hopeful as I know that he prefers a smooth one when he's home on leave, but nothing ventured, nothing gained, and so I went for it anyway. Unfortunately the Colonel was in a meeting with the Home Secretary when my call was put through and he was unable to comment in person, but his secretary nipped in to ask him on my behalf and apparently he replied that he is well acquainted with the odd rough shag and will be home on Friday to show me.

In the meantime, however, there are alternatives to 'British Oak' out there which I am aware of. I wonder if you might not be able to amuse yourself with 'Three Nuns' or a little 'Presbyterian'? The former isn't to everyone's taste and can be habit-forming, something which might make one a little cross, but the latter is really quite rough round the edges and thus might serve to minister to your needs until you can get round to a decent bit of shag?

I hope you're able to enjoy a quick puff or two whilst waiting for the merchant fleet to make it back home. Those seamen are hardy types and I'm sure there will be plenty of British Oak to go around when they make it back into port.

Do let me know how you get on.

Yours,

Hilda Ffinch
Hilda Ffinch,
The Bird with All The Answers

P.S. Avoid stuffing bay leaves into your pipe at all costs, there's nothing remotely attractive about a gentleman who goes about the place smelling of oxtail soup.

VIII.

Hard Times: Getting A Decent Mouthful

"This is an interesting one, Cook!" remarked Colonel Ffinch, gingerly poking his spotted dick. "Not sure it will be to Mrs F's taste, though?"

"Of course it will," Cook replied confidently, "and anyway, if it's not, there's a jam roly-poly in the pantry..."

My Kingdom for a Hog!

Marjorie Butterworth
3 Agincourt Street
Little Hope

16th March 1940

Dear Mrs Ffinch,

Through tears I write you, I am most definitely 'on the edge'.

You see, since Mr Butterworth has been away seeing to Mr Hitler, I've been finding it increasingly difficult to put food on the table for my children and for Mrs Butterworth senior. To date, we have worked our way through our eight chickens, two geese and the children's pet rabbit and now all we have left is my beloved pet pig, Hamlet.

The mother-in-law is putting increasing pressure on me to do the dastardly deed and is being most insistent that I turn Hamlet into pork chops, but I just can't bring myself to do it. When I look into my dearest Hamlet's eye (singular, he only has the one since the unfortunate incident with a peashooter last year) I well up inside – and I…I just *can't* do it!

What should I do?

Yours desperately,

Marjorie Butterworth (Hamlet's Mother)

𝕿𝖍𝖊 𝕷𝖎𝖙𝖙𝖑𝖊 𝕳𝖔𝖕𝖊 𝕳𝖊𝖗𝖆𝖑𝖉
Saturday, 23rd March 1940

Dear Mrs Butterworth,

Now, if your pet were to be say, an anonymous hedgehog, would this still be a prickly problem for you? If he were a nameless deer, would you have issues with passing the buck around the dinner table?

I think not.

It is my opinion, my dear, that you have fallen into the time-honoured trap of giving a familiar name to an undomesticated animal, one which – in nature – habitually lumbers about the place on all fours sniffing cowpats before defecating in a haystack.

It's all very well becoming attached to wild beasts, Mrs Butterworth, but it is not in the nation's best interests to stand in the way of such a creature as it meanders through life en route to its final destination – a Wedgwood dinner plate on one's dining table – as we are after all, a country at war, and where should we be without bacon?

I do have a little sympathy for you, but you really do need to man up and set that upper lip to 'stiff as a board' if you are to put a decent meal on the dinner table for your family. Perhaps strengthen your resolve a little by easing yourself gently into the 'process of dispatchment' by having a stab at a less vocal and not quite so reproachful looking mammal? Hedgehog is jolly tasty, my Cook caught an old gypsy stuffing one in the Bell End Wood a year or so ago, adapted the recipe a little and has been serving up 'Prick on a Plate' at Ffinch Hall ever since. Delicious. We love it!

I truly believe that your problem is self-induced and has its root in the realms of the subliminal, my dear, wholly on account of your pig's romanticised moniker. Let me explain further:

Were I to espy you coming out of the Yorkshire Meat Emporium in the High Street and call out to you *"I say! Mrs Butterworth! How is dear Hamlet?"* then I suspect that your thoughts would immediately turn to a noble head beneath a golden crown in the faraway kingdom of Denmark. Your subconscious mind might then bring to your attention a well-turned calf (human, obviously) in a beautifully ladder-free white stocking and then it would all go pear-shaped for you as you subconsciously added a snout to the fair face of Shakespeare's doomed hero and a pair of trotters where his hallux ought to be.

Please do endeavour to desist from your faux intimacy with this beast of the field, Mrs Butterworth, I implore you. Look your succulent porker in the (one) eye and see the delight on the faces of your little Dickensian ones as they suck on a tasty trotter reflected back at you!

You'll be waiting forever for Pigling Bland to recite a soliloquy to you, Mrs Butterworth, so do have at it and get that sausage inside you!

Yours,

Hilda Ffinch
Hilda Ffinch,
The Bird with All The Answers

P.S. If I might just point out the sole exception to the 'give a pig a name' rule in these trying times: several of the villagers have clubbed together and formed a pig club and the object of their heart's desire – destined for many a festive table this Yuletide – has been named Herman Goering. 'Churchill' was mooted briefly, but Mr Trotter the butcher made it very clear that under no circumstances would he agree to stuff the Prime Minister over the Christmas period.

How Do I make It Rise?

Doreen Pennywhistle
17 Mafeking Terrace
Little Hope

21st March 1940

Dear Ms Ffinch,

Why don't my eggless cakes rise? What am I doing wrong?

Yours,

Doreen.

The Little Hope Herald
Saturday, 23rd March 1940

Dear Doreen,

Given that you've neglected to give yourself a title I'm assuming that you're a spinster and have never seen anything rise in your life (bar the sun and the price of gin). I suspect that your problem is actually due to a streak of bitterness and sexual frustration festering deep within you, and it's now beginning to boil over into your baking.

Do stop blaming it all on the war and rationing, if you can't make an eggless cake rise then you really are in trouble. I suggest that you find yourself a suitable beau and let him get his leg over (put your baking bowl down first though for health and safety reasons), thus enabling you to *both* have your cake and eat it.

Yours,

Hilda Ffinch
Hilda Ffinch,
The Bird with All The Answers

My Old Man's Sausage…

Violet Bell
Harpy Cottage
Bushy End
Little Hope

1ˢᵗ May 1940

Dear Ms Ffinch,

I am sure I'm not the only one with this problem, but how am I supposed to make my old man's sausage last a bit longer?

I only get it once a week (and that's because Mr Trotter the butcher manages to be a bit generous with his Tuesday banger special every now and then) but it really doesn't last very long at all – and it makes my old man so miserable. I used to enjoy a bit of sausage every day at breakfast myself but I fear that those days are gone for good.

What's a girl to do?

Yours,

Violet Bell

The Little Hope Herald
Saturday, 4ᵗʰ May 1940

Dear Violet,

I suspect that your old man's sausage would last a darn sight longer if you stop gnawing at it quite so ferociously at every available opportunity! I'm aware that you're quite often at it in the back kitchen when you think no one's looking following a conversation which I had last week with my lame gamekeeper Dick Scratcher's wife, Fanny, who had called to your cottage to enquire after pig bones. When she found no signs of life in your front garden or back passage, Mrs Scratcher peered in through your pantry window and caught sight of both Mr Bell and yourself going at it like a pair of deranged beavers.

Now, we all know that Mr Bell has not yet fully recovered from the severe knock on the head he received during the course of his now infamous altercation with the travelling strong man in the boxing booth at the Christmas Fair last year, but I'm quite sure that he can be made to understand that unless he keeps his sausage to himself and out of harm's way then inevitably it's going to end up in completely the wrong hands.

Further to Mrs Scratcher's report and ongoing surveillance, I can't help but think that you yourself really ought to know better than to take advantage of your husband's concussed state, Violet. Exhorting Mr Bell to 'get it out again' several times a day – even though the poor fellow is clearly not at all with it and in need of a bit of peace and quiet – certainly isn't going to improve the situation.

To this end, and for the sake of all involved (Mrs Scratcher is in danger of developing Sherlock Holmes Syndrome, she's already asked Dick for a magnifying glass for Christmas) why not just give the sausage in question a quick lick after breakfast and then put it back in the pantry until teatime?

Do make the effort dear, before you have an entire posse of Baker Street Irregulars peeping in through your pantry window.

Yours,

Hilda Ffinch
Hilda Ffinch,
The Bird with All The Answers

Spam...

Mrs Cross
Sunshine Cottage
Agincourt Street
Little Hope

1ˢᵗ June 1940

Dear Mrs Ffinch,

I'm at my wits' end as my child refuses to eat spam, I've tried everything but he's not having any of it. I hope you can help me with this problem.

Yours hopefully,

Mrs Cross

The Little Hope Herald
Saturday, 8ᵗʰ June 1940

Dear Mrs Cross,

Cross? I would be Mrs Jolly-Furious (hyphenated) were I to suddenly find myself in your shoes (which, incidentally, I suspect probably wouldn't be to my taste). Doesn't the ungrateful little brute know that there's a war on? What does he expect for dinner, vermicelli soufflé followed by Poire Jacqueline? Perhaps you could further pander to his desire for haute cuisine and the high life by adding some charming canapés and a string quartet to the family dinner table?

Really, Mrs Cross, I'm surprised that you have let it get this far. You must put your foot down very firmly at once and impress upon your delusional offspring that small children who do not eat their Spam with grateful gusto are ten times more likely to fall victim to Otto Von Hungergobbler, the twelve-fingered demon who creeps into the bedrooms of pernickety eaters (particularly those under the age of ten) at night and devours them whole saving for one rib, which he uses as a toothpick afterwards.

Fairly certain that this will do the trick.

Yours,

Hilda Ffinch
Hilda Ffinch,
The Bird with All The Answers

Crab Paste...

Mrs W Slack
16, Titley Close
Little Hope

10th June 1940

Dear Mrs Ffinch,

Recently, during a charity tea party which I held for the local 'Saucepans for Spitfires' campaign, I was most disconcerted to receive a number of complaints about the crab paste sandwiches which I carefully cut and served up on my best china tea plates. I don't mean to complain but there is a war on and times are hard, and I'm quite hurt that some of the villagers saw fit to spit rather than swallow, as it were.

Where did I go wrong?

Yours dejectedly,

Mrs Winifred Slack

𝕿𝖍𝖊 𝕷𝖎𝖙𝖙𝖑𝖊 𝕳𝖔𝖕𝖊 𝕳𝖊𝖗𝖆𝖑𝖉
Saturday, 15th June 1940

Dear Mrs Slack,

I myself attended your slightly unusual soiree; might I suggest that you purchase your crab paste from the village shop next time rather than the chemist?

Yours (still gargling with Jeyes Fluid),

Hilda Ffinch
Hilda Ffinch,
The Bird with All The Answers

Rabbit Pie...

'AJ'
A fellow of Little Hope

16th November 1940

Dear Mrs Ffinch,

I read with interest your letter of 7th October and the dilemma of Dorothy Doe and her numerous offspring and your suggestion of rabbit pie has me salivating!

However, I do not have a good austerity recipe – could you please assist me with this or should I just chuck the meat into a pot with some rhubarb roots and hope for the best?

Yours,

'AJ'

The Little Hope Herald
Saturday, 23rd November 1940

Dear 'AJ',

Many thanks indeed for your missive, it's always nice to hear that one's letters are actually being read following publication in *The Little Hope Herald* and are not simply either being cut up into squares for use in the outside privy or quickly donated to Mr Trotter at The Yorkshire Meat Emporium in the High Street for the purposes of packaging his meat.

My hairdresser was saying only the other day that when she was last on our dear butcher's premises waiting for her weekly ration she caught sight of my face wrapped around his much-admired sausage, adding that I appeared to have been well fingered beforehand, which is always rather satisfying.

Now, to the subject in hand – rabbit pie! Whilst I myself obviously only set foot in the kitchens up at Ffinch Hall twice a year on average – Christmas (to look for figgy pudding) and Shrove Tuesday (Huzzah! Pancakes!) the Colonel and I are rather fortunate in that we have been able to retain the services of a fine old kitchen type even in these difficult times. Now, Cook (who may or may not have another name, I'm not sure) is often wont to prepare what she calls 'Poor Old Peter Pie' in honour of Mr McGregor's furry adversary – she's a great admirer of Miss Beatrix Potter – and I have to say, it's jolly delicious. Disappointingly for you however, I am not privy to Cook's closely guarded recipe. But I can tell you that 'Peter' is devoid of fur before going into said pie and is, rather ironically in my opinion, accompanied in death by a number of carrots, the odd bit of turnip, quite a few peas and a delicious gravy.

Cook is very secretive where the contents of her culinary arsenal is concerned and would probably give a good account of herself were Herr Himmler himself to try to get his hands on her spotted dick, but I believe that your best chance of cracking the old trout is to contrive a chance meeting with her in the snug of The Royal Oak on a Tuesday evening. If you ply her with alcohol and chance your hand at covert interrogation there is a slight chance that you'll make it home alive.

This formidable mistress of matters culinary also occasionally serves up something called 'Prick on a Plate' here at Ffinch Hall, it contains – to the best of my knowledge – well-seasoned choice cuts of Mrs Tiggy-Winkle the hedgehog, so perhaps try and wrestle that one out of her too?

Other specialties of the house in Cook's 'Pottering About in the Kitchen' arsenal are 'Pigling Bland in a Blanket' (sausage rolls), 'Aunt Pettitoes' Trotters in Aspic' (fairly obvious) and 'Squirrel's Nutkins' (don't ask). If you can wangle any of those recipes out of her then I'll personally ask Colonel Ffinch to have a word with the chaps at the War Office and recommend your transfer to the MI19 Interrogation Unit at once, as you must clearly possess a charm and guile which may yet win us the war.

Good luck, 'AJ', don't over-force that rhubarb, now!

Yours conspiratorially,

Hilda Ffinch
Hilda Ffinch,
The Bird with All The Answers

A Bit Windy…

Mrs Agnes Bottomly
Juniper Cottage
Windy End
Little Hope

26th November 1940

Dear Mrs Ffinch,

Since the rationing of meat, I find that I'm having to consume a lot more vegetables. As a result, I find that I'm suffering rather badly with a lot of flatulence and am finding it difficult to keep my little indiscretions under control when out and about – especially whilst in Church!

Obviously, I'm sure you will understand my rather rancid predicament and any help or advice would be gratefully received.

Sincerely,

Mrs Agnes Bottomly

The Little Hope Herald
Saturday, 30th November 1940

Dear Mrs Bottomly,

You are not alone in your predicament, my dear! With the advent of meat rationing and the rise in consumption of root vegetables, half the country is afflicted with pernicious windy spasms, the like of which we, as a nation, have not hitherto known. Indeed, had this state of affairs occurred during the age of sail then one is confident that our merchant fleet would have serviced the empire in double quick time, and previous to that even we might well have seen off the Spanish Armada in under an hour.

Flatulence, my dear, is never acceptable in decent society and you must take steps to control your offensive emissions at once, lest you unnerve horses in the street or cause a major incident in Sheffield by accidentally igniting the steelworks when passing.

Remember: Methane + hydrogen + a naked flame = an impressive but short-lived bird's eye view of the coast of France.

All is not lost, however. Might I suggest that when cleaning out your hearth of a morning, you seek to collect several little clinkers and put them to one side? Charcoal tablets are known to put quite a damper on those susceptible to accidentally 'shooting a fairy' after ingesting a Peter Rabbit sized helping of cabbage, but these are now difficult to come by and so the charred remains in your grate will have to do until we win the war.

Now, although coal clinkers are not particularly appetizing, my dear, if you set too with a will and follow my instructions, all will be well. You might try grating your embers and mixing them with your tea ration, or perhaps sprinkling a pinch onto your solitary bacon rasher. A teaspoonful added to your weekly jam ration shouldn't cause you too much distress and if used as a topping on a well charred slice of toast it should prove barely noticeable at all. A tablespoon or two stuffed into a spotted dick will bulk it out nicely, giving it an impressive girth, and if added to a stiff gin one might digest as much as one likes without discomfort.

A word of warning however, please do *not* endeavour to crush and inhale your clinkers in place of snuff as was the case with Mr Percy Pottinger, the ARP Warden from Kitchener Close, who was apprehended by the long arm of the law following a misunderstanding regarding his exhortation to the few remaining men of Little Hope to go forth and 'sniff a bit of slag'.

Should the above suggestions fail to impress you then Mr Leach, the chemist, will be only too pleased to supply you with a packet of Doctor Cassell's Tablets. Take two at night time, but for heaven's sake be sure to leave your bedroom window open and fire a warning shot (munitions, not emissions) before retiring for the night to alert nocturnal passers-by of the clear and present danger posed by your fully primed posterior.

Finally, please do refrain from attending church until you have your posterior firmly under control again, Mrs Bottomly. Our stained-glass windows are sixteenth century and history will not thank you if they might have survived the Luftwaffe but instead fell victim to your rectal utterances.

Fragrantly yours,

Hilda Ffinch
Hilda Ffinch,
The Bird with All The Answers

My Hens Are Barren…

Mrs N. Batt
36 KOYLI Terrace
Greater Hope

1st December 1940

Dear Mrs Ffinch,

My hens have stopped laying and my beloved is not enjoying powdered egg at all. I think I may have spoiled him a tad in the past, he didn't used to be this fussy!

Should I be eating the hens or giving them a chance to start laying again?

Any advice would be ever so helpful with this difficult decision.

Yours,

Mrs N. Batt

The Little Hope Herald
Saturday, 7th December 1940

Dear Mrs Batt,

Your chickens may not be aware that there is a war on but your ARP warden of a husband certainly is! Why, only two nights ago I espied him making his way up Violet Millington's back passage presumably on account of the plainly visible and well-lit crack in her kitchen window. I don't have to tell you how dangerous an oversight this was on her part, surely? It's a good job that your spouse was in the vicinity and quick to act.

Half an hour after entering Miss Millington's much-admired thatch, dear Mr Batt emerged in quite the state of disarray, clearly disorientated and quite without his helmet. He had just turned on his heel to go back in to collect it when Miss Millington appeared in the doorway wearing the titfer in question at a dangerously jaunty angle. As if that were not bad enough, she was lit up from behind like the Statue of Liberty on the fourth of July. Back in went your conscientious man, this time for a good hour or so, slamming the door tight shut behind him to ensure that Miss Millington definitely got his point.

I admire your dear spouse, a man who is always out and about after dark, keeping his pecker up and servicing this community in our hour of need. Who knows how many bombs old Jerry might have dropped on Little Hope nightly were it not for perennially upstanding gentlemen like your husband searching for cracks in the darkness and barking their shins on boot scrapers whilst feeling for knockers in the blackout?

I do hope that with this in mind, you might reconsider your position in regard to Mr Batt's dislike of powdered egg. Really, one wonders how the fellow manages to keep his mind on the job at all with you henpecking him at home!

Cut the man some slack, as the Yanks say, and encourage your chickens to start laying again by leaving a steaming bowl of sage and onion stuffing outside the hen house door every morning for a week. If that doesn't encourage them to get on with it then the sight of a gleaming hatchet and a pair of gumboots definitely will.

Yours,

Hilda Ffinch
Hilda Ffinch
The Bird with All The Answers

Beetroot...

Mrs Gloria Golightly
Rorke's Drift Cottage
Goose Lane
Little Hope

3rd December 1940

Dear Mrs Ffinch,

I am an avid fan of the excellent advice which you dish out to we mere mortals and I wonder if you might be able to help me.

My Bill has always liked a bit of sugar in his morning tea to start the day off proper. He lost a leg at Mafeking but keeps buggering on and now works wonders with a bit of yew between his legs and a sharp knife in his hand. He whittles walking sticks and longbows, you see, and it does my heart good to see his excitement mounting over the breakfast table of a morning when in possession of a good bit of wood.

My problem though lies in rationing. How am I to keep Bill's enthusiasm at a peak if he can't have sugar in his tea? It's a known fact that a little of what you fancy does you good and if Bill's energy levels drop then there is no way he will be able to show his longbow off at the Christmas Fair.

I know how busy you must be, Mrs Ffinch, and I have tried to address the problem myself, really I have. I was having a small lunchtime libation the other day with my friend Mrs Pentecost from Sheffield and we were discussing how to overcome the problems rationing is causing us. It was a noisy affair, even tucked away in the snug, and I must have misheard my dear friend's advice on how to keep one's man sweet.

Mrs Pentecost mentioned the use of beet which, when cut into little cubes, could easily be added to my Bill's morning cuppa. Apparently if I turn my back on him whilst I slip it in and give it a good old stir he'll never know the difference when I put it onto the table in front of him. This sounded like the perfect solution and so the following day I nipped off down to the Bell End Market and purchased a quantity of beetroot which I then boiled up and cut into sugar cube sized lumps and the following morning I popped two into Bill's tea as directed.

Thinking that all was well, I then went over to see my elderly mother, to help her with some old lady things, but as I made my way home just before lunch I came across my brother-in-law Harold in the High Street. He said he'd seen Bill in his workshop not ten minutes since, sporting a lovely shade of red on his lips and that Bill wasn't at all amused, on account of several of the village boys queuing up and asking him for a kiss. I realised at once that it was on account of the beetroot and rushed home at once to put the rest into a Woolton pie before Bill came home and had a chance to reapply his lip colouring.

I do hope that with your wealth of knowledge you can help me with the correct way to sweeten tea, Mrs Ffinch, I'm a bit too embarrassed to go back and ask Mrs Pentecost.

Thanking you in anticipation,

Mrs Gloria Golightly

The Little Hope Herald
Saturday, 7th December 1940

Dear Mrs Golightly,

Many thanks for your letter, the safe arrival of which has certainly cleared up a little mystery for me as I was passing your husband's workshop on Tuesday last (in the Bentley, obviously) when I espied a number of small boys parading about outside like catwalk models and pouting their lips at one another. One was holding two tennis balls against his chest and had quite mastered the art of the raised eyebrow (singular). I did rather wonder what the devil was going on.

"You, boy!" I called through my opened window, "What are you *at*?"

"It's Rita Hayworth, Mrs!" came the reply, from a red-haired tyke in neatly patched short trousers. "She's in 'ere tuggin' like buggery on old Golightly's longbow!"

Obviously, I let the matter drop immediately and poked my ancient chauffer in the shoulder with my umbrella, instructing him to put his foot down at once. I took the encounter to be nothing more than childish nonsense which is endemic in the under-tens. If Miss Hayworth *had* been at large in the Old Armoury on Quiver Lane then I'd certainly have known about it. Clearly however – and with the benefit of hindsight – the incident ties in quite nicely with your brother in law's account of events.

Now, to address and get to the root of your problem (root being the operative word as you have, I fear, managed to confuse one member of the genus *Amaranthaceae* with another).

Sugar, my dear Mrs Golightly, is extracted from sugar *beet*, which we've been growing here in Blighty in gargantuan quantities since the Great War. You must have come across it in the market, it looks very much like an over-indulged parsnip. It's as pale as porridge and as rotund as the Bishop of Rotherham.

Your husband's lip rouge, Mrs Golightly, has come about on account of you slipping the unfortunate fellow a Mickey Finn full of beet*root*.

I am somewhat at a loss to understand how you have managed to confuse the two as, after all, the clue is in the name. But let us press on and endeavour to resolve the matter before you follow through and accidentally garnish the poor man's porridge with catnip.

I have, on your behalf – and to save Miss Rita Hayworth the embarrassment of ever learning that she has been confused with your husband – made a few enquiries of my Cook as to how you might save the day by extracting the juices of the humble sugar beet in your own kitchen. To wit, I have the following to impart:

- Clean your kitchen floor and please do put the cat out whilst you're at it. Mrs Agnes Wildgoose was overheard in the Meat Emporium in the High Street on Monday last saying that you don't appear to have done so since the Relief of Mafeking and the poor thing's forever scratching at your parlour window trying to get out.
- Wash a large copper thoroughly. I'm not sure how this will help, I can only assume that Constable Clink may come into his own when required.
- Have at your raw sugar beet with a meat cleaver, taking care to wrench the blade out of your chopping board or table after each blow.
- Put the resulting mess into a pan with some water and leave it to boil for a minimum of twenty-four hours. Actually, come to think of it, this is where Constable Clink may come in handy as I'm sure that the good man will be more than happy to keep an eye on it for you in recompense for your having given him a good wash down earlier.
- After boiling for the specified amount of time, remove the resulting black pulp from your saucepan and give it a jolly good wringing with a firm hand. Keep the liquid to one side.
- Take a car jack to the solid remains in order to extract the last drop of moisture but do mind your fingers.

- Boil the liquid once more (I have no idea how long for but presumably until it sets or does something unusual) and then bottle the resulting gloop.
- Use sparingly in your husband's tea. Please note that any floating black bits may well be engine oil as the result of the battering with the car jack, but these can easily be scooped out with a spoon and put to one side for use in the war effort later.

Alternatively, should this all prove a little too much and the urge to keep using beetroot regardless of its stain on both your husband's lips and his reputation overcome you, then why not pop round to see our local beekeeper, Mr Godfrey Cantrell at Trafalgar Cottage and ask if you might relieve him of a little of his much sought after 'Hive Nectar'? He's usually only too pleased to give a bit to the ladies of the village and it is rumoured to be the finest in the district on account of the use of hand pollination, regarding the application of which Mr Cantrell is known to be something of an authority.

I do hope that this helps. Should confusion overtake you again dear, and poor Mr Golightly find himself inadvertently 'doing another Rita' then you might diffuse the entire situation by putting it about that he's playing the lead female role in the Dreary Lane Players production of 'Withering Frights' which opens on Friday night next at the Village Hall.

Yours knowledgeably,

Hilda Ffinch
Hilda Ffinch,
The Bird with All The Answers

How Do I Make It Stretch?

Peggy Plump
28 Armistice Avenue
Little Hope

5th December 1940

Dear Mrs Ffinch,

I know there is a war on, but I am simply not getting enough. How can I make the little I do get stretch further?

Yours,

Peggy

The Little Hope Herald
Saturday, 7th December 1940

Dear Peggy,

One would hope, my dear girl, that you are *not* alluding to matters of a sexual nature! If you are then do please remember that the newspaper in which these letters are published is purchased on a regular basis by – amongst others – the Bishop of Rotherham and the three surviving nuns of St Candida's Leper Infirmary on the Poxwell Road. I'm fairly certain that no good will come of any of those people being exposed to your fascination with *smut* – in particular poor Sister Agnes Nonpubis – who is now so terribly afflicted by her malady that she was accused last Christmas of having 'fingered the mince pies' at the Church fete, although that unfortunate turn of events was hardly the poor girl's fault.

On this occasion however, and for the sake of appearances, I am going to give you the benefit of the doubt and assume that you are, like the rest of us nearly always hungry and that this is what is at the root of your somewhat perplexing missive.

Now, chin up, all is not lost. Mr Trotter the bachelor butcher is always in need of a helping hand at home and recompenses his ladies handsomely for their services by giving them 'a bit off ration' as it were. The dear man is known to be very generous with his meat and likes to make sure that his sausage allocation goes as far as possible in these lean times. True, it's jolly hard for him and the man's permanently exhausted with his labours – forming those bangers really takes it out of him – but he nearly always manages to come good in the end. My housemaid Daisy is a regular visitor to the backroom of The Yorkshire Meat Emporium in the High Street where she goes to "Blow the cobwebs off" for Mr Trotter on her day off, I could ask her to put a word in for you?

Failing that, have you thought about getting off your rump and starting to dig for victory like the rest of us? Mr Thorne, my gardener, is at it from dawn till dusk most days to such an extent that I find it quite exhausting just watching him from the terrace and have to go inside and sit down for a bit. The fishing docks at Hull might also prove useful to you, should you wish to consider waiting winsomely on the quayside for the fishing fleet to limp back into port and offering to give those brave men of the sea a helping hand unloading their pollocks?

Yours helpfully,

Hilda Ffinch
Hilda Ffinch,
The Bird with All The Answers

IX.

Anderson Shelters and Associated Erections

*"I'm not at all sure that I'll be home in time to get it up for you,"
Colonel Ffinch explained somewhat ruefully down a terribly
crackly telephone line from somewhere in occupied France, "but
I have a man who can, shall I send him round at once?"*

*"Oh, please do," replied Hilda, glancing at the cocktail cabinet.
"Do you think he might like a stiff one on the terrace?"*

Should He Have It Up in The Living Room?

Mrs Agnes Piggott,
Sod's Bottom,
Little Hope,

24th September 1939

Dear Mrs Ffinch,

My husband and I recently acquired our lovely new Anderson Shelter but found that the volume and consistency of clay in our garden made it quite impossible to dig a hole for it.

Mr Piggott has since given up with that idea and has instead erected his rather glorious construction in our living room. I am of course rather concerned that should we be unfortunate enough to find ourselves subject to a direct hit, that our corrugated iron haven may in fact implode and prove to be quite insufficient for our safety.

Please could you advise me on how to address this issue with my husband as he is adamant that the current set up is adequate for our needs when quite obviously it is not?

Sincerely yours,

Mrs Agnes Piggott

The Little Hope Herald
Saturday, 26th September 1939

Dear Mrs Piggott,

Might I congratulate you, dear lady, on being married to such an enterprising fellow? There are very few men these days who – unable to get one up in the great outdoors – choose to take the matter in hand in the front parlour instead and pull off a perfectly adequate erection in the privacy of their own home. I applaud your spouse enthusiastically, I having failed in *all* attempts to persuade Colonel Ffinch to have a bash himself in the blue drawing room at Ffinch Hall and, as a result, having had to deal with his damp and musty attempt at getting one up behind my well-trimmed acacia bush in the old rose garden which is now given over to eight rows of cabbages and a pig bin.

I am assuming that in his haste to get it up, your husband's pride and joy is not on display too close to the fireplace? Corrugated iron does rather tend to conduct heat and whilst a little warmth is desirable on a cold night no one particularly wants to learn from the newspapers that your spouse and yourself have been conveyed to the Sheffield Infirmary on account of heat-stroke and shock (the latter being occasioned by exposure to – *shudder* – lightly boiled gin).

Now, on to the positive. Do take heart, Mrs Piggott, and remember that an Anderson shelter suits the house every bit as well as the garden! Why not make yours a little more gay with the addition of some cheerful wallpaper, a small cherry wood drinks cabinet and a brightly coloured peg rug? That, and a little Noel Coward number on the gramophone, is a sure-fire way to lift one's spirits when Jerry's going at it hammer and tongs in the skies above you with enough vigour to make your teeth rattle in your head (or in their glass on the bedside table, as the case may be). Perhaps also consider including in your interior decoration a small, tastefully framed photograph of His Majesty the King and at least two volumes of the collected works of Charles Dickens?

Might I also point out that a sure advantage of having your Anderson shelter inside the house is that you don't have to grab your pussy and run as soon as the sirens sound? You might as well leave it stretched out on your favourite armchair in front of the fire, where it is at a sufficient distance from your bedding to stop your sheets smelling of kippers but close enough to be able to seize and sprint with should push come to shove, as it were.

Perhaps, as a footnote, you might consider attaching a large Union Jack to the interior shelter ceiling above your bunk? That way if you *do* happen to come a cropper one dark night then at least the last thing you will see before being flattened like a pancake by a fine oak wardrobe from two floors above will be the finest flag in the free world. Just a thought.

Press on, Mrs Piggott, press on! The Women's Institute are always looking for a guest speaker and you might perhaps consider putting yourself forward to discuss your husband's unusually placed erection?

Chin up, dear. Make Do and Mend!

Yours,

Hilda Ffinch
Hilda Ffinch,
The Bird with All The Answers

I'm Struggling to Get It Up…

'Tad Risqué'
In Hiding

25th September 1939

Dear Mrs Ffinch,

I've tried erecting an Anderson shelter in the back garden but I'm struggling to get it up. Mrs Risqué thinks it may be due to the draught around the back but I'm not sure – I've managed to get it up outdoors before (August Bank Holiday Monday, Taunton, 1933 to be exact). My wrists are quite weak, and I find the screwing particularly difficult.

I just don't know what I'm doing wrong! Please, could you give me some advice, or even better come and give me a hand?

Yours dejectedly,

Tad Risqué

The Little Hope Herald
Saturday, 26th September 1939

Dear Tad Risqué,

Really! I have to say that this is the first time since the war started that I've come across a fellow who wasn't able to get one up in the great outdoors. Look around you, the village is <u>full</u> of men of your age going at it hammer and tongs and displaying some very fine erections indeed. Why, Colonel Ffinch and Mr Percy Mountjoy managed five between them on Saturday last and might have got another one up if the sun hadn't gone over the yardarm and it was time for tea!

Put your back into it, man, for heaven's sake! If you do find tightening your nuts particularly difficult then I'm more than happy to send my lame gamekeeper Dick Scratcher round to help you with the screwing on Tuesday, assuming that he's not still up at Mrs Agapanthus Crumb's.

Battle on and think of England then! Never mind the wind round the back, just get it in the hole and you'll be well away!

Yours,

Hilda Ffinch
Hilda Ffinch,
The Bird with All The Answers

How Deep is Too Deep?

Capt. Godfrey Fitznicely
Harbinger's Cottage
Gallows Lane
Little Hope

30th September 1939

Dear Mrs Ffinch,

Like all of our neighbours in Little Hope, and indeed the rest of England, my old wife Sibyl and I set too with a will when our Anderson shelter was delivered, and had it installed in next to no time. Sibyl, who was in the Land Army during the Great War, is still a dab hand with a pickaxe and spade and she dug the hole to put it in all by herself whilst I was queuing up outside The Yorkshire Meat Emporium in the High Street waiting for a bit of sausage. Whilst I can't fault Sibyl's enthusiasm or technical expertise it does, however, lead me to ask you this question: How deep is *too* deep?

You see, thanks to Sibyl's deep mining activities, one now has to go down a flight of twenty-two hidden steps (accessed via a covered manhole) in order to actually get into our shelter and – now that she has put the earth back in place on top of everything again, banked it up and topped it off with an impressive assortment of winter vegetables – the whole thing is invisible to the untrained eye and is more like a sniper's bunker than a garden shelter, truth be told. On the off chance it should cave in, we should probably never be found.

Did I ought to bite the bullet and tell her to start again?

Yours faithfully,

Godfrey Fitznicely, M.M. Capt. (Retd) King's Own Yorkshire Light Infantry.

𝕿𝖍𝖊 𝕷𝖎𝖙𝖙𝖑𝖊 𝕳𝖔𝖕𝖊 𝕳𝖊𝖗𝖆𝖑𝖉
Saturday, 7ᵗʰ October 1939

My dear Captain Fitznicely,

Thank you for your letter dated Saturday last, I have perused its contents with care and believe that the following advice is in order.

First of all, were I in your shoes and married to such 'une dame formidable' as the French say, I think that the very last thing I should be silly enough to do would be to tell her that she's gone overboard and needs to start all over again. One suspects that should you take this course of action, then the next time you return from the butcher's it may well be to find your good lady digging a much smaller hole in the garden, one which corresponds approximately with your own vital statistics and only goes down to a depth of six feet. Do think before you act, dear sir, do think!

Secondly, in answer to your question 'How deep is too deep?' I have to report that Colonel Ffinch and I quite often disagree on this very point, he being a firm believer in getting stuck in up to the hilt, as it were, whilst I tend to err on the side of caution and frequently urge restraint. I am assuming however that in this case Mrs Fitznicely, unlike my husband, 'knows her onions' and has taken measures to ensure that going down with such enthusiasm and gay abandon will not result in suffocation or another equally unfortunate complication.

Now, dear man, your spouse's impressive engineering prowess aside, I suspect that the *real* reason for Mrs Fitznicely having gone quite so berserk with her pickaxe and spade, is that the good lady intends removing her gin supply from house to shelter as soon as possible – common sense dictates that in these trying times one ought to take such a measure, given half a chance – for where better to store the elixir of life than in

Mother Nature's very own frigid bowels? I do not think that I need to point out to you that the temperature of one's tipple when indulging in a little after-dinner snifter is linked indelibly to the degree of enjoyment derived from the same. Gin must be cold, Captain Fitznicely and ice cubes are, of course, an essential component part of a decent gin and tonic in peacetime. In wartime however, I'm sure that I don't have to remind you of how difficult it can be to fill one's ice bucket when one is standing directly beneath a hail of falling incendiary bombs and other associated pernicious pyrotechnics, and so shifting your cocktail cabinet into your shelter and freezing your corks off underground is a sterling idea.

Do buck up and be of good cheer, Captain Fitznicely! If you must fixate on something, then let it be the positive aspect of spending your evenings considerably closer to the earth's core than the rest of mankind. You will surely come to thank your dear spouse for her good sense and foresight when the next bombing raid finds you reclining comfortably in your extreme subterranean shelter with a little Noel Coward on the gramophone and a desirable stiff one in your hand, interrupted by nothing more than the occasional gentle growls of a disturbed badger sett hard by.

Far better be singing along to 'Mad Dogs and Englishmen' below ground than to be listening to Herman Goering's 'Midnight Symphony in A Flat Outhouse' up above – yes?

Keep Calm and Carry On, Captain Fitznicely, Keep Calm and Carry On!

Yours,

Hilda Ffinch
Hilda Ffinch,
The Bird with All The Answers

He Sank His Teeth into my Wicker Bottom…

Mrs Dilly Down
8, Crecy Street
Little Hope

6th November 1939

Dear Mrs Ffinch,

Prior to the outbreak of war, our family dog Mr Waggs had his own lovely little kennel in the backyard where he lived quite happily. True, the roof leaked a little bit and it was prone to the odd visit from an uninvited mouse, but he took it all in his stride and was no trouble at all.

Our problems started however when – having only a small back garden here in Crecy Street – we had to demolish the kennel to make room for our Anderson shelter. We made room for Mr Waggs under the sink in the back kitchen but it seems that he prefers to err on the side of caution and has taken up residence in the Anderson shelter and isn't too happy about having to share it with us – he's even taken to you know, 'relieving himself' on my husband's bunk and snapping viciously at my sandwiches!

It might be thought that being such a small creature, a Jack Russell can be easily put in its place but at ten in the evening with Jerry thundering overhead and a basket of insurance policies on my arm, this is definitely not the case. The little blighter jumped up and sank his teeth into the bottom of my wicker basket the other night and added considerable weight to the aforementioned documentation by refusing to let go.

Please help! I'm not sure how much more my nerves can take!

I look forward very much to your reply.

Yours faithfully,

Dilly Down, Mrs.

𝕿𝖍𝖊 𝕷𝖎𝖙𝖙𝖑𝖊 𝕳𝖔𝖕𝖊 𝕳𝖊𝖗𝖆𝖑𝖉

Saturday, 11th November 1939

Dear Mrs Down,

I have to tell you from the outset, my dear, that you have an uphill battle on your hands here as your problem touches on a well-known male proclivity – irrespective of whether the creature in question was blessed by the Good Lord with two legs or four – and that is the overwhelming desire for territorial gain. Additionally, if that were not already enough to be going on with, you have a *small* dog on your hands which – in human terms – means that essentially you are having to share an Anderson shelter with Napoleon Bonaparte.

Think for a moment, Mrs Down, about those infamous dictators who have curdled the printer's ink in many a history book over the years with tales of their shameless rampages. Every last one of them lacked manners, height and good looks. I do not for a moment imagine that you will be able to bring to mind a single historical despot who, from the contemporary portraits which remain, could be described as being even *remotely* attractive or indeed much taller than the average garden gnome (the exception to the rule being Caesar Augustus who apparently had a fine pair of legs on him and was blessed with supremely well-situated ears – but that particular 'tiger in a toga' aside, they've all been short and cosmetically challenged). Each and every man jack of them has been little more than a small dog in fancy clothing, trotting about on its hind legs, nose in the air, yapping relentlessly. Do you follow my correlation?

Do not despair however as all is not lost. In my experience, (should I ever choose to publish my memoirs, please do look up the bit about Senor Mussolini and I coming to blows in the Colosseum in 1926 as this will serve to clarify my credentials in this department) the only way to deal with a dictator or as in your case, a '*dogtator*', is to brush aside its posturing and show it what a real 'big boy' can do!

Now, in order to achieve this you will need three things:

- a chamber pot
- a stirrup pump
- a gas mask

Predatory males (mainly but not exclusively the four-legged variety) are wont to mark their territory, as it were, by the indiscriminate spraying of urine against that which they either hold dear or should very much *like* to – as per Mr Waggs' inappropriate behaviour on your husband's bunk. The only means by which this behaviour can be discouraged is:

a)   by use of a blunderbuss or

b)   by the liberal sprinkling of the headier working-class trouser cologne of a slightly more dominant male directly onto the area of contention.

Now, I'm not for a moment suggesting that you take measure (a) with Mr Waggs, a little extreme under the circumstances one feels, even if he has sunk his teeth into your wickerwork, but I do believe that measure (b) may prove to be your salvation. To this end, might I suggest that you take the following steps:

1.   Encourage Mr Down to relieve himself of a morning into a chamber pot, sacrifice your own cup of morning tea if you must in order to have him pass as much water as possible. (Don't be tempted to hold the chamber pot yourself whilst he's at it though, it takes Colonel Ffinch

at least five minutes to make his mind up as to whether "That's it!" or not and as such there's a danger that you might whip it away too quickly and spoil a favourite rug.)

2. Put the full chamber pot out of harm's way for the remainder of the day in a warm room (the milder the temperature the more pungent the contents of the chamber pot will become, this is essential if you are to put Mr Waggs off his stroke, as it were).

3. Wait for the evening siren to sound and then casually collect said chamber pot en route to your shelter.

4. Don your gas mask before leaving the house (the chamber pot and its contents will have been festering for quite a while by this time and the intent is to unnerve your four-legged foe with it, not render yourself insensible).

5. On approaching the shelter, hold the chamber pot in front of you and brandish it in Mr Waggs' general direction ere he starts his nightly performance. This just may be enough to calm the beast down and put him in his place, with any luck he will have a quick sniff, sneeze heavily and then slink off with his tail firmly between his legs.

6. Should (5) prove to be ineffective, then place the chamber pot securely on the floor of the shelter – I suggest that you put a foot either side of it and get a good grip with your ankles – and insert the end of the stirrup pump before going at it hell for leather in the general direction of your nippy little Napoléon Bone-apart. No self-respecting Jack Russell will stand for this and he's sure to bolt past you and take cover under the kitchen sink as per your previous generous offer.

I am fairly sure that this will do the trick. If it doesn't, I'll have my housekeeper bring Colonel Ffinch's brimming chamber pot down to Crecy Street for you when he's home on leave next. Worked a treat at the siege of Tsingtao following a particularly riotous night on the lash, apparently. The locals still refer to the liberation of the town as "Ffinch's Relief".

Do let me know how you get on then Mrs Down, and remember to cover your sandwiches and cup of tea with an impermeable object before doing the stirrup pump thing, lest your entire evening be ruined!

Yours confidently,

Hilda Ffinch
Hilda Ffinch,
The Bird with All The Answers

Am I Safe in Akela's Saucy Den?

Miss Ena Carstairs
9, Kitchener Terrace
Little Hope

21st November 1939

Dear Mrs Ffinch,

Being a lone female and unable to put up my Anderson shelter without help, I was fortunate enough to attract the attention of my next-door neighbour, who happens to be the Akela of the Little Hope Scout Troop. He offered to undertake the task for me with the help of some of the boys who are working towards their Dig for Victory badge and I gratefully accepted.

Whilst the shelter was under construction though, on the second night when the scouts had gone home for their tea, the air raid klaxon on top of the Village Hall went off. There was no possibility of my sheltering in a big hole with just a tin hat between myself and a stick of incendiaries and so when Akela's head popped up over the garden wall and invited me into his shelter for the evening I was cock-a-hoop.

Now I am no prude, Mrs Ffinch, but I was dismayed to discover on entering Akela's lair that the walls were papered with images of scantily clad ladies from what I can only describe as a rather racy gentlemen's magazine. Akela was quite the gentleman and blew out his candle so that I wouldn't have to sit looking at them – he even offered to hold my hand to calm my nerves – but I'm not sure that I quite believe his explanation as to why the pictures are there. Do boy scouts do a Female Anatomy Badge in case they are called upon to administer emergency first aid in the High Street?

I look forward to your response.

Yours faithfully,

Ena Carstairs

𝕿𝖍𝖊 𝕷𝖎𝖙𝖙𝖑𝖊 𝕳𝖔𝖕𝖊 𝕳𝖊𝖗𝖆𝖑𝖉
Saturday, 25th November 1939

Dear Miss Carstairs,

I really wouldn't worry too much about the décor, dear, the ogling of risqué images of the female sex has long been a favourite pastime of the red-blooded male and besides, I think if Akela had been Little Hope's answer to Dr Crippen then we'd probably have heard about it by now.

No indeed, rest assured that this is nothing unusual as far as the male of the species is concerned. Why, even Colonel Ffinch is in possession of a fine collection of saucy French postcards which he evidently came across during his time in the trenches of France and Flanders. He's still loath to part with them. Not wishing to offend the sensitivities of the average British postmistress at the time of their acquisition, he decided against sending them home to Blighty but instead kept them tucked away inside a pair of his underpants in the false bottom of the steamer trunk he took everywhere with him in those days. I would not necessarily have known about the existence of the erotica in question had my dear spouse not invested in a new trunk for his present war service and inadvertently left the lid of the old one up whilst answering a telephone call from Mister Churchill at the War Office. Thinking myself helpful I set to emptying it where he'd left off and, having retrieved three ancient packets of Player's Navy Cut, a Bible with a bullet lodged in it and the spike from a Jerry helmet, I discovered the loose bottom and consequently the lewd images and underpants in question.

"Oh, don't mind those, dear," said Colonel Ffinch coming back into the room at that very moment. "Special training material for officers. 'How to spot a Mata Hari when you see one' and all that. Very hush-hush. Terribly tiresome business. Had to keep them out of sight for reasons of national security, you know."

"Why are they wrapped in your underpants?" I asked, not unreasonably.

"The last place anyone would look, old dear."

"Oh," I knocked on the underpants in question which were as stiff as the cardboard postcards within, before adding "They appear to have *set*."

"Over-starched at the front, that's all."

"Over-starched all over, by the looks of it," I replied thoughtfully. "Didn't you have a man to see to your smalls back in the day?"

Colonel Ffinch shook his head and held out his hand "No dear, things were terribly hard back then, we all had to keep our own end up and just get on with it. Came good in the end. Might you pass those here, they're still classified?"

"Of course," I handed over the articles in question, unable to help noticing the rather hirsute sepia nether regions of a French female just visible through the unbuttoned flies, "I do hope that you're not using those for...you know...*nefarious*...purposes, dear. You know it isn't good for your eyesight."

"No indeed!" replied my spouse confidently, "Merely intelligence in the field, dear, intelligence in the field."

And that was that.

Now, given that we have established that your Akela is not a sex beast, Miss Carstairs – after all, he did blow the candle out whereas I suspect Doctor Crippen wouldn't have bothered and using my husband's feigned disinterest in naked French doxies as an example which does rather prove the point – I think it best that you just come to accept that men will be *men* and that a little visual stimulation is something which they can't help but indulge in from time to time. Looking at the mantelpiece doesn't always mean that they're desperate to poke the fire and so you should be alright.

Do buck up therefore and, should your own Anderson shelter not be finished before the next raid and you again find yourself bunked up with Akela, then perhaps consider taking a copy of *The War Cry* and a tambourine into his den with you? The word of the Salvationists is terribly powerful, even on the printed page and that together with half a dozen quick choruses of 'What A Friend We Have In Jesus' and a little rattle of the aforementioned tambourine should certainly serve to reinforce your message. Perhaps eat plenty of cabbage beforehand as well, I assure you that that will carry the day if nothing else does.

Yours confidently,

Hilda Ffinch
Hilda Ffinch,
The Bird with All The Answers

P.S. About the cabbage – don't overdo it and please be sure to blow the candle out yourself upon entering the shelter lest the naked flame/methane ratio prove to be even more problematic than the Luftwaffe.

A Bit of a Problem 'Down Under'…

Edna Mulch
17 Armistice Avenue
Little Hope

7th January 1940

Dear Mrs Ffinch,

Since the bombing started, my husband and me have been spending most nights in the Anderson shelter. George has taken an information film he saw at the picture house very seriously indeed and once we're in the shelter, that's it, we're in for the duration and nothing will shift him until his cock crows at dawn. Problem is, by then both gazunders are full and frankly I'm green around the gills and cross-eyed from the honk.

What can I do to resolve this?

Yours hopefully,

Edna

The Little Hope Herald
Saturday, 13th January 1940

Dear Edna,

Might I begin by drawing your attention to the fact that we live on an island? In times of national emergency my dear, our ancient moat (the English Channel) becomes both our salvation and our foe; yes, it's doing a sterling job of keeping Jerry at bay but unfortunately given that it's currently infested with U-boats, sea mines and the odd German battle cruiser intent on causing havoc it has rather left us high and dry as far as international trade is concerned. We are, in short, marooned.

Now, in order to compensate for this unfortunate state of affairs, we Anglo-Saxon types are – for the most part – pulling together and exercising the gentle art of self-sufficiency. We are constantly being encouraged to 'Dig for Victory!' and practically all of my friends and acquaintances who are in possession of an Anderson shelter are making the best of their unexpected hump in the garden and are carrying their horticultural endeavours to new heights on the back of it.

Just yesterday, Mrs Marjorie Thrift was overheard by my lame gamekeeper Dick Scratcher (in the Union Jack Tea Rooms on the High Street) extolling the advantages of Mr Thrift's well-tended wartime erection behind the front hedge and the subsequent triumph of his early rhubarb on top of it. The secret of Mr and Mrs Thrift's success? A surfeit of Woolton pie, consumed at lunch and converted into manure at the first rising wail of the air raid siren after supper.

With this in mind and in light of your predicament Edna, my advice to you is to get your hands on some Webb's Wonderful Lettuce and go berserk! Plant parsnips, cauliflowers, carrots and the odd turnip – the main ingredients for (the still terribly dashing) Lord Woolton's pie – all about your backyard in order to ensure that input enables output as it were. Dig for Victory by day, produce your own manure by night and decorate your vegetables with it when the all clear-sounds!

Failing this, badger your husband into joining the local ARP gang, they're out and about most nights and with him actually doing something practical for the war effort (as opposed to simply mooching about and relieving himself into a porcelain plant pot occasionally) of an evening you'll be able to settle down in the privacy of your own shelter with your feet up and a mug of cocoa in your hand. A little peace and quiet (the Luftwaffe notwithstanding) will enable you to get stuck into your *Woman's Weekly* without let or hindrance and you'll feel so much the better for it.

Yours,

Hilda Ffinch
Hilda Ffinch
The Bird with All The Answers

P.S. Don't over fertilise the lettuce as it's generally eaten raw.

Two Is Company, Six Is
A Married Woman's Nightmare...

Mrs Agnes Roper
6, Omdurman Terrace
Little Hope

6th June 1940

Dear Mrs Ffinch,

I know that we all have to pitch in and, where necessary, 'go without' in order to win the war and free occupied Europe, but I do feel that there's a limit to what a married woman can reasonably be expected to endure.

At present, my husband Albert and I are sharing our Anderson shelter with his mother, my mother, two maiden aunts and a cat named Kipper and – obviously – this means that we are unable to you know, '*do it*'. If I thought that the war would be over by Christmas, I might be able to grin and bear it, but as things stand I'm worried that we'll both be too old to indulge in a bit of 'the other' by the time the victory bells finally ring.

Please don't judge me too harshly or think me unpatriotic, I'm only human and 'going without' for such a long period of time surely isn't natural and I do know that I'm not the only married woman caught up in this dreadful state of affairs. But short of sending our old folk back to their own homes (where they may well come a right cropper) and putting the cat out to take his own chances of an evening I really can't see a way forward?

What, oh what, can we do?

Yours despairingly,

Mrs Agnes Roper

𝕿𝖍𝖊 𝕷𝖎𝖙𝖙𝖑𝖊 𝕳𝖔𝖕𝖊 𝕳𝖊𝖗𝖆𝖑𝖉
Saturday, 8th June 1940

Dear Mrs Roper,

You are not the first to write to me regarding this rather delicate subject and I do not think that you will be the last, given that Jerry is now becoming rather tiresome with his bombing campaign and endeavouring to flatten as many of us as he possibly can. But whilst his attempt to bomb us into submission and crush the indomitable British spirit is proving to be somewhat futile, he *is* succeeding in getting a few danders up (whilst leaving everything else where it is) on account of familial overcrowding. Jerry is no fool, my dear, and he knows only too well that people who have either already 'copped one' or are likely to if they stay where they are will totter off in the general direction of close family in order to get out of his way. He's also aware that welcoming hosts will immediately put the kettle on and fold themselves up like out-of-season deckchairs in order to make room for their kith and kin in their Anderson shelters!

Now I know that the European perception of the British is that we are a breed who replicate asexually like hollyhocks or lupins, and that we do not possess much of a capacity for sentiment (apart from our fondness for tea and macaroons, obviously) and nor do we indulge in a great deal of social intercourse, never mind getting round to taking one's shoes off in company. But the fact is, we *do* rather enjoy the occasional bit of coitus, and Jerry is proving to be a most annoying sexual chaperone.

With this in mind, I have put together the following strategy for couples such as yourself and your husband. It has thus far proved to be rather successful and has resulted in three children being conceived in Greater Hope, two in Little Hope and one up in Trollop's End:

1. When tucked up in the Anderson shelter with your extended family (having eaten plenty of cabbage for dinner so as to make yourself mildly unpleasant to the olfactory nerves of your companions), strike up a conversation with your husband about a (spurious) spate of burglaries in the vicinity which have been taking place during air raids. Be sure to mention that the felon responsible targets the households of large, extended families, and particularly those who all squeeze into an Anderson shelter together, as the greater the volume of people within the longer it takes them to get out should they hear a burglary in progress.

2. Ask your guests (casually) if they've left any valuables in the house.

3. Ask your spouse if he's sure that he's locked the front door.

4. Ask your spouse if he's sure that the bedroom window is securely closed.

5. Ask your spouse if he just heard the sound of breaking glass 'round the back'.

6. Tell your spouse that it's far too dangerous to go out there now and that if your guests' valuables are gone, then they're gone. Perhaps also throw in the phrase "It's not worth the risk! There's a madman out there!"

7. Repeat the above for several nights until your guests are thoroughly unnerved and are quivering visibly. Should they show signs of regaining their lost nerve then perhaps add that you heard in The Yorkshire Meat Emporium in the High Street that the rogue in question has at least one accomplice and appears to be 'upping his game' and stealing the underwear of old ladies' and houseguests.

8. Quietly order a Morrison shelter.

9. Wait for the Morrison shelter to arrive, keeping the pressure on until your husband has managed to get it up.

10. Have your spouse announce (manfully, if at all possible) that he has decided that it's best if you and he stay inside the house during a raid, in order to protect the property and its contents from the Fagin of Little Hope, adding that now you have a Morrison shelter you will be quite safe. Everyone else should carry on as usual and use the Anderson shelter, which will now be much more spacious and comfortable, making knitting and Ludo much less hazardous a pastime.

11. Do not take 'No' for an answer!

12. When the sirens sound, have your spouse escort your mother, his mother, the maiden aunt and Kipper the cat into the Anderson shelter and secure them within whilst you meanwhile 'slip into something comfortable' and crawl into your Morrison shelter.

13. Await the arrival of your husband, as it were, and indulge in that which the French claim that they alone excel at, in the reasonable comfort of your own home.

There is no reason, if you adhere stringently to the above, why your spouse and yourself should not once again have the privacy to indulge in that for which you so crave. Do be careful however if sharing a cigarette afterwards, that the raid hasn't ruptured your gas mains, as a naked flame combined with a leakage of the latter will once again cause the earth to move under you, but not in a good way.

I do hope this helps.

Yours confidently,

Hilda Ffinch
Hilda Ffinch,
The Bird with All The Answers

I Found Something Terribly Interesting in My Hole…

'Miss Ethically Challenged'
Living in Little Hope, like my neighbours

8th July 1940

Dear Mrs Ffinch,

When I was in the garden digging the hole for my new Anderson Shelter, I found a small cache of tarnished silver pieces that may be very, very old. Must I turn them over to the local authorities, or should I polish them and wear them to the next Little Hope church dance?

Yours,

'Miss Ethically Challenged'

𝕿𝖍𝖊 𝕷𝖎𝖙𝖙𝖑𝖊 𝕳𝖔𝖕𝖊 𝕳𝖊𝖗𝖆𝖑𝖉
Saturday, 13th July 1940

Dear 'Miss Ethically Challenged',

Long ago, Lord Elgin registered mild concern about a similar issue when he was halfway up the Parthenon, as it were, with my dear grandmother. Having followed the titled gentleman for a good half-mile on foot on the premise that she'd get to see the finest erection in Greece if she kept up, Granny was quite taken aback when his Lordship suddenly stopped mid-stroke and admitted that he didn't have a clue what to do with his marbles. He'd seemed quite confident up until then and this defining moment was, Granny always said, the beginning of the end for his lordship.

Now, there are those amongst us who are quite simply the natural guardians of all things excavated, shiny and worth a bob or two and then there are the Lord Elgins of this world who simply cannot cut the mustard, so to speak. Why, the fellow fannied about for far too long and ultimately – as we all know – lost not just his marbles but also several well-hung nudes to the British Museum and the parties of ill-bred schoolchildren with sticky fingers, nose candles and mouths like goldfish who frequent it these days.

Do you wish to follow suit, Miss Ethically Challenged? Turn your cache over to the local authorities and you will be talked about in this village for all the wrong reasons for some time to come, principally because you will find yourself hand-bagging the wife of a local dignitary when she turns up to the Little Hope Church Dance wearing your silver trinkets and claiming that they are 'on loan' from the British Museum. Lord Elgin may have lost his marbles, dear girl, but I strongly advise that you keep your hand on your recently discovered ha'penny, as it were!

That said, I also feel it incumbent upon me to remind you that there is a war on and that looting, even here in Little Hope, is positively endemic. I cannot impress upon you enough how perilous your situation has become since your fortuitous discovery and – following the publication of this letter – danger will abound for a young unmarried lady living alone with no man around to keep an eye on her assets of an evening.

Might I therefore – in the spirit of female camaraderie and Christian fellowship – suggest that you have two of your least impressive and most damaged little silver pieces made into earrings? This will crush the hopes and ambitions of prospective beady-eyed vagabonds who will think them worthless on the open market and forego their plans to break into your house at midnight and murder you in your bed. Quite a relief for you, I should imagine.

Meanwhile, might I suggest that you quietly deposit the remainder of your cache with my good self for safe-keeping in Colonel Ffinch's strongbox until the war is over? It's possible that I may have to decamp to India at some point to shore up the Vicereine should things become a little fraught and the Japanese appear on her tennis court intent on disrupting play, but rest assured that your little cache will travel with me and will remain perfectly safe.

Do think it over, Miss Ethically Challenged, there's a travelling fair arriving in Little Hope on Tuesday week and with it will come some jolly unsavoury roustabouts who will not think twice about wangling your swag given half a chance!

Yours,

Hilda Ffinch
Hilda Ffinch,
The Bird with All The Answers

The Bristol Bomber...

Mr D Twitch
2, Crecy Street
Little Hope

9th July 1940

Dear Mrs Ffinch,

The other evening whilst taking cover in the Anderson shelter at the bottom of our garden, my second cousin Maureen took fright on account of a very loud bang outside, so much so that lunged at me and nearly suffocated me with her rather large bosoms.

I really don't mind, I know it was an accident, but I actually would have felt safer taking my chances outside with incendiaries raining down left, right and Chelsea!

What do you advise that I should do during the next air raid? Take my chances outside the confines of the bunker, or risk suffocation by Maureen's excitable chest?

I earnestly await your reply

Davey Twitch (Mr)

The Little Hope Herald
Saturday, 13th July 1940

Dear Mr Twitch,

It is my belief then, given the circumstances you have outlined, that you would probably be better off out in the open air, where the chances of one of Jerry's diabolical whizz-bangs actually landing on you is minimal, as opposed to being cooped up in a confined space with a set of bosoms which are clearly not under their owner's control and are likely go for you at the drop of a hat! Do please endeavour to give your Anderson shelter a wide berth whilst still it contains your buxom relative, as I'm quite sure that at no stage during the proceedings would you wish to look up from your bunk just in time to see Maureen the Bristol Bomber bearing down on you from a great height. My feeling is that should that occur, you really wouldn't stand a chance.

Think, my dear fellow, should the worst come to pass, how history might record and judge your untimely demise. Would you not prefer a tombstone which reads 'he fell under enemy fire' to one which announces to one and all (for the next two hundred years or so until it crumbles away completely) that you are the fellow who was 'flattened by a loaded brassiere'?

Should you decide to heed my advice and take your chances alone behind the outside privy or in your rhubarb patch, please do remember to keep your mouth open should Jerry happen to drop one nearby. Better still, pop a cork between your teeth to allow the blast to pass through you and chances are you'll probably make it.

Good luck in the trenches, Tommy!

Yours,

Hilda Ffinch
Hilda Ffinch, The Bird with All The Answers (and the reinforced shelter with the gramophone, Persian rug and double bed in it)

How Might I Drench the Stench?

Mrs Amy Armitage
'Verdun'
18 Mafeking Terrace
Little Hope

6th August 1940

Dear Mrs Ffinch,

I have a bit of a ripe problem. My old man, I love him to bits but between you and me his feet smell worse than pig slop. Anyways it wouldn't be so bad but with all the air raids, we've been going down the shelter and he will insist on taking his blummin' boots off. Mrs Perkins from down our road almost fainted last time round.

What can I do to drench the stench?

Yours hopefully,

Amy Armitage

The Little Hope Herald
Saturday, 10th August 1940

Dear Mrs Armitage,

Oh dear, you are in a pickle, aren't you? If there's one thing worse than an empty gin bottle on a shelf it is the curse of the honking-hoofed husband! Nothing prepares a girl for this and I have lately begun lobbying several Finishing Schools in an effort to persuade them to include this very subject in their curricula.

Now, although my own spouse, Colonel Ffinch, habitually smells of either *'Fougere Royale'* (Tonka beans always do it for me) or a decent shag, I did encounter an issue similar to your own many years ago when stepping out with a young officer in the Horseguards. Far too much time in the saddle and mincing about in the stable meant that frankly, the poor fellow smelled like the King's racehorse from the derriere downwards. Balls were a nightmare – there wasn't a string quartet in the entire county of Buckinghamshire that would draw a bow within twenty yards of the man. He could clear a dance floor quicker than Herman Goering.

After much thought, and to spare my beau (read: myself) further embarrassment, I applied myself to the task in hand at once and drilled a series of small holes into the soles of his riding boots. This done, I lined them with finely shaved mothballs encased in bombazine pads and finished the enterprise off with a light sprinkling of Grossmith's 'Phul-Nana' fragrance – *Instant relief!*

Although we parted company soon afterwards (I had other fish to fry in the shape of Colonel Ffinch coming onto the scene rather suddenly, as it were) my foray into the world of olfactory chiropodial alteration proved to be so successful that the aforementioned young officer was last seen galloping like buggery up the Silk Road with two dozen romantically inclined Tuareg horsemen hot on his tail.

I suggest that you use this example as your blueprint. Should it prove to be too problematic then Plan B is to pour gum Arabic into your spouse's boots, apply a little more to the soles and pass them to him when he's seated in the outside privy prior to the sirens sounding. He'll put them on immediately, without a second thought and will be out of your hair – and stuck in the best place – for the duration of the raid.

I do hope this helps.

Yours,

Hilda Ffinch
Hilda Ffinch, The Bird with All The Answers

I've No Coal in My Hole but There's Lots in The Shed...

Mrs E Entwhistle
8 Omdurman Terrace
Little Hope

1st September 1940

Dear Mrs Ffinch,

My son-in-law was home on leave recently from the RAF and, after much prompting from myself, he agreed to dig a hole for our Anderson shelter in the backyard (my husband's always struggled a bit with holes, but is a dab hand when it comes to the actual erection bit).

My son-in-law is a strapping lad and no stranger to hard work and I thought he'd have my hole sorted in next to no time but after eight hours of watching him buggering about with a pickaxe and shovel, I lost all patience with his efforts and cleared out the coal shed instead. Took me all of fifty minutes. It's not that I wasn't grateful, it's just that night was fast approaching and there was a bomber's moon on the go and I had a Woolton Pie in the oven.

My problem is now though that I have half a ton of coal stored in the outside privy, a coal shed full of muck from the hole my son-in-law dug, a gaping hole in the yard waiting for my husband to get his act together, an Anderson shelter still in pieces in the best parlour and nowhere to 'go' when nature calls.

What am I to do?

Yours frantically,

Ethel Entwhistle

𝕿𝖍𝖊 𝕷𝖎𝖙𝖙𝖑𝖊 𝕳𝖔𝖕𝖊 𝕳𝖊𝖗𝖆𝖑𝖉
Saturday, 7th September 1940

Dear Mrs Entwhistle,

Hmmm…

Do you, perchance, like to engage in games such as the 'hokey-cokey' or musical chairs at social gatherings to such an extent that your fellow guests/combatants eventually tut and go off in a huff and leave you to it?

As a child were you particularly adept (read: prone to nervous aggression) when playing 'red rover, red rover, come over, come over' and did sparks fly from your heels whilst engaging in a quick round of hopscotch?

You see, I think that the root of your problem lies in your inability to 'come second', as it were (Colonel Ffinch has been known to level a similar accusation at me, upon his returning unexpectedly on leave and surprising me in the oratory, but that's another matter) and I feel that it is something which you must address with some urgency, before you inadvertently kill someone with a rolled-up newspaper during the course of a quick round of 'Are you there, Moriarty?'

You must learn, my dear, to relax a little and be less critical of the snail's pace at which men in general go about their business. Had you left your son-in-law to it and retired to your parlour for a nice cup of tea and a chance to read your *Women's Weekly* then your hole would have been in a perfect state of repair by dinner time, requiring only your spouse's erection to complete the job.

The entire enterprise is, as they say, a piece of cake really. Both Mr Scratcher (my gamekeeper) and Mr Thorne (my gardener) have recently been engaged in the self-same tasks – I've been renting them out at a very reasonable hourly rate to close friends whose spouses are away on active service – with jolly pleasing results. Dick Scratcher had Mrs Bunty Buckridge's hole excavated in an hour and a half and Aloysius Thorne wasn't far behind him with Mrs Violet Cummings' burrow. Both men had their subsequent erections in hand in time for tea with the minimum of fuss and bother.

As things stand with you however, you are clearly going to need a little help in rectifying the muddle (read: carnage) which you have visited upon your own backyard, and to this end I have passed your letter on to the Brown Owl of the local Girl Guides group. Swallow Patrol will be round to empty your outside privy tomorrow morning, Thrush Patrol will then clear out your coal shed and a couple of Blue Tits will be round to sort out your parlour at lunchtime.

I do hope this helps. If not, then might I suggest a nerve tonic from Doctor Proctor or a brief stay at the Sheffield Asylum, where they do an excellent cream tea and have their own shelters well and truly sorted.

Yours,

Hilda Ffinch
Hilda Ffinch,
The Bird with All The Answers

X.

Giving it to Jerry
(or, "Follow me, I'm right behind you...")

"Do you think that there are any spies amongst us?" Hilda whispered into Colonel Ffinch's ear as Lord Shagg-Pyle ushered his guests into the dining room that evening. "I've heard they're everywhere!"

"Oh I expect so," the Colonel replied, fingering his weapon confidently. "But don't worry, old dear, the alcohol in Shagg-Pyle's spotted dick will have them singing like canaries in no time at all..."

The Fifth Columnist...

Mrs Dolly Grey
6 Passchendaele Row
Little Hope

2nd June 1940

Dear Mrs Ffinch

Last Tuesday night I found a man with a pair of binoculars in my back passage, just behind the pig bin. When I confronted him – with a large frying pan and no teeth in – he claimed to be from the War Office and said that he was on the lookout for fifth columnists. I told him to go away before I called a constable.

Should I be worried? You read about these things in the papers, but what if he was a spy and he's been watching the goings-on in our village?

Nervously yours,

Dolly Grey

P.S. I've tied the pig bin lid with string, just in case it was that he was after.

The Little Hope Herald
Saturday, 8th June 1940

Dear Dolly Grey,

You're absolutely right, my dear, to be vigilant in these trying times and to keep the lid tightly on your pig bin – after all, we're all looking forward to a half-decent banger come Christmas.

Fifth columnists are everywhere at the moment. One hears that in London and the provincial cities there are indecent numbers of them loitering in alleyways and public conveniences, eavesdropping on everyday conversations in the hope of picking up a little covert intelligence. I heard only last Tuesday – and I have this on good authority – that one such fellow was apprehended flashing shamelessly in the general direction of Wapping from the rooftops of the Bank of England. These people have no integrity whatsoever, and will go to any length to spy on the activities of dear old John Bull and his honest countrymen with a view to ingratiating themselves with that dreadful little man in the Reich Chancellery who, apart from anything else, is an abysmal watercolourist.

It's no use to ask me why, Dolly Grey, but there's a murmur in the air, one can hear it everywhere and so it's time to do and dare and perhaps take a rolling pin or a wet tea towel to any suspected miscreant whom you might find making their way up your back passage after dark?

I myself will have a word with Constable Clink when he calls here tomorrow for a good stuffing from Cook, he's usually up at about two in the afternoon, I'll be sure to mention your concerns when I give him his handcuffs and truncheon back – he likes to leave them on the hall table when he comes.

It's nigh on one o'clock here at Ffinch Hall now, and so I'm afraid that it's goodbye Dolly, I must leave you, there's macaroons and bisquits on the go. Something tells me I am needed, for there's lunch and gin to stow. Hark! I hear the Vicar calling, and his call is oh so gay, he's come at last for tea and crumpets, so goodbye, Dolly Grey!

Yours,

Hilda Ffinch
Hilda Ffinch,
The Bird with All The Answers

Fanny by Gaslight...

Mrs C Arbuthnot
1 Mafeking Terrace
Little Hope

12ᵗʰ June 1940

Dear Mrs Ffinch,

Recently, whilst fingering *Fanny by Gaslight* in the Little Hope Library, I came across a page where certain words, letters and numbers had been underlined. I mentioned this to my friend from two doors down and she said that there's a good chance that we have a fifth columnist in our midst who is using the book to leave coded messages for a Jerry spy.

Do you think it's possible, and if so, what should I do about it?

Yours sincerely,

Cynthia Arbuthnot

The Little Hope Herald
Saturday, 15ᵗʰ June 1940

Dear Mrs Arbuthnot,

Just to be on the safe side, I popped into the Little Hope Library and looked at *Fanny by Gaslight* myself this morning and I am now certain that you were attempting to decipher the booking out slip at the front. I double-checked with our dear librarian Mrs Hinge and she confirmed that you and a friend spent twenty minutes examining the self-same page on Tuesday last with, as she put it, a very quizzical look on your faces 'as though you may have been at the Cooking sherry again'.

I note from your address that you live at number 1, Mafeking Terrace, which puts your neighbour from two doors down (Miss Dilys Still the interesting barmaid from The Rose and Crown who is blessed with breath like a crumbling French wine cellar) into the frame as your alcoholic accomplice. Little wonder that she encouraged you in this nonsense. Really, Mrs Arbuthnot, do try to reign it in a bit and save a little for our inevitable victory celebrations when the time comes!

And on that same subject, do please try to remain sober when handling the very few tomes which are left on the library shelves. We've already lost *Little Dorrit* and *Moby Dick* to a paper drive and whilst I'm sure that none of us begrudge their noble sacrifice for the war effort I'm quite sure that nobody wishes to see *Fanny by Gaslight* come to a sticky end on account of your heavy-handed fingering.

I am sending you (by second class post) a small tin of Andrews Liver Salts, Mrs Arbuthnot, please do feel free to indulge heavily.

Yours,

Hilda Ffinch
Hilda Ffinch
The Bird with All The Answers

A Terribly Secret Service...

Mrs Betty Hall
Honeysuckle Cottage,
Hangman's Lane
Little Hope

22nd July 1940

Dear Mrs Ffinch,

I'm a bit worried about my husband, Albert. He's been acting very oddly over the last few weeks, ever since he had a letter in a brown envelope from someone in London. Two days after the letter arrived, he went off to the Smoke to 'see a man about a dog' and hasn't been the same since. Last Monday I found him writing a letter in onion juice in the washhouse and my old mother said she found him stuffing a fuse into a mouse in the pantry.

Has he lost the plot? What should I do?

Yours,

Mrs Betty Hall

The Little Hope Herald
27th July 1940

Dear Mrs Hall,

You may be surprised to learn that there is quite a lot of this sort of thing going on at the moment and that you are not alone in your curiosity. In times of adversity, such as those in which we find ourselves at present, the Government launches a myriad of little schemes to take people's minds off the worst-case scenario – which in our case that is almost certainly the prospect of Herman Goering munching his way through the last of the madeleines in Miss Titty Henderson's cake shop in the High Street – and my intelligence suggests that one of these marvellously diverting government schemes is none other than a recruitment drive by the Boy Scouts!

In his (slightly) younger days, my own spouse was wont to pull on a pair of khaki shorts, straighten his woggle and sally forth for a bit of a dib-dib-dib in the scout hut himself in his capacity as Scout Leader of Little Hope. He gained this position initially on the back of being a personal friend of the then Prince of Wales but later thoroughly deserved it on his own merits for displaying an excellent bit of wood whilst endeavouring to impress the Baden-Powell examining board whilst going for his 'Man About the House' badge.

Other skills which the Colonel learned 'under canvas with the lads' as it were, included semaphore, trout tickling, sonnet composition, giving a fellow a decent bunk up and the gentle art of flashing across a minimum distance of twenty-five yards with the aid of a hand mirror.

Such forays into the world of alternative methods of communication lead me to believe that your husband is engaged in the exact same thing as the Colonel's previous pastime, albeit with some new and exciting high jinks which were clearly added *after* the Colonel found himself up the proverbial creek without a paddle on account of an altercation with the Prince of Wales about Mrs Wallis Simpson. The two never did speak again and still avoid one another like the plague at social gatherings.

So fear not, Mrs Hall, for I believe that your spouse is gainfully engaged in the sterling task of egging on the downy-cheeked youth of today in the hope that they'll become the stubble-chinned British warriors of tomorrow!

Be proud, Mrs Hall, be proud! God save the King!

Yours,

Hilda Ffinch
Hilda Ffinch,
The Bird with All The Answers

P.S. There is a slight chance that your spouse has not been grabbed by the Akela at all and that he may well have joined the Secret Service. Should this prove to be the case then don't assume that he's just pleased to see you when he returns from work, he might actually have a loaded service revolver in his pocket and making amorous overtures towards it might startle him and set it off. You might also want to keep an eye out for men in raincoats slipping up your back passage when you're asleep and take care to avoid batting mice in the pantry with your broom, as they may be primed and a good thwack could easily take out half of the High Street. Just a thought.

I Long to Give It to Jerry...

Miss Gertrude Bunion
9, Mafeking Terrace
Little Hope

8th August 1940

Oh Mrs Finch!

Why can't we girls go to war like our men do?

I know we can do our bit and I dig for victory, knit balaclavas and generally try to keep everyone's spirits up here at home, but I do so long to really give it to Jerry! It is so unfair! I may seem to be a weak and feeble woman, but I am roaring with rage and passion inside and can just imagine myself charging, bayonet in hand and giving Fritz a good seeing to!

I am so frustrated, and I am thinking of cutting my hair, binding my chest, dressing up as a boy and signing myself up on the spot. Do you think it would work?

Yours patriotically,

Miss Gertrude Bunion

The Little Hope Herald
Saturday, 10th August 1940

Dear Miss Bunion,

Giving it to Jerry, dear, is something we'd all like to do given half a chance. I said as much to Colonel Ffinch in an idle moment over his billiards table the other night, to which he replied that giving Jerry a good seeing to was a real man's job and could I please remove my hand from his end pocket as it was hindering the intended trajectory of his balls. I was loathe to do so as – with yarn being in such short supply at present – I was actually endeavouring to covertly detach the dangling bit in order to convert it into a snood, but alas the Colonel has eyes like a hawk and requested that I cease fiddling with his bits and pieces at once.

Now, cutting one's hair, Miss Bunion, is not generally recommended (even today) unless one is able to retain the services of a decent hairdresser with a minimum of ten years' experience and – ideally – a salon in Mayfair.

Imagine the *shame* one might bring upon one's self were one to put one's ambitions regarding Jerry into motion only to find oneself staring directly into the lens of the Berlin paparazzi whilst sporting a particularly bad hairdo? If one is to be at the forefront of the action, my dear, then one needs to look one's best and have the foreign press comment on one's impeccable appearance under fire. There's little or nothing to be gained by bringing the collective reputations of the hairdressers of the British empire into disrepute by appearing in public looking as though the gardener has cut one's hair with a knife and fork, they won't forget about it when the war is over I can assure you! Why, one might as well be caught short with one's 'lower thatched cottage' on display for all to see as perambulate about sporting a rough and ready short back and sides, my dear. Please, please do think of your reputation!

In a similar vein, binding one's chest receives an unequivocal 'No!' from yours truly – where else should one contrive to keep one's Craven A cigarettes and a hip flask full of gin if not safely within the confines of a well-constructed brassiere? Think before you act, dear girl, *think*!

As things stand however, I do empathise with your patriotic ambitions and to this end might I suggest that you perhaps give a trial membership at the local Women's Institute some consideration? They really are top end militant and if their May Day Parade up the High Street is anything to go by then one suspects that they'll certainly give a Panzer Division or two a run for their money should push ever come to shove.

God Save the King, dear, God Save the King!

Yours,

Hilda Ffinch
Hilda Ffinch,
The Bird with All The Answers

The Dickin Medal...

Mr Benn
Chancer's End
Greater Hope
Yorkshire

26th August 1940

Hallo Mrs Ffinch,

I have a dilemma. I found a pigeon in the garden and it has some kind of medallion around its neck with the words 'Dickin Medal' on it.

My dilemma is do I put it in a pie or let it go?

Times are hard, Mrs Ffinch, and we are all hungry. What do you advise?

Regards,

Mr Benn

The Little Hope Herald
Saturday, 31st August 1940

Dear Mr Benn,

I wonder could you double-check around the side of the medal in question to ascertain whether or not a name, rank and number are inscribed thereon? I ask simply because two days before he went back to his regiment, Colonel Ffinch was rampaging about the house shouting "Where's my dickin' medals?" at all and sundry and they never did turn up. I'm wondering if perchance he left them on the terrace after getting them out for Lady Shagg-Pyle when she called for a spot of tiffin the previous afternoon and perhaps this led to them being misappropriated by your feathered friend?

Should it transpire that the gong in question does indeed belong to the Colonel, I'd be most grateful if you would drop it off at the manor in person rather than entrust it to the postman who has anger management issues with military trinkets on account of flat feet.

Bring the pigeon with you and my Cook will give you a good stuffing.

Yours,

Hilda Ffinch
Hilda Ffinch,
The Bird with All The Answers

What If Jerry Comes?

Miss Cecily Petticoat
Juniper Cottage
Gin Lane
Little Hope
Yorkshire

8th September 1940

Dear Mrs Ffinch,

During the course of a recent meeting of my weekly book club the topic of conversation veered away from the Industrial Revolution in Mrs Gaskell's Cranford and onto the subject of what might occur here in Little Hope should our defences fail us and Jerry arrive. What concerns my fellow bibliophiles and myself most is this – is our Home Guard up to it and did we ought to start taking precautionary measures now, you know, *just in case*?

We are not defeatist by any means, but watching old Mr Oddfellow tottering into the Village Hall with a tray of macaroons for the local platoon the other night has made us wonder if we might not be better off reading up on sabotage, trinitrotoluene and semaphore before our next meeting?

I, and my fellow club members, look forward very much to your reply (we meet every Tuesday evening at six, here at my cottage. You are most welcome to join us should you be interested?).

Yours curiously,

Miss Cecily Pettifogger

𝕿𝖍𝖊 𝕷𝖎𝖙𝖙𝖑𝖊 𝕳𝖔𝖕𝖊 𝕳𝖊𝖗𝖆𝖑𝖉
Saturday, 14ᵗʰ September 1940

Dear Miss Pettifogger,

Back in the days when that dreadful little despot Napoleon Bonaparte was jumping up and down and rattling his sabre at us from yonder side of the English Channel, it was the duty of every Englishman to have his musket ready, should push come to shove, as they say. The musket makers of England, although going at it hammer and tongs, were simply unable to keep up with the surge in demand and so many an older armament was given a quick rub down with a damp cloth and made ready for action. There was really no cause for alarm on the home front back then, as even in the tremulous hands of the over forties the weapons in question would have given Boney's henchmen *'une course pour leur argent'* as they say.

Similarly, when the King of Spain sallied forth (by spineless proxy) and had a bash with his ill-fated Armada during the reign of Elizabeth, it was the ordinary fellows of this sceptered isle, armed with pitchforks and cudgels who stood ready at the coast to defend their homes, families and alehouses, come what may.

With this in mind, and although I share your trepidation regarding the great and manifold dangers facing Mr Oddfellow's precariously balanced macaroons, I do believe that if Jerry were to come at him then the dear old gentleman would still give a jolly good account of himself, albeit with the aid of an ear trumpet and a baking tray.

Up at Ffinch Hall, we are also ready to face the threat of invasion in the unlikely event that that day should ever dawn, and to that end we have stashed away enough ingredients for Cook to rustle up one of her infamous Trench Cakes to feed the first infantry division to goosestep up the drive. Whilst this may appear to be an overtly friendly gesture, indeed some may suspect us of outright collaboration, the dangers of ingesting this seemingly harmless offering are incalculable. Cook is still wanted in the Reichstag for war crimes committed in the trenches of the Great War where – disguised as a field kitchen helper named Klara von Krapp – she laboured tirelessly on behalf of the British government to have the Hun bought to his knees, literally, by English home cooking. The dear woman narrowly missed out on being awarded the Croix de Guerre by the French Government for her extraordinary devotion to culinary espionage in the field on account of Monsieur le President accidentally trying one of her Belgian buns at a soiree the night before the ceremony and being bedridden with thunderous bowels for a week afterwards as a result.

Forewarned is forearmed, Miss Pettifogger! To this end I have on your behalf conducted a survey of the measures which some of the villagers of Little Hope are themselves taking in order for them to be able to defend King and Country in the unlikely event that the hand of God should fail to deter Jerry from crossing the English Channel. If Fritz ever does manifest in the High Street he will have the following to deal with:

- Mrs Nellie Mint of The Farthings on Gallows Hill Lane has been busy crocheting 'Jerry bells' from old 'pulled down' cardigans and jumpers and is handing them out to her neighbours in exchange for a small donation to The Spitfire of Little Hope fund. Mr Teesdale the village vet has kindly donated his collection of cat bells to Mrs Mint and thus might the traps be set – simply stretch the gaily coloured chain stitch length across one's gateposts at shin height of an evening and attach to little hooks screwed into the wood on either side. Should Jerry endeavour to open the gate then the gentle tinkle of said cat bell should alert one to his close proximity and allow ample time for one to put one's teeth in before answering the door.
- Mr Tiberius Pickering, the village archaeologist who is so

old – legend has it – that he actually knew Caligula, has invested in a gaggle of particularly grumpy geese, on the grounds that the Romans habitually used them instead of guard dogs. One hears that he has yet to train them to distinguish friend from foe however and that the Postman has taken to delivering Mr Pickering's mail from behind his privet hedge, having secured said correspondence to a house brick before lobbing it into his cabbages. Should Mr Pickering succeed in curbing the killer enthusiasm of his geese however, one wonders whose side they might come down on should a troop of Italian parachutists – the heirs of the Roman empire and unparalleled exponents of the goosestep – ever chance to descend upon us.

- Mr Clarence Attenborough, late of the Natal Mounted Rifles and currently resident at Kimberley House on Bell End Lane, has apparently dug a tiger trap behind his runner beans which – until the church bells sound the alert – is being used to store his gin and tinned goods, the extreme cold at depth being an excellent alternative to an inhouse Frigidaire.

- Mrs Enid Tweedy of Badger's Nook has, with the aid of her Girl Guide troop (she being their Brown Owl) been hard at work building a mediaeval trebuchet in her front garden just to the left of her chicken coop. Although built to scale and technically capable of hurling a load of heavy rocks some 1000 feet, Thrush Patrol have encountered significant problems calibrating the thing and have, to date, succeeded only in catapulting Mrs Tweedy's cat onto the roof of the Post Office.

- Finally, bringing up the rear as it were, my very own lame gamekeeper, Dick Scratcher, has finally finished work on a prototype exploding faux barn owl which, he is hopeful, can withstand a resounding thwack with a cricket bat in the general direction of an advancing German panzer division before exploding on impact.

I look forward very much, Miss Pettifogger, to seeing you and your bespectacled amigos top that lot, and to this end accept your invitation to the meeting at your cottage on Tuesday evening next. I thought I might bring along the Vicar and the verger too, if acceptable, as they're both at a loose end that night and do look very much like a pair of bookends themselves when sat either end of a church pew of an evening twiddling their thumbs.

Yours,

Hilda Ffinch
Hilda Ffinch,
The Bird with All The Answers

I Can't Bring Myself to Eat the
Duke Of Normandy...

Mr Benn
Chancer's End
Greater Hope
Yorkshire

9th September 1940

Dear Mrs Ffinch,

Very sorry for the delay in replying to your very good advice about my pigeon.

I have been in Normandy of late – it's all been a bit 'hush-hush' you know – "Careless talk costs lives" and all that. However, the French resistance informed me whilst I was over there that my pigeon's nickname is 'The Duke of Normandy' and that the medal was presented to him for his service with the 6th Airborne Divisional Signals.

After finding out the above information I feel it would be wrong to eat this pigeon, and therefore it is with deep regret I will have to decline the invitation to the manor for a good stuffing.

Yours,

Mr Benn

𝕿𝖍𝖊 𝕷𝖎𝖙𝖙𝖑𝖊 𝕳𝖔𝖕𝖊 𝕳𝖊𝖗𝖆𝖑𝖉
Saturday, 14th September 1940

Dear Mr Benn,

Thank you for your latest missive. I have talked this matter over with Cook and we both entirely agree that serving the Duke of Normandy up for lunch is utterly unacceptable, even if he is round, plump and potentially jolly good with parsnips and a redcurrant sauce.

Cook said that the offer of a good stuffing is still on, however. Leave the bird at home and she'll meet you at the back of Trotter's Yorkshire Meat Emporium in the High Street at seven-thirty on Friday evening. The blackout will be in force so watch out for the kerb and the dustbin full of pig scraps destined for our communal porker, Goering the Wessex Saddleback.

Should you happen to be away on 'hush hush' business on the evening in question, please ask those jolly nice SOE people to relay the following message via the BBC Home Service: "Sorry Fanny, Dick being held by Jerry" and she'll completely understand.

Yours,

Hilda Ffinch
Hilda Ffinch,
The Bird with All The Answers

XI.

How to be
Fit and Fabulous Under Fire

*"Mrs Ffinch! Mrs Ffinch!" called Cook from the bottom of
the stairs, just after eleven that evening, "you'd best come
quick, Jerry's overhead!"*

*"I couldn't possibly!" replied Hilda, raising a well-groomed
eyebrow at Colonel Ffinch, who was still struggling to get his
Sam Browne off, "I'll be a good three-quarters of an hour, yet!"*

*"I think she means it's time to go into the shelter, dear,"
interjected Colonel Ffinch, reaching for his jacket with
a disappointed sigh…*

A Pressing Problem...

Mr Charles Bottomly
Handyman Cottage
Bushy Gap
Little Hope
Yorkshire

19th February 1940

Dear Mrs Ffinch,

My sister Violet has a rather delicate problem on account of an ever-increasing growth on her backside. I initially advised her to apply a poultice to the offending boil without much success, and now she is insisting that I lance the beast. Apart from being mortified at being asked to do such a thing, I simply do not have the stomach for such a procedure and don't relish the thought of being in such close proximity to my sibling's derriere.

Please could you help by advising me?

Yours, a very worried,

Charlie Bottomly

𝔗𝔥𝔢 𝔏𝔦𝔱𝔱𝔩𝔢 𝔥𝔬𝔭𝔢 𝔥𝔢𝔯𝔞𝔩𝔡
Saturday, 24th February 1940

Dear Charlie,

Fear not, my dear fellow, fear not! Whilst one commends your good care and concern for your festering sibling, I bring tidings of great joy on behalf of the Reverend Aubrey Fishwick and the choristers of Little Hope!

Your sister Violet has – as you will no doubt be aware – been keen to 'cut the mustard' as it were, within the ranks of the St

Candida's Church Choir for some time now and as such has been practising with them regularly on a Wednesday evening. My sources tell me that the general consensus of opinion amongst those already frocked up and caterwauling their heads off at the rafters above the quire on high days and holidays was that although Violet's voice wasn't *offensive* to the ear, it wasn't particularly remarkable either. She was, they said, definitely experiencing significant difficulties hitting some of the higher notes on the scale.

"She was endeavouring to bring Joy to the World," choir mistress Vera Flynn informed the Vicar and I over gin and macaroons barely a week ago, "But dear Lord and Father of mankind it was hard work…"

Miss Flynn went on to say that she feared that your dear little songbird's dreams of soaring up to the rafters were in danger of fluttering no higher than the top of Miss Titty Wainwright's hat, and that your poor sibling – painfully aware of her shortcomings – had been ready to throw the towel in once and for all last Wednesday evening after a particularly disastrous attempt at 'Jesu Joy of Man's Desiring'. Having whipped off her chorister's frock (fortunately she had something on underneath) she gave a rather melodramatic sigh before sitting down heavily on the altar steps.

"Hallelujah! Sing to Jesus!" Vera Flynn ejaculated loudly over her third macaroon in as many minutes, causing both the Vicar and I to jump violently as she went on relaying the tale to us "Violet rose up suddenly with amazing grace and hit a note so high that the verger's Alsatian went berserk and sank its teeth into a hymn book. After that, there was no stopping the girl."

It seems that the festering aberration on your sibling's rump, when sat upon heavily, had freed her voice.

"Praise my soul, the King of Heaven!" Miss Flynn concluded, "I wonder now that I ever asked 'what child is this?' when first she came to sing with us. Might I have another macaroon?"

And so you see, Charlie, lancing the beast – so to speak – is *not* in your sister's best interests. Might I suggest therefore, in the hope of Violet keeping her place within the ranks of the warblers of Little Hope, that you instead shepherd the girl in the direction of the frequent application of goose grease to the offending/holy area and mention that the wearing of hand-knitted (and slightly rough) undergarments might go some way towards ensuring it's longevity?

Praise the Lord and pass the rectal ammunition, Charlie!

Yours,

Hilda Ffinch
Hilda Ffinch,
The Bird with All The Answers (and an empty macaroon tin on account of Miss Flynn's voracious appetite)

Death by Aspidistra...

Mrs Bathsheba Pidcock
'Seaman's Rest'
19, Jutland Terrace
Little Hope

29th February 1940

Dear Mrs Ffinch

I'm all of a tizzy and don't know what to do. My husband Hector, home on leave from the Navy, has only gone and come down with a bout of something a bit nasty and is laid up in the attic bedroom. I've isolated him as best I can in case it's, you know, something catching, and he seems to be holding his own.

My worry is that friends and neighbours, meaning well like, keep calling round with bunches of flowers and the odd potted plant from the florists in the High Street and my old mother happened to remark that plants in a sick room like to suck the life out of the afflicted after nightfall. Is this true, and if so, should I chuck them out?

Hoping you can help.

Yours,

Bathsheba Pidcock (Mrs)

The Little Hope Herald
Saturday, 2nd March 1940

Dear Mrs Pidcock,

Let me begin by reassuring you that it is not at all uncommon for a matelot to take to his bed and hold his own when back in port – my cousin Crispin, a gay young lieutenant aboard HMS

Nancy being a case in point – hardly ever did the fellow arrive back at the family seat on leave but he would immediately dash upstairs to his bedchamber with indecent haste and close the door firmly behind him. His relief at being home was audible even out on the front terrace and it twice startled the hounds of the Belvoir Hunt. That said, Crispin was always down in time for afternoon tea, although his mother – my late Aunt Maude – was very much against him touching the sandwiches on such occasions and always had the footman transfer two cucumber and salmon ones to his plate with tongs.

The seaman's relief, my dear, is a curious thing and unless your husband has come home covered in spots or wailing like a banshee when confronted with a chamber pot, I'd be inclined not to worry too much. Like all sailors he'll know his onions and will surely have the matter in hand.

Now, with regard to your concerns about killer houseplants and the bouquets of death pedalled by our very own Mrs Ivy Potter of The Potting Shed of Little Hope in the High Street. Plants, both the potted variety and those living on borrowed time in jam jars and vases in homes the length and breadth of this sceptered isle, breathe in carbon dioxide and exhale oxygen as a rule during the hours of daylight.

This is a hard fact and cannot be disproved, and was explained in some detail to me by the renowned botanist Mrs Beever-Blackburn during an almighty thunderstorm several years ago in Kew Gardens, when a bolt of lightning hit an exotic greenhouse door, melted the lock and provided her with a captive audience for two and a half hours as the London Fire Service fought to free us.

After a brief foray into the sex lives of plants (which caused a lot of tittering at the back and a mighty rustling of leaves from two yuccas and an African palm), Mrs Beever-Blackburn went on to explain that at night, the breathing process of plants undergoes a reversal process and they breathe in oxygen and exhale carbon dioxide giving rise, in some quarters, to fears that one might be suffocated during the hours of darkness by one's own houseplants.

"What about an aspidistra?" whispered a tall, thin lady at the back (who looked as though she'd already had the life force sucked out of her after dark by Nosferatu), "Are they wont to go for one, too?"

"Good lord no!" barked Mrs Beever-Blackburn testily, "The only death by aspidistra I ever came across was as a result of the pot it was in making contact with the skull of an errant husband! Of course it won't kill you!" before adding "Idiot!" under her breath, which I don't think the skeletal lady at the back quite caught.

And so there you are, dear Mrs Pidcock, you may take comfort from the words of an expert, and also from those of an eminent botanist. Fill your attic with flowers to your heart's content! Be sure to knock before you enter however, just in case Mr Pidcock is still hard at it, and with any luck a bout of hay fever or a greenfly infestation will have your spouse out of his hammock and back on his feet in no time at all.

Yours knowledgeably,

Hilda Ffinch,
Hilda Ffinch
The Bird with All The Answers

P.S. Is your husband's life insured? Maybe just check before taking any more flora and fauna up there? Best be safe, rather than sorry when turning the light out tonight and leaving him alone in there with all those tubers, tendrils and intriguingly robust stamen.

A Delicate Matter…

'Mrs Exasperated'
'Purgatory, Frankly'

11th March 1940

Dear Ms Ffinch,

I do hope you can help me with a terribly worrying problem. Ever since his granddad was blown clean off the privy by the blast from a very near miss during a recent air-raid my Albert (who is seven years old) simply won't, well, you know – he won't *go*!

I have tried prunes, I have tried ghost stories, I have tried everything! He is starting to turn a funny colour and I'm very concerned that he might explode!

Yours,

'Mrs Exasperated'

The Little Hope Herald
Saturday, 16th March 1940

Dear 'Mrs Exasperated',

Firstly, dear lady, did your boy's grand sire survive the blast and is he quite recovered? If he is currently still above ground and once again ensconced on your best sofa, nibbling on a biscuit then might I suggest that you give young Albert a good clip round the ear and tell him to man up?

Explain to your boy that there's a war on and that patriotic grownups (such as sewer men) have jolly important jobs to do, and that by him not doing at least one daily 'job' of his own your child risks hampering the war effort, and who knows where such selfish and underhand behaviour will end?

Tell him that without his regular contribution to the rivers of slurry currently coursing through the sewers beneath England a large plug will form and next Saturday (at about six in the evening) there will be an almighty bang as pipes rupture left, right and Chelsea. The Ovaltinies, Rin Tin Tin and 'Uncle Arthur' from Children's Hour will then be carried away to their doom in the cruel North Sea by the sludge, cursing your thoughtless and selfish child roundly as they go.

That, my dear, ought to do it. Should your child still persist in filling himself up with his own manure however then perhaps call round to Fox Manor and beg a slab of Trench Cake from my Cook. The woman's been baking that full-bodied bowel-encourager since 1915 and is still wanted for war crimes in an enemy soup kitchen on the western front during the Great War. I'm confident that it will do the trick!

Yours,

Hilda Ffinch
Hilda Ffinch,
The Bird with All The Answers

A Bad Case of the Short and Curlies...

Miss Edna Privet
Badger's Nook
Bushy Gap
Little Hope

9th April 1940

Dear Mrs Ffinch,

I seem to have misplaced my tweezers and have been unable to source a replacement in the shops since the war began. As a result, I have an unruly growth of hair above my top lip and am now looking more and more like my grandfather by the day.

I have tried tugging on my short and curlies with my fingers but to no avail and have even resorted to a bit of sticky tape hoping that it would un-root my ginger bush. I have very probably not helped the situation by trimming my new moustache with a pair of scissors – when all it has done is encouraged further growth.

I fear that if this should continue, I may be in danger of being kidnapped by a travelling circus as a thing of curiosity. Please could you advise me on how I can sort this rather embarrassing issue out?

Yours faithfully,

Edna Privet

The Little Hope Herald
Saturday, 13th April 1940

Dear Miss Privet,

A stiff upper lip, dear girl, is a sure sign that one is British, made of sterling stuff and is absolutely not the sort of person that

Jerry ought to upset.

In a man, it's often supported/held in place/petrified by way of a heavily waxed moustache (Colonel Ffinch sports a marvellously stiff one at all times) which also adds a look of good breeding and derring-do to a fellow's general appearance, but in a woman it really is most unfortunate.

I note, my dear, that you are also ginger which can only queer the pitch further, as it were, as your sort are prone to sport a slightly more wiry and pubic-looking mane if cropped too close. I speak from personal experience, having once been familiar in the Biblical sense with a young Lieutenant in the Royal Flying Corps. The dear fellow sported two identical ginger wire-wool rugs, one at either end (if you follow my meaning) and would never consent to being naked with one in the dark lest the upper brush be mistaken for the lower one, or vice versa and – having seen him in 'a state of nature' by the light of an oil lamp – I could certainly see where he was coming from.

Do not – whatever you do – resort to trimming your lip bush with a pair of scissors. My young Lieutenant attempted that and ended up looking (and feeling) like a ginger tom that had been caught on an electrified fence. Nor is plucking the answer, by now you would probably need to use a stout pair of pliers rather than tweezers anyway, and a broken pair of those may well cost us a spitfire and indeed the war.

No, the answer, dear girl, comes in the shape of a dainty little tube of hair removal cream which – when applied as per instructions – will melt away your facial fleece and leave your top lip smooth and starkers. I am enclosing a newspaper cutting for you to have a look at. Perhaps take it to the chemist's shop with you to ensure that you get the right thing and don't inadvertently come away with a jar of mustard poultice which, with your colouring, would really put the tin hat on you ever daring to venture out of the house again.

Price 2/6!

Happy withering!

Yours,

Hilda Ffinch
Hilda Ffinch,
The Bird with All The Answers

P.S. Please do not take the poses of the models in the enclosed newspaper cutting too literally. Stick to your moustache. My young Lieutenant had me do the other end for him and was quite unfit to fly for some time afterwards and consequently missed his chance at potting The Red Baron from behind.

Keeping Up Appearances…

Mrs Agnes Piggott,
Sod's Bottom
Little Hope

13th May 1940

Dear Mrs Ffinch,

Even though we are at war with Germany, I feel it of vital importance to 'keep up appearances'. I believe that we must try to look our best and to show Hitler that we continue to be a glamorous people in spite of his best efforts to have us look otherwise and that we are not terribly plain like that sour-faced lady friend of his.

Anyhow, I have recently run out of lipstick and am now resorting to beetroot juice in its place. The problem I have is that yesterday after applying the aforementioned root vegetable, instead of my lips being transformed into luscious red – they instead turned a purplish blue and my appearance is now that of a corpse.

I have washed and scrubbed my lips with little effect and was wondering if you have any suggestions as to how I might remove the dye from my lips so that I may once again be seen in public without being looked at in a peculiar way.

Yours most desperately,

Mrs Piggott

The Little Hope Herald
Saturday, 18th May 1940

Dear Mrs Piggott,

Were you, perchance, passing the churchyard at approximately twenty minutes past eleven last night? I ask because upon calling at the Vicarage this morning to enquire after the Vicar's health (following the unfortunate incident on Tuesday last when one of his bell clappers came loose, bounced off the vestry floor and briefly rendered the poor man quite insensible) I found him in a state of some agitation.

It seems that on setting out on his nightly fire watching round (which begins in The Rose and Crown and progresses on to The Dun Cow and The Cat and Cabbage before taking him back to the roof of St Candida's via a quick one at The Three Jolly Bishops) he chanced upon – and I quote ad verbatim – "A spectre! Quite loathsome of visage! A female form displaying lips as blue as nightshade!" pottering about in Deadman's Close, the little snicket adjacent to the graveyard.

As I say, to be fair to the man he had had a sociable swift half in each of the aforementioned hostelries in the course of his nightly civil defence perambulations (in order to foster a feeling of congenial camaraderie with his fellow fire watchers), and so his description may have been a tad more Shakespearian than usual.

Anyway, it seems that 'the Loathsome Lady', whoever she may be, was wearing an ARP helmet, a snug fitting siren suit and a pair of highly polished – and very unusual – crocodile skin boots, such as I have seen your good self-sporting outside Trotter's Yorkshire Meat Emporium in the High Street on a Wednesday afternoon whilst you are waiting in line for Mr Trotter the butcher to get his sausage out.

For goodness sake, Mrs Piggott, if my suspicions are correct and you are indeed the blue-lipped spectre of Deadman's Close then you really are in a beetroot pickle! Has it not occurred to you that being out and about in that state might cause hens to stop laying, cows to yield curds and that it might turn the village water supply quite brackish?

I'm sure that you are aware that due to Little Hope's success in the county 'Chinese Whispers Championship' last year it's just a matter of time before rumour has it that a blazing comet has been seen in the sky over the Bell End Wood and fish have fallen from the heavens above the dairy! No doubt it will then just be a matter of time before a riotous mob (comprised primarily of the militant wing of the Little Hope WI and egged on by Mrs Agapanthus Crumb in particular) gather to encircle the rectory and put the Vicar off his stroke whilst he's fiddling with his canticles.

Dearie me, Mrs Piggott, dearie me!

Please do *not* despair however as I assure you that this situation can be resolved without too much ado and you can probably avoid the added embarrassment of having a burning cross appear on your lawn.

Now, my Cook (who may or may not have another name, I'm never entirely sure) is in possession of a large and terribly impressive bit of beaver. She generally only gets it out during the winter months but is quite happy to rent it out for two shillings and sixpence a week during the summer. True, it does have a slight whiff of mothballs about it and displays a few bald patches here and there (due to its advanced age, you understand) but it's been stuffed again recently and – if positioned correctly about your lower face – is sure to keep your lips well covered until they're back in the land of the living again. Do let me know by return of post if you're interested, and I'll have Cook get the brute out for you.

Should this plan not be to your satisfaction, then I fear that your only course of action is to stay indoors with the curtains drawn until a severe vitamin D deficiency renders you pallid from head to foot.

I do hope that this will be a lesson learned for you, my dear, times may be hard and we may have our backs against the wall but that is no reason to go berserk and satisfy ourselves quite so inappropriately with root vegetables.

Yours,

Hilda Ffinch
Hilda Ffinch,
The Bird with All The Answers

The Black Hole of Mrs Cutter…

Mr Albert Cutter
Moorcock Cottage
Grouse Lane
Little Hope

5th June 1940

Dear Mrs Ffinch,

I have recently returned home on leave from the front and, on being reunited with my wife Meryl, I have been confronted with what can only be described as a big black hole.

Meryl tells me that she has done everything in her power to sort it out – it's giving off quite a nasty niff – but that she's finding it very difficult to put right on account of our village dentist having been called up.

Do you have any advice or suggestions which could help? I only have a few days left until I return to duty and quite honestly our dog Bella has sweeter breath!

With very best wishes,

Albert Cutter

The Little Hope Herald
Saturday, 8th June 1940

Dear Mr Cutter,

Mr Grunting, the local dentist prophesied events such as these when his call-up arrived a few months ago. It was the third attempt at the delivery of said papers, the previous two efforts by the War Office to draft him into the King's Own Yorkshire Light Infantry having come to nothing on account of the papers in question going astray. They were later discovered stuffed into a hollow tree in the depths of the Bell End Wood – much to the consternation of an incumbent screech owl who had made herself quite at home on top of them.

"You'll see!" Mr Grunting bellowed, still clutching a pair of well-used dental pliers and smelling slightly of Colgate luxury tooth powder as he was hauled up onto the back of an army lorry by two rather beefy military policemen, "You won't be able to carry on without me! No! Toothless hags you'll be! It'll be Waterloo Teeth for the lot of you!"

Clearly, he had a point.

Now, rather than embarrass Meryl by drawing attention to her dental odour which, it is clear from your letter is offensive enough to stop a bull elephant in its tracks, might you perhaps consider inserting a small and innocuous nosegay into each of your nostrils as a temporary measure until you are safely back with the colours?

I wouldn't recommend anything too conspicuous, such as a sprouting bit of mint or a stem of basil, but perhaps a gentle sprig of fennel (or rosemary, at a push) which might easily be mistaken for unruly nasal hair?

Should such herbs not be abundant in Meryl's garden, so to speak, then why not pop down to the local ARP post and have a quiet word with Mr Grimshaw the head warden? The dear fellow is always eager to please and will doubtless be able to let you have two short lengths of rubber tubing which you can stuff with bombazine pads soaked in Jeyes Fluid. Insert one into each nostril and explain to Meryl that you are afflicted with a summer cold – the Jeyes Fluid will make your eyes water quite convincingly – and that you'll be fine once the contagion passes. Please do remember to breathe through your mouth at all times however, as the extraction of foreign bodies from the nasal cavities can be somewhat costly and one good sniff could well cost you your life savings.

I do hope this helps. Enjoy your leave as best you can, Mr Entwhistle, and the very best of British luck to you when you return to the front.

Yours sagely,

Hilda Ffinch
Hilda Ffinch,
The Bird with All The Answers.

P.S. How big is Bella's kennel? If all else fails, then a gay little hideaway might be made in a small space for very little outlay.

A Bad Case of 'The Yellow'...

Miss Fanny Millord
Whizzbang Cottage
Bushy End

4th July 1940

Dear Mrs Ffinch,

I have been working in the factory up at 'You-Know-Where' for this past year and for some reason I've begun to turn yellow. I don't want to be mistaken for a Japanese spy, can you please help me?

Yours frantically,

Fanny Millord

The Little Hope Herald
Saturday, 6th July 1940

Dear Miss Millord,

Firstly, might I ask if 'Fanny Millord' is actually your name, as it does rather sound like a risqué question aimed at one's gentrified host after a dinner party?

If it is indeed your name and should you wish to sue your parents for having saddled you with it, then the Colonel and I retain the services of a beastly good lawyer, Sir Gerry Mander. The fellow specialises in personal injury claims (both genuine and spurious) and I'm fairly certain that he would relish the opportunity of bellowing "Fanny, Millord?" across a crowded Sheffield courtroom at Mr Justice Poppycock at some point during the course of his career. I should be more than happy to recommend you to him if needs be, his spirited defence of the so-called 'Anderson Shelter Chopper Man' was masterful if a little misguided.

Now, to the matter in hand.

I'm assuming that 'You-Know-Where' is the rather badly camouflaged former 'You-Know-What' factory nearby where they used to make 'Those Rubber Things' before war broke out?

If so, it's common knowledge that they're manufacturing 'You-Know-What's' there to drop on Jerry, and that in order to make 'You-Know-What's' they have to use some frightfully odd things with peculiar side-effects which 'Thingummy-bob' workers are rather susceptible to.

This being the case, my dear, being mistaken for a Jap is probably the least of your worries, after all – there isn't exactly an abundance of wild bamboo in the Bell End Wood and as such you're unlikely to be mistaken for a sniper and bumped off by the Home Guard, the Boy Scouts or indeed the Little Hope Women's Institute.

No. Frankly. Yellow or not, I'd be more concerned about the possibility of an accidental spark-induced solo flight in the general direction of Berlin than anything else, given your occupation. I mean, should such an event occur then you may well find yourself clinging to the top of Herr Hitler's Chancellery Building and desperately trying to attract the attention of a passing spitfire for the duration of the war. I'd be far more inclined to lose sleep over this possible scenario than over the Japanese thing, if I were you. Do you have a German phrase book? Maybe start swatting up, just in case?

But look on the bright side. If you're utterly sick and tired of working 'You-Know-Where' and aren't blown clean across the English Channel by a rogue spark anytime soon, then perhaps you might consider crossing the Atlantic (a bit risky, but it can be done) and presenting yourself nude at the Hollywood Oscars Ceremony this year? Nobody would notice your affliction there, and there's every chance that you'll inadvertently end up being awarded to Mr Clark Gable as the award for the Best Actor. The fellow's on form, well-endowed (allegedly) and *Gone With The Wind* is a surefire bet this year apparently.

Just a few possibilities there for you to mull over.

Yours,

Hilda Ffinch
Hilda Ffinch,
The Bird with All The Answers

XII.

Affairs of the Heart

"War does funny things to people, but then so does love. Both have us at their mercy. On that note, I think I have my foot stuck in your trouser pocket…"

(Hilda to Colonel Ffinch over the billiards table,
4th June 1940)

An Annoying Fokker...

Nora from the NAAFI
RAF 'Somewhere in England'

5th July 1940

Dear Mrs Ffinch,

I'm not local to your village but came across your problem page whilst travelling from A to B on the Great Western Railway. During the course of my journey we stopped three times on account of dodgy signals, twice while the guard shooed cows off the line and once because of a very annoying Fokker who just wouldn't give up and go home. Fortunately, the latter was seen off by a nippy little Spitfire which appeared out of nowhere, took care of the business and then did two victory rolls, a heart-stopping sideslip, a slightly antiquated yet nonetheless perfect Immelmann Turn and a wing-wiggle-waggle before disappearing into the clouds again.

The thing is, Mrs Ffinch, I think I may have fallen in love with the pilot, but how ever will I find one knight of the air amongst so many?

I do hope you can help; I'd hate to pine away over my tea urn and Malted Milk biscuits.

Yours hopefully,

'Nora'

The Little Hope Herald
Saturday, 7th July 1940

Dear 'Nora',

Firstly, let me congratulate you on the sterling war work which you have undertaken in volunteering to staff the RAF NAAFI canteen. An army may march on its stomach (as that bounder Napoleon once said) but the Royal Air Force flies on fried egg sandwiches and whilst you may not be beavering away at a top secret government installation cracking codes and saving lives, your efforts at cracking eggs and saving the RAF's bacon are equally commendable.

Now, with regard to your mysterious flying ace. I do, as my readers know, have connections with most branches of the Armed Forces, and I'm fairly certain that from the description of the aeronautical display you gave that the pilot of the 'Fokker-off-er' is none other than Group Captain Rupert 'Blinkers' Blenkinsop, who used to fag for my brother Charles at Eton.

Young Blinkers was a fine upstanding and very well-connected lad with a talent for polishing boots, ironing cricketing whites and – crucially – making the finest paper aeroplanes in the dorm. Even back then, he had such an understanding of aerodynamics that he was able to launch a quick one off the wrist at such a trajectory that it would fly twice round the quad and buzz the sundial before invariably coming to rest on the headmaster's windowsill. It's difficult to do that with a paper plane, and Blinkers was often to be found in detention after such a stunt but no matter, the seed of greatness had already been sown.

After Eton and Cambridge and a brief spell in The City – where paper planes were banned on the grounds that far too many compromising missives were floating out of his office window and landing on the hats and in the baskets of old ladies sitting on the steps of St Paul's, badgering passers-by to feed the birds for tuppence a bag – Blinkers followed his heart's desire and joined the Royal Air Force, where he took to the skies like a great swallow and was finally able to unleash his pent-up aeronautical prowess.

The 'two victory rolls, heart-stopping sideslip, slightly antiquated yet nonetheless perfect Immelmann Turn and wing-wiggle-waggle' which you mention in your letter, Nora, comprise what is without doubt the aerial signature of Group Captain Blinkers Blenkinsop. It is a routine he perfected along the boulevards of Paris prior to the occupation, when a chap might still swoop low enough in his Spit to snatch two French sticks, a bottle of Bollinger and *la plume de ma tante* from the table of an unsuspecting mademoiselle and leave her with a packet of Players Navy Cut and a lightly smoked kipper by way of recompense. Your Fokker foiling hero, my dear, is one of Blighty's most renowned defenders and is, as such, rather high on the wish list of Herman Goering and every female under the age of ninety in the Home Counties.

My advice to you therefore – should he come into your NAAFI – is to act fast lest another woman get her equally keen talons into him first, Nora!

With this in mind, why not throw on a nice gay pinny and ask him if he'd like a bit of crumpet or something a little spicy for supper, or perhaps consider looking him in the eye and whispering "Meat and two veg, Sir?" into his ear in your most seductive voice?

Should Blinkers still prove difficult to snare after that (and he shouldn't, I've known him to go weak at the knees and grasp the mantelpiece at the very mention of toad in the hole), then perhaps hint that a little tossed salad might be on the menu later or that you yourself would kill for a decent finger roll or some slightly salty (but not stale) nuts?

Avoid mentioning chocolate fingers at all costs, but a raised eyebrow and a breathy "Chocs away, Group Captain?" accompanied by a quick flash of your Kit Kat might be just the ticket. Similarly, asking whether he'd like you to hold his

Bertie Bassett's whilst he reaches for a napkin may prove to be felicitous. Should he still fail to twig then I can only suggest that it's probably time to get your dumplings out and hope for the best dear, as even the finest of fellows can be a little dense at times.

Rest assured, that should I run into Blinkers at The Savoy Spitfire Ball on Saturday next, I'll mention your name to him.

Tally Ho for now, Nora!

God save the King and bless our Boys in Blue!

Yours confidently,

Hilda Ffinch
Hilda Ffinch,
The Bird with All The Answers

The Pussy Fiddler...

Violet M.
Harpy Cottage
Bushy End
Little Hope

12th May 1940

Dear Mrs Ffinch,

Now my Jim is away at war I am finding it very difficult to sleep at night. The bed is so cold without him in it and I miss my special cuddles. We'd only been married a couple of months before he went away you see and I have taken to snuggling with the cat at night, but she isn't keen, and is ripping my sheets to pieces with her claws when I'd much rather Jim was ripping my nightie to pieces with his teeth.

How do other girls cope?

Yours hopefully,

Violet M.

The Little Hope Herald
Saturday, 18th May 1940

Dear Violet,

First of all, might I suggest that you desist from any kind of nocturnal activity which involves fiddling with your pussy? Cats are predatory creatures, particularly after nightfall and so unless you're actively involved in wrestling an unfortunate rabbit from the jaws of your rampant British shorthair then do leave it well alone, dear!

Secondly, might I suggest that you pay Doctor Proctor a visit and ask for a prescription of bromide and 'Veronal' which – if taken at bedtime as prescribed will give both yourself and your pussy a bit of peace and quiet for a good eight hours or so.

Don't get any funny ideas about your Jim's propensity for ripping at your nightie with his teeth either, there's nothing sexual about that at all – according to Colonel Ffinch (who is a dab hand at it) – it's merely standard commando training for first aid in the field.

Yours,

Hilda Ffinch
Hilda Ffinch,
The Bird with All The Answers

The Problem with Roger...

Mrs Jean Prick
Bleak House
Trafalgar Road
Little Hope

17th June 1940

Dear Mrs Ffinch,

I am feeling ever so slightly silly writing to you about this, but I have this nagging feeling that just won't go away.

My husband and I had only been married for a couple of days before he had to go off to do his bit. We hadn't been courting for very long but you know, wartime and all that, and so when he asked for my finger I was glad to let him put his ring on it. He has been very good and writes to me as often as he can. I know it is sometimes difficult to make sense of his letters as there are lots of bits crossed out by the censor, but he does seem to be talking about his chum Roger, rather a lot. It's Roger this, Roger that, Roger the other. Roger all over the place! And I must admit to feeling a bit jealous that Roger is getting all his attention. He keeps saying how wonderful it is to have Roger and they do seem to be terribly close; he has even mentioned that they sometimes hold each other for comfort when they are lonely or afraid.

I know that war must be a terrible thing to be involved in, but should I be concerned about him and Roger? I mean, it doesn't seem at all manly and more than once I have had to throw away a letter I have been writing which has included the words 'Bugger Roger!' as it does seem a rather uncharitable sentiment.

Am I being silly?

Yours,
Jean

𝕿𝖍𝖊 𝕷𝖎𝖙𝖙𝖑𝖊 𝕳𝖔𝖕𝖊 𝕳𝖊𝖗𝖆𝖑𝖉
Saturday, 22nd June 1940

Dear Jean,

Might I begin my response by advising you *never* to include the phrase 'Bugger Roger!' in any of your responses to your husband, no matter how frustrated you may feel? The phrase is not only uncharitable but could also be construed as being somewhat provocative and may well lead to the censor who is absorbed in reading your letter getting a little hot under the collar himself and having to disappear into the W.C. for an inordinate length of time, thereby delaying release and delivery of your missive.

Now, let me ask you this: Did your husband attend public school? If he did, then you have absolutely nothing to worry about with regards to his closeness to Roger (assuming that the latter is of a similar social standing, of course). Boarding schoolboys have long been renowned for their closeness and 'cuddling up', it's all par for the course, as it were. Colonel Ffinch often mentions the spanking good time he and his chums had at Eton, not to mention the 'highjinks in jodhpurs' he still talks about and which apparently refers to the close camaraderie of some members of his polo team in the communal baths following a match back in the day. I myself was never privy to any of this joshing around, principally on account of being female but also as the bathhouse was windowless and had only one door and so I've had to take the Colonel's word for what went on, but he talks of it fondly and always keeps his back to the wall when he bumps into Tristan Bellenderby and Crispin Wentworth-Crump at his Club. Should your husband and Roger fall into this general category, Jean, all is well and there's really nothing for you to worry about.

A problem might arise however if your husband and Roger are polar opposites who might never have met under normal circumstances but who have been thrown together by the fortunes of war with such force that one of them has perhaps been rendered unconscious by a shell from a Panzer tank or something and has woken up in a state of matrimonial confusion. These things usually blow over without too much ado though, and as long as your husband doesn't confuse your matrimonial ring with Roger's I'm sure everything will be tickety-boo.

Please do try not to read too much into your husband's closeness to another man at this point, Jean. Just a few days ago I witnessed Mr Peabody the greengrocer giving my lame gamekeeper Dick Scratcher a bunk up over the garden wall. There was no way the latter could have achieved it on his own on account of his limp appendage. It took three or four big pushes before Dick could get his leg over properly, and afterwards I noticed that he hugged Mr Peabody gratefully before loosening his grip and plummeting headlong into my vegetable patch where he landed uncomfortably on a rhubarb forcer and bounced off into the undergrowth. As luck would have it, Mr Peabody was still on hand to help and between us we were able to get Dick out of the hole he'd found himself in, clean him up a bit and point him in the right direction. All entirely innocent.

Hold fast with your suspicions then, my dear, you're probably getting all hot and bothered about nothing. The bottom line is though, do write to me again should your husband return with Roger in tow and you find yourself relegated to a tent in the garden, unable to find your lipstick and haunted by the delightful smell of a roast chicken dinner for two wafting out of the kitchen window.

Yours reassuringly,

Hilda Ffinch
Hilda Ffinch,
The Bird with All The Answers

The Pheasant Plucker...

Captain Everard Faithful
Salvation House
TrafalgarRoad
Little Hope

6th July 1940

Dear Mrs Ffinch,

Do please excuse my contacting you on what must seem such a trivial matter, but I am at a loss as to what to do.

My reason for writing is that I am somewhat concerned about my wife Emma. She is of a shy and retiring disposition usually but recently she has taken to wearing gaudy head apparel garnished with, of all things, the tail feathers of deceased pheasants. Quite out of character. When I broached the subject with her, she informed me that she has a friend who is a pheasant plucker and that they sometimes get together to do it, and that rather than waste the late bird's plumage she's happy to wear it about the place.

This is all well and good, but I don't know any pheasant pluckers, and am at a loss to explain how these feathers so often appear in our bedroom and behind the sofa in the best parlour. My wife denies plucking at home with her friend when I am away banging my cymbals together in the High Street, but I am perplexed and don't know what to do.

Please help!

Your servant,

Everard Faithful.

𝕿𝖍𝖊 𝕷𝖎𝖙𝖙𝖑𝖊 𝕳𝖔𝖕𝖊 𝕳𝖊𝖗𝖆𝖑𝖉
Saturday, 13th July 1940

Dear Captain Faithful,

Might I first of all congratulate you on your choice of religious affiliation and take a moment to sing the praises of your congregational preference?

I have had a soft spot for the Salvation Army since a terribly unfortunate incident at my family home in Belgravia on the evening of December 20th, 1921. It was then that a very heavy fog occasioned a slightly inebriated junior officer in the Blues and Royals to career off the road, clatter across the pavement and plummet headlong down the steps of our servants' quarters at precisely the moment that a kitchen maid was ascending them with two French sticks and an under footman. Needless to say, chaos ensued, exacerbated by the fact that the aforementioned junior officer was dressed as Father Christmas and had a live reindeer and a full sack in tow.

Fortunately, a passing Salvation Army band, happened to hear the commotion (an angry reindeer is terribly loud indeed) and groped their way through the fog to the railings above the steps and proceeded to play a rousing medley of Christmas carols as a rescue operation was mounted by the Commissioner of the Metropolitan Police and the Bishop of Truro, who – as luck would have it – both happened to be having tiffin with my mother in the drawing room at the time.

As it happened, no great harm had come to the slightly inebriated junior officer (I married him three years later and he's currently giving Jerry a good seeing to somewhere in the European theatre), or to the housemaid, the under footman nor indeed to the reindeer, but sadly both French sticks were rendered inedible during the course of the incident and Father Christmas' sack was quite badly crushed. Those marvellous people from the Sally-Bash however finished their concert, came in and made us all a nice cup of tea before disappearing into the fog once again leaving the strains of 'It came upon a midnight clear' hanging in the icy vapour behind them. Marvellous people. Truly marvellous.

Getting back to the matter in hand, however. It's clear to me (and indeed half of the village) that Mrs Faithful has been indulging in rather a lot of pheasant plucking in the Bell End Wood on a Tuesday evening just after the blackout. My lame gamekeeper, Dick Scratcher, had a nasty altercation with a terribly angry badger which had been startled from its set by your dear wife's enthusiastic plucking just last weekend, and he has now has to fortify himself with a proper stiff one of an evening before setting out on his rounds.

I'll say no more, Captain Faithful, I'll say no more. But I must just mention the blackout curtains up at your bedroom window of an evening when you are out lecturing the Women's Institute on the evils of alcohol. That visible crack of light isn't accidental, you know, ask Mr Pointer the ARP Warden, he'll explain everything!

I will be sure to pop a tanner into your collection box next time I come across you in the High Street, keep your pecker up, dear man.

Yours,

Hilda Ffinch
Hilda Ffinch,
Bird With All The Answers

A Clerical Crush...

Miss Virginia Hotfoot
Harriet House
Fanny Hands Lane
Hampton Upon Mott

20th July 1940

Dear Mrs Ffinch,

I seem to have developed a slight infatuation with our new parish Vicar – the Reverend Gabriel Longbottom.

I am sure he has realised that I have taken a fancy to him and is slightly unnerved as a consequence, as he takes flight to the vestry and bolts the door behind him whenever he sees me. I am not generally this forward; indeed I have no idea what has come over me, I can only put it down to the fact that with all the able-bodied (and handsome) men of the village being away giving Jerry a good seeing-to, the dashing reverend has become something of a tempting proposition.

What can I do to still my beating heart?

Sincerely,

Miss Virginia Hotfoot

The Little Hope Herald
Saturday, 27th July 1940

Dear Miss Hotfoot,

I'm very much afraid, my dear, that the Reverend Longbottom – currently on loan to the parish of Hampton Upon Mott from Rotherham as their own Vicar is in the Sheffield Infirmary recovering from a particularly debilitating bout of genuflector's palsy – is a man of superbly firm thighs and great moral fibre and is therefore most unlikely to even think of returning your affections.

No. Not if you were Mary Magdalene herself offering to wash his feet with a fluffy towel in one hand and a pristine bar of Camay in the other. The man will not succumb to your feminine wiles no matter how fast your heart is beating, and should you contrive to hyperventilate and pass out in the aisle when he's up in the pulpit then please be aware that the verger of Hampton Upon Mott, the redoubtable Mrs Nellie Stocks, is fully primed and well trained in first aid and will be at you like a starving alley cat on a particularly succulent kipper.

Now, I myself have witnessed the Reverend Longbottom shinning up the ladder into the church tower of Saint Venereal's on several occasions when he has a mind to polish his much-coveted bell clappers. All credit to the man, he's up there like a ferret up a drainpipe and masters an impressively firm grip on the ladder rungs with those delightfully manly hands of his. Being the Christian woman that I am, and out of concern for his personal safety, I have often stood directly underneath his dangling hatch with my eyes raised heavenwards whilst he's getting up there. Let me assure you therefore, that I am well placed to confirm that the dear man asserts his authority over the temptations of the flesh by wearing a pair of jolly tight hand-knitted wire-wool underpants which, I am sure, completely eliminate all thoughts of a sexual nature on his part in the most efficient and uncomfortable manner. So efficient and uncomfortable in fact, that I hear that Mrs Maureen Grocock has taken to leaving a small pot of her calendula ointment 'for the relief of severe chafing' on the Vicarage doorstep of an evening, along with a couple of spears of asparagus and a small dish of oysters.

I am also reliably informed that our very own Reverend Fishwick has been on hand to offer his dashing colleague some sound advice on the gentle art of fending off sex-starved harpies. Lord only knows that the good man has suffered enough of that nonsense himself. To this end, please note that the electrical work in the church at Hampton Upon Mott last week has resulted – on the advice of our own Vicar – in the wiring of the pulpit steps to the mains for the purposes of self-defence once the Reverend Longbottom is firmly ensconced and has his psalms out. Please therefore resist any attempt to have at him mid-flow as it were, lest you be shot through with an electrical charge of Biblical proportions and catapulted clean through the church roof and into the centre of Sheffield.

Anglican Men of God, Miss Palpitating Hotfoot, are put on this earth to lead us away from temptation and not into it. Utter shame on you for thinking any different. To this end, might I suggest that you have a firm word with yourself and take a cold bath whilst wearing a hair shirt and a chastity belt on a Sunday morning before kneeling with bowed head on the Reverend Longbottom's hassocks? You might also like to consider taking a drop of holy water with your gin, I'm eighty percent certain that it won't cause you to choke or disappear in a puff of smoke, thunderbolts being rare in St Venereal's since the erection of the Bishop's splendid lightning rod in 1926.

Yours judgingly,

Hilda Ffinch
Hilda Ffinch,
The Bird with All The Answers

P.S. Mrs Grocock's ointment is available from the Jubilee Stores in the High Street for tuppence a jar should the chastity belt start chafing a bit, but if you are truly repentant for your lascivious thoughts then you really ought to just grin and bear it for at least a week. Do make the effort, there's a dear.

And Then There Were None...

Anonymous of Knob End
Greater Hope

1ˢᵗ August 1940

Dear Mrs Ffinch,

My lover from the RAF base up the road says he can't get any more prophylactics as they are all being used by the army to stop water getting into their rifle barrels. I suspect he is lying but I really cannot afford to you know, end up 'in the family way', as my husband is away at the front. I don't want to deny my 'Flyboy' his little bit of pleasure either though, as he's such a long way from home (Chipping Sodbury, wherever that is) and I really quite enjoy it myself.

Can you please offer me some advice as I cannot speak to anyone in the village about this delicate matter?

Yours in desperation,

'Anonymous'

The Little Hope Herald
Saturday, 3ʳᵈ August 1940

Dear 'Anonymous',

Although the temptation to remonstrate with you for taking a lover whilst your husband is away serving King and Country is upon me, might I at least congratulate you for having taken a (presumably) dashed good-looking airman as a lover and not – as is the case with Mrs Edith Muff-Hawker from The Cat and Cabbage in Hampton Upon Mott – a Jerry POW? She's been at it quite openly with the fellow for at a good three months now much to the chagrin of the Vicar who was wont to call round at said hostelry for lunch on a Tuesday until Mrs Muff-Hawker tried to interest him in two tins of Iron Ration Meat, a pair of lederhosen and some very questionable sauerkraut. A shocking state of affairs indeed.

I do rather suspect however that you are right in your assertion that your lover is lying to you about running out of prophylactics – I myself (pre-war and pre Colonel Ffinch, obviously) was acquainted with two Field Marshals, a naval Commander and a frightfully exciting gun-slinger from Minnesota, all of whom it seemed were major shareholders in a variety of the aforementioned products and sales were excellent.

Might I therefore suggest that you explain to your airman that unless he is able to magically produce a quick Sheik in the alleyway behind The Majestic after next Saturday's showing of *Gone With The Wind* he'll be taxiing back into his hangar alone with his landing gear stuck in neutral?

Trust me, if you proffer this ultimatum, you'll find yourself in possession of two dozen prophylactics in the blink of an eye. Should you have any to spare later in the week, then do feel free to pop them into the post and send them to Ffinch Hall, as my gardener will almost certainly be able to put them to good use on the occasional early marrow.

Yours,

Hilda Ffinch
Hilda Ffinch,
The Bird with All The Answers

I'm in Love with the Most Wonderful Man…

'Ethel of Little Hope'
Pining Away in Yorkshire

8th August 1940

Oh Mrs Finch, oh Mrs *Ffinch!* – What can I *do*?

I am afraid that I am desperately in love with the most wonderful man, but he doesn't even know that I exist. Ever since I first heard Winston Churchill on the radio, with his deep, slow, rumbly voice I have been awfully smitten, and to see him on the newsreels with that cigar and his beautifully erect fingers flourishing the V for Victory sign – my heart swells and I go all wobbly.

Oh, what a man! He definitely makes me want to do my bit (well, his bit really) for England!

I have written him several letters but have had no reply so I can only think that someone is plotting to keep us apart – and I think I may be being watched. (there has been a very dodgy looking fellow loitering in my street lately) so I know it isn't going to be easy for us to be together but I *know* that if we could just meet he would realise that I am the only woman for him!

I am on the verge of packing my best flannel nightgown and trotting off to London to try and slip him a note, but I know he is terribly busy – do you have any tips on how I may be able to win his heart?

Yours, desperately,

'Ethel'

The Little Hope Herald
Saturday, 10th August 1940

Dear Ethel the Desperate,

Hormones, my dear girl, are the curse of womankind! Let me begin however, by reassuring you that you are not alone in your plight and are, in fact, two-thirds of the way down an enormous queue of love-sick fillies all champing at the bit and eager to indulge in a bit of horseplay with Mr Churchill, our glorious leader.

Colonel Ffinch – my 'significantly absent other' – spends a great deal of time at the War Office and is often invited for a game of 'Old Maid' on a Tuesday afternoon between three and five, at the Cabinet War Rooms with Mr Churchill. He has confirmed that that particular card game is a favourite with the Prime Minister on account of its association with the dozens of love letters which he receives daily. The poor man is inundated with them and, were he to even consider a dalliance with a small percentage of the senders, he would find himself considerably more occupied than France for the next three hundred years or so.

I myself had the privilege of meeting Mr Churchill, quite by accident, on Tuesday last at the Savoy where we were both staying. Having fainted over the Concierge desk just before dinner (on account, I believe, of the price of caviar) I somehow managed to appropriate Mr Churchill's room key with my flailing left hand and lifted it clean off the hook. Revived and upright, but still in a state of shock, I then quite inadvertently took Mr Churchill's key to be my own and accidentally let myself into his suite, where I was not unpleasantly surprised to find the great man taking a bath. Terribly embarrassed and quite unable to take my eyes off his cigar (as you mentioned in your letter, he does display it rather well) I found myself in danger of fainting again, into the bath with him this time, and I am quite sure it would have been so had he not bellowed rather abruptly "Good God, Madam! Watch me brandy! Sit over there and take a letter, would you?"

One French letter– this one to Charles de Gaulle – and a lecture on the history of the English speaking peoples later, we were rather rudely interrupted by General Smuts and a small bespectacled man from the Admiralty and I was forced to depart, which was a terrible shame as we had been getting on so well. That said, the Colonel and I have been invited to lunch at Chartwell on Saturday week and I have strict instructions to take a portable typewriter, a siren suit and the Colonel's sleeping tablets. My suitcases cases are already packed and standing in the hall.

And so you see my dear, the Prime Minister really is a terribly busy man, hard at it and rising to the occasion even when taking his bath and I really do not think that he'll have time to indulge you in your romantic fantasy – flannel nightgown or no. Set your sights a little lower for your own heart's sake.

Now, I wonder, have you thought much about seamen? There are submariners aplenty out there desperate to get their periscopes up and head into port. Failing that, get yourself off to Doctor Proctor's and ask him for an industrial strength dose of Bromide.

As for the dodgy fellow you've espied loitering in your road of late, I suspect that he may well be from the Secret Service and will disappear as soon as you've stopped harassing poor Mr Churchill with your thrice daily missives.

Yours,

Hilda Ffinch
Hilda Ffinch,
The Bird with All The Answers

A Dangerous Crush...

Miss Veronica Prigg
14 Kitchener Close
Little Hope

19th August 1940

Dear Ms Ffinch,

My sister Gertie seems to have a bit of a crush on an American journalist who frequents our local pub. She has become infatuated with him since he gave her a pair of nylons (which are obviously of poor quality on account of them not being French). The silly girl has it in her head that he will make an honest woman of her and that his intentions are sincere on account of him having trimmed back her foliage the other day.

What can I say to her to make her realise that the bush trimming was just his opening shot and that once it has had a good seeing-to, he will be off like the clappers?

Yours faithfully,

Veronica Prigg (Miss)

The Little Hope Herald
Saturday, 24th August 1940

Dear Miss Prigg,

You're quite right my dear in your assertion that a once-trimmed bush doth not Kew Gardens make. Quite the reverse in fact. If this fellow has trimmed your sister's foliage willy-nilly (so to speak) then it will probably look like the Hanging Gardens of Babylon – post irrigation failure – at this very moment and she will bitterly regret not relying on gravy browning to colour her legs until Hitler is defeated and Europe's supply of stockings are liberated from Herr Goering's lingerie drawer.

One assumes, Miss Prigg, that given the inanely lustful nature of certain sections of society at present that your sister is aware of the dangers of letting unqualified fingers fiddle about in one's shrubbery? It's invariably a prelude to something altogether more familiar and she may find herself in sole possession of an unexpected seedling if she isn't careful. I recommend therefore that you telephone the Hack in question (anonymously, of course) with a cock-and-bull story about Herman Goering having been spotted tottering about in a green jumper on Portland Bill. Trust me, the cad will decamp immediately and disappear off into the sunset, never to return. Your sister may be peeved with you for a little while, but she'll soon cheer up when Mr Trotter the butcher puts his thrice stuffed porky banger on show in his window on Tuesday.

All credit to you for your moral stance, Miss Prigg and for the horsehair vests which I hear you've been running up on your Singer sewing machine for members of the clergy and visiting dignitaries. If Herr Hitler ever does make it across the Channel and into Yorkshire then one is confident that the ceremonial presentation of a set of your 'special underwear' to him will have him begging for mercy, scratching like an old bear and back in Berlin in no time at all.

Yours,

Hilda Ffinch
Hilda Ffinch,
The Bird with All The Answers

I'm in the Family Way!

'Titty the Worrier'
Somewhere in Yorkshire

25th August 1940

Dear Mrs Ffinch,

Please could you give me some advice?

Following a dance in our Village Hall a few weeks ago, a rather friendly and over amorous pilot (from somewhere in Europe) and I had a brief dalliance and as a result I find myself in the 'family way' as it were. I am wondering how I might approach Mother about this as my ever-increasing bosom and waistline will surely give me away soon!

What should I say? Mother is bound to be most disgruntled.

Sincerely,

'Titty the Worrier'

The Little Hope Herald
Saturday, 31st August 1940

Dear Fatty the Wrongdoer,

You may recall the advice given to the villagers of Little Hope by Mrs Lavinia Fox at a gathering in the Village Hall earlier in the year just prior to the arrival of our dear friends and allies from the continent, when she said very clearly that "We ought to be friendly and hospitable but know where to draw the line. Sensible shoes at all times, a quick handshake and then it's back home to pull the parsnips and churn the butter."

If memory serves me correctly – and I think that it does – at no point during the course of her (admittedly rather long and somewhat rambling) speech did the chatelaine of Fox Manor suggest that you and the other young ladies of the village should feel free to indulge in a 'bit of the other', as it were.

What, oh *what*, were you thinking of, Titty?

Now – before I offer the only sensible piece of advice available to you at this time – would you please be so kind as to pop into the local library and have a quick flick through Miss Virginia Creeper's excellent little tome about the facts of life. It's entitled *A Fiddle in the Haystack and a Bun in the Oven* and is to be found on the top shelf of the 'Ladies Only' section between *The Man in the Iron Basque* and *Little Women In The Workhouse*.

Do have a good read, Titty, in order to ensure that you're on the right track and haven't just overeaten or are incubating our 'Village Fete 'Flu', which is prevalent in the district at this time and which most likely had its genesis in the interesting composition of Miss Mildred Sparrow's homemade cider.

That out of the way, if your suspicions are confirmed and the cider is off the hook, might I suggest that you have a quiet word with your mother and explain to her that she is going to be a grandmother sometime this side of Christmas? Throw in a cock-and-bull story about three wise men, a couple of shepherds and a bright star in the east (you might consider pointing to the anti-aircraft flares over Sheffield next time Jerry comes in for a night run to add some credence to your tale). Ply your mother with a glass or two of the aforementioned alcoholic beverage from the illegal still of the erstwhile Miss Sparrow (she's still hawking it about the place, in spite of warnings from the village council) and with any luck your mater will see the light and ship you off to live with a maiden aunt in Tooting

Broadway until your Holy Child of Little Hope arrives and no one here will be any the wiser.

This ruse will only work once, so I strongly recommend that upon your return you keep your knees clamped tightly together and avoid men of the opposite sex altogether for the next thirty years or so. That should do the trick and avoid the possibility of a repetition of this reprehensible state of affairs.

Yours very judgingly,

Hilda Ffinch
Hilda Ffinch,
The Bird with All The Answers

P.S. Was the airman terribly good looking? Asking for a friend.

Is He 'At It'?

'Beryl of Little Hope'
Yorkshire

9th September 1940

Dear Mrs Ffinch,

I'm a little worried that my husband may fall prey to a lady of the evening whilst away on active service, what measures might I take to allay my fears?

I do realise that it's difficult for a chap when he's away and in the thick of it, but I'm so worried that chewing my nails no longer suffices, last week I accidentally took a bite out of a china teacup.

Yours frantically,

'Beryl'

The Little Hope Herald
Saturday, 14th September 1940

Dear Beryl,

Most married men, my dear, are in danger of falling prey to the call of the siren – the bane of Odysseus and his seamen that is, and not the air raid klaxon on top of the Village Hall – from the moment they set foot outside of the marital home and there isn't a great deal one can do about it.

I myself invariably have a 'frank and fearless' on this very subject with Colonel Ffinch when he's home on leave and I tend to follow it up when he returns to the front by waving him off with a handkerchief in one hand and a jolly sharp pair of gardening shears in the other, taking care to point the latter in the general direction of his 'gentleman's equipment' whilst mouthing "Snip! Snip!" before he gets into his staff car. As far as one is aware, this seems to do the trick and one is reasonably confident that the only time that the Colonel actually gets Percy out beyond the confines of Ffinch Hall, it's to point him at the porcelain, as it were.

The only way one can ever be certain that one's spouse is being unfaithful with a lady of disreputable morals Beryl is to look for the tell-tale signs of a cheating heart when he comes home on leave; Is he boz-eyed on mercury tincture and smelling as though he's been had at by a pox doctor's apprentice? Does he scream at the sight of a cocktail umbrella? Is he scratching his nether regions like an old bear at every opportunity? And the absolute giveaway – has he rather gone off afternoon tiffin?

At the end of the day, dear girl, men will be men, they're not so very different to the average tomcat spraying all over one's hollyhocks at the drop of a hat, and so it has been for time out of memory. Sir Francis Drake was all over the Plymouth Hoe like a rash and don't imagine for one moment that 'Mad Carew' didn't have a wife and six dependent children at home in Chipping Sodbury either.

To this end, I am enclosing a beautifully framed poster detailing the inevitable consequences of infidelity for you to hang above your mantelpiece when your spouse is next home on leave. The beautifully illustrated spectre of blindness, insanity, sterility, itchy snooker balls and baldness ought to put him off his stroke if he *is* at it. Happy to send you some of the aforementioned garden shears too if it helps.

Yours fragrantly,

Hilda Ffinch
Hilda Ffinch,
The Bird with All The Answers (and the Husband on
a Very Tight Leash).

I Can't Hide it for Much Longer…

'Joan'
Somewhere in Yorkshire

21st September 1940

Dear Mrs Ffinch,

I have a boyfriend, well he's like a man friend really as all the boys are gone at the moment, he's nineteen years older than me and works as an aeroplane tester. The thing is you see we seem to have developed a little problem, well its quite a big problem now, and I'm beginning to show.

The thing is, Mrs Ffinch, how am I going to tell my father?

Yours in a slight panic,

Joan

The Little Hope Herald
Saturday, 28th September 1940

Dear Joan,

My dear girl, if you are – as I suspect – Miss Joan Swallow from Frosty Hollow Bottom, then I'm surprised that your aeroplane engine tester is able to develop anything other than rheumatism and dropsy given his advanced age. Having calculated your own birth date (and had it double-checked and verified by three members of the Women's Institute, the Vicar's housekeeper and my fellow Thursday night whist players) it occurs to me that you must be at least fifty-six, making your 'beau' at least seventy-five years of age and a contemporary of Charles Dickens, Arthur Conan Doyle and Benjamin Disraeli.

One has to wonder, what sort of aeroplane is the randy old codger testing? The prototype Aerial Steam Carriage? A Sopwith Camel? A *Blimp*?

The chances, my dear, of your expanding girth having anything to do with procreational matters are slim – much, *much* slimmer than you are. I think it more likely that Orville Wright's brother Wilbur has been treating you to an excess of peas and pigs trotters at the British Restaurant on Canal Street and that if you can possibly desist from eating an entire herd of Wessex Saddlebacks at each sitting then you might drop a marquee size or two and give the rest of the village a fighting chance of getting their hands on a bit of pork this side of Victory in Europe.

Don't bother your Father with any of this, dear girl, given that he's even older than the randy old goat you've been fiddling with, it may well be the end of him. Take up knitting and keep those knees tightly pressed together instead, presupposing that your thigh girth allows you to.

Yours very judgingly,

Hilda Ffinch
Hilda Ffinch,
The Bird with All The Answers

The Unfaithful Politician...

Gertrude Jones-Smyth
Flat 1 The Mansion House
London

9th October 1940

Dear Mrs Ffinch,

Several years ago, my husband decided that a dalliance with his secretary was an excellent political manoeuvre for him and would enhance his chances of being elected as an MP. 'She Cow' (as I call her) was younger than I and extremely attractive and as my husband kindly pointed out to me, as well as to all of our friends and acquaintances and half of the Liberal Party, I had 'let myself go' after the children (eight in total) and 'lost my looks'. I'm sure you can understand how this made me feel. Totally without hope or the will to carry on.

Well to cut a long story short, he divorced me on the grounds of unreasonable behaviour (his, not mine, but he had a top barrister whilst I could barely afford my own legal representation) and I'm sorry to say that I took solace in gin and rarely left the little flat I ended up living in. The children – who were almost grown up by this time – took it all splendidly and accepted 'She Cow' which caused me great distress at the time although I now appreciate they were being quite 'canny' and were merely safeguarding their own future inheritance.

Now, here is my problem. When the bounder first mooted divorce, I went into a flat spin and I didn't know what to. I was terrified and so I confided in an old friend – the Honourable Fanny Featherstone – who suggested that I find a reputable jeweller, preferably many miles away from here, and get pastes made of my enormous stash of diamond jewellery, which included a priceless tiara which had been made by Faberge for my husband's grandmother and had been worn on by her many an occasion of state. Apparently, Fanny's own mother had done exactly the same thing when her husband began his philandering and had got along rather nicely on the back of it.

When our divorce came to court, my husband demanded the return of all my jewellery, including the gifts which he had given to me over the years. I fought him tooth and nail, but his barrister won out claiming it was all investment and merely on loan to me. I couldn't prove that any of it was a gift given with love because after all, who keeps a gift card? A salutary warning if ever there was one.

Needless to say though, I followed Fanny's advice and whilst the contents of my jewellery safe are worth a fair bob or two, the trinkets which my jezebel of a replacement has been parading about in for years might as well have come out of a Christmas cracker.

I have, thank God, remarried now and my jewellery has been remodelled, I really couldn't be happier with life for the most part. But this is where I need sound advice as my conscience is beginning to prick a little.

The 'She Cow' is currently in the process of divorcing our former husband on account of his indulgence with yet another floozie in another adulterous liaison and the heifer in question is, apparently, 'taking him for everything'. The divorce settlement which she is seeking includes the pile of paste jewellery in our ex-husband's possession which both he and she believe to be genuine. Should she win her case, then our mutual former spouse will be on his uppers and at risk of losing his seat in the House of Commons.

Should I sell some of the jewellery to help him out (after all the tiara was rightfully his) or just leave him to his fate? What do you think?

I very much look forward to your reply.

Yours,

Gertrude Jones-Smyth

The Little Hope Herald
Saturday, 12th October 1940

Dear Mrs Jones-Smyth,

Firstly, may I congratulate you on having so rightly concentrated on the important matter of ensuring that you weren't left completely high and dry by The Right Honourable Member for Bordello Passage and Iniquity Lane (and his shameless doxy) and for managing to put 'a little something' away for the future in the shape of your re-modelled sparklers? The Honourable Fanny Featherstone's advice was, in my opinion, sound, sensible and sterling.

Colonel Ffinch once asked me – in an idle moment over the billiards table – what I might do should he fall sway to the thrall of a playhouse doxy to which I replied "Good luck with her sort pulling one of your balls off, my dear." which certainly put a stop to any notion which he may have been entertaining, given that I only bother hosting a foxtrot when the Duke of Wellington and Lord Uxbridge are able to come too, which Colonel Ffinch seems to quite like.

Philandering husbands, my dear, and particularly those of the parliamentary persuasion, really are the curse of womankind and I commiserate with you on having plighted your troth with a twit.

Prior to the present coalition (led, of course by the still terribly attractive and upstanding Mr Churchill), there has never, in the entire history of these islands, existed such a thing as a well hung Parliament. There are, of course, some fine upstanding members in the House and one or two of the constituency representatives aren't bad either, but they really are the exception as opposed to the rule.

My advice to you, my dear, is to cut and run! Leave your bounder of an ex-husband to stand atop his car shouting promises he won't be able to keep through a dented megaphone at candle-nosed urchins and women with gin-soaked muffs. The lot of an MP isn't generally as hard as they make it out to be, you know, so you've probably had a fortunate escape. Don't be bamboozled by the preening occupants of the corridors of power, they're not all that which they would have us believe and generally lack the nerve and capacity to fire anything but blanks at weekend house parties during the grouse season.

Yours,

Hilda Ffinch
Hilda Ffinch
The Bird with All The Answers

9 781913 340889